DEATH ON THE CANAL

Chapter One

Even the most meticulously planned operation could go wrong. I had surveyed the area previously to identify the optimal position and had found a location that would allow me plenty of warning. As I cycled there across the wide tarmac bridge with two lanes of cars shooting past, I could feel the nerves jangling at my fingers.

According to the calendar it had been summer for five weeks, but only today had the weather in Amsterdam woken up to this fact. Following a miserable couple of months, with limited sunshine, now people could finally sit outside in T-shirts and jeans and be pleasantly warm even though it was coming up to half past seven in the evening. I chained my bike to a lamp post and thought the weather was a mixed blessing. On the one hand I could be situated at my selected spot without attracting any attention – had it rained I would have had to abandon the plan – but on the other hand more people were still outside and the place might be occupied. I walked quickly because a few seconds could make all the difference.

I wanted one of only six tables on a tiny terrace where the city had forgone three parking spaces. The one I preferred

1

was right at the canal's edge and only protected from falling into the water by a shin-high rusty-red metal railing.

It was still vacant.

I jogged the last couple of steps and sat down quickly with the bridge to my back so that I faced the direction he would be arriving from. My breathing was faster than the little run warranted. I'd managed to stop myself from checking my watch until now. Maybe he wasn't going to turn up. Maybe this time he wasn't going to come.

The waitress crossed the narrow one-way street that separated the bar from the terrace. A different woman had served me yesterday. I ordered a glass of rosé and said that it was surely the perfect way to celebrate the arrival of summer. It barely drew a smile. The bar's door was open and Ricky Martin's music drifted out to mingle with the hum of traffic behind me and the quacking of a pair of ducks to my right. Everything was in place. A sultry breeze tickled my bare neck where I'd had my hair cut that afternoon. He should get here soon.

My mouth was dry and I took a sip of my drink. This wasn't a bad place to be. It was the height of tourist season but here you wouldn't know it. Amsterdam's canals formed concentric half-circles and, like year rings on a tree, the further away from Centraal Station they were, the more recently they'd been dug. But also the further away from the centre you were, the fewer tourists you found. Here, about ten canals out, Amsterdam was a different city. I threw a quick glance at the menu. They served decent food. If he wasn't going to turn up, I would finish this glass of wine and order something to eat.

Then I saw his tall shape. He was walking slowly with his hands in his pockets. He wasn't looking my way. During the minutes that I monitored Mark Visser strolling along the canal, my heart must have thumped a thousand times. I got ready to act.

'Mark,' I shouted when he was close to the bar. I waved at him. 'What a surprise. Good to see you.' I fought to keep the smile on my face in this instant when failure and success were balanced on a knife-edge.

He hesitated but came over. 'Hi, Lotte, how are you?'

I stood up and we kissed three times on the cheek like old friends. 'Have a seat.' I pointed at the vacant chair on the other side of the table. 'It's such a nice evening. Join me for a drink.'

He didn't refuse. He looked at his watch but then drew out the chair.

'How are you?' Now my smile was real.

'I'm well.' He sat down opposite me. He stretched out one of his long legs and it touched the inside of mine. For that second, the world shrank until all that mattered was us in this moment. It wasn't that I didn't see the street; it just didn't signify any more.

'Sorry,' he said, and pulled his leg back.

I looked down. The tables had been reclaimed from an old school building. I could imagine lifting up the lid and finding space for pens and books. Even the chairs were not that dissimilar to those we had, only bigger. It seemed appropriate, as Mark and I had first met at primary school before losing contact for over thirty-five years.

There was grey in the stubble hugging his jaw, more than there was in his dark hair, and the lines around his eyes were noticeable even behind his round glasses.

'What's with the stubble?' I said.

'I had to rush out this morning.' His long fingers rubbed his face. 'Doesn't it make me look strong and capable? That's what I was going for.'

'Smooth as sandpaper.' I broke off a piece of wax from the outside of the candle, held the long strip over the flame and watched the molten drips return to their source. 'Let me get you a drink.' I gestured at the waitress to come over and ordered Mark a beer.

'I've nearly finished the house,' he said. 'I'll have to put it on the market in a few weeks.' He pushed his glasses higher up his nose. 'I still won't get what I'd hoped for.'

When I had first gone there, three months ago, it had been a building site with just two rooms habitable: Mark's office and a bedroom. My mind flooded with memories of that time. Of us together.

Before.

'House prices have dropped again,' he said.

A large moth buzzed over our table. I shooed it away from the candle. It should sup from the red hollyhocks flowering along the bar's wall, not burn its wings in the flame. Then the creature's hum was drowned out by the unusual sound of a car turning off the main drag over the bridge. An Audi drove past and parked further down the canal, partially shielded from view by the heart-shaped leaves of the plants crawling over a trellis. Two men and two women got out. One of the women went into a side street, probably to pay

4

for parking, and the others took the table next to us. They were about our age, maybe a little younger, and smartly dressed.

A moment later, the other woman joined them. She carried a beautiful orange handbag with a large silver clasp. She put it down on the floor and I could imagine the leather complaining about having to touch the dirty pavement. You could fit a slim laptop in there. It was exactly the kind of bag that I'd been looking for. It would probably be way outside my budget. Also it might not be wide enough to hold a gun. She jolted their table as she sat down and moved her chair forward. 'Sorry,' she said.

'No need to apologise,' one of the guys said loudly in accented English. He had bronzed skin and his beard was so neat it looked as if he'd laid a ruler along his cheek to decide where to stop shaving. The hairline on the back of his head was equally straight, but hair was creeping up from the collar of his shirt where it escaped upwards from his back. 'You always do that. For everything. I guess you're just more empathetic, you . . . you women types.'

'Women types?' I mouthed at Mark with raised eyebrows.

He smiled and shook his head. He enjoyed listening to other people's conversations as much as I did.

The Beard insisted on ordering a pitcher of cocktails. 'Moscow mules,' he said to the waitress. 'They sound great.'

The women, sitting opposite each other, started talking in Dutch and excluded the men from their conversation.

'Don't go,' the Beard shouted loudly after the waitress. 'We want to get food as well.'

The woman who had jolted the table translated the menu. At this bar, the menus were in Dutch, as mainly locals frequented it. The outdoor seating area was too small to get the place featured in any guidebooks. The Beard ordered for everybody. When the woman complained in a soft voice that it was far too much food, he ignored her and added another dish. He must be the one picking up the tab at the end of the evening.

'Is excess food a new way to impress?' Mark said.

'It's never done it for me,' I said. I stopped watching the table next to us. 'Do you want to eat something?'

Mark didn't answer.

'Did you hear the news this morning?' he said. 'That guy got eighteen months.'

I lifted my wineglass and washed down the lump that had suddenly appeared at the back of my throat.

'The cop who fired at that getaway car and hit the passenger,' he said.

As if I hadn't known who he was talking about. I pulled my hair away from my face. I still felt so guilty. And not just about the man I'd shot. It didn't matter that it had been self-defence. 'I was cleared.'

He rubbed his forehead. 'I know. You had no choice. You had camera footage to back everything up. I'm sorry. I shouldn't have brought it up.'

So why did you, I wanted to say, but I hadn't planned this evening only to get into an argument. Talking about guilt wasn't making either of us feel any better. 'Do you want another drink?'

'Sure. Same again.'

I could have ordered from the waitress, but I was keen to get up. Mark probably wouldn't leave while I was buying another round, but if he wanted to I would allow him an easy escape. I carried our glasses inside.

The café was dark and half empty apart from a group of men in yellow T-shirts and a young couple at a table by the window who were deep in conversation. Their voices were little more than a murmur floating above the sound from the speakers. The music had changed to Abba. The woman wore a flowery sleeveless summer dress; she had matched it with a denim jacket that now hung over the back of her chair. Her dark hair was pulled back into a small ponytail and she had a muscular solidity that reminded me of one of the nurses who'd looked after me in hospital. The kind of girl who would have been the goalie in the school hockey team.

The man stared at her like a sniper focusing on a target. It went with his khaki-green T-shirt. Only his white jeans were incongruous. The woman reached behind her and fished a piece of paper out of the pocket of her jacket. Her shoulders were tense as she pushed it abruptly across the table. I craned my neck but I still couldn't see what it was. Maybe a photo. It was the right size. The man looked down and smiled. He was in his early thirties, but his wide grin transformed his face and gave him a quirky, boyish charm.

The woman's shoulders didn't relax and she didn't return the smile.

Then the Beard arrived next to me with the waitress at his side. 'No, no, I'll choose one myself,' he said. Moscow mules hadn't kept him happy for long. He got behind the bar and made a show of studying every whisky bottle on the shelf. The barman exchanged a look with the waitress, who gave a helpless shrug. The Beard finally found one he liked and handed the bottle to the waitress. 'This one. Large measure.' She poured.

The barman came to take my order.

'A rosé and a beer, please.'

'Sure.' He pulled the pint and then unscrewed the top of a bottle of unknown origin. I didn't care enough to study bottles. Holding both glasses, I walked back to our table.

My arm brushed Mark's as I put his beer down. That he didn't flinch was a victory.

The evening sun turned the sky the colour of my wine and it would have been absolutely perfect if only the people next to us had left. I tried and failed to tune out their conversation, which revolved around pharmaceuticals of varying kinds. Then the Beard asked his companion how he'd go about scoring some drugs around here. The other man told him to shut up and stop being stupid. I looked over because it annoyed me when people came to Amsterdam for just one reason. I didn't even try to be subtle about it. The woman who'd earlier apologised for jolting the table now mouthed 'sorry' to me. She called the waitress over and managed to bring the focus back to alcohol.

Mark and I chatted about uncontentious topics and ordered some snacks from the waitress. He seemed better than me at blocking out the Beard, who went into the bar a few more times, once accompanied by the woman. I thought Mark enjoyed the evening and maybe even my company.

My glass was almost empty when the couple who had been inside the bar came out and walked along the canal, away from the bridge, turning left into the first sideroad, towards the houses. Stars started to appear in the evening sky and the fat candle in the middle of the table threw shadows on to Mark's cheekbones.

'It's good to see you,' I said.

My heart pounded as I waited for him to respond that it had been good to see me too.

But before he could say anything, a shout pierced the evening. It was a man's voice. It took me a few seconds before I identified the source of the sound: a young black man, a Surinamer, with dark-rimmed glasses. He came running out of the side street. 'Help!' he screamed. 'Help!' He waved his arms above his head but he already had my attention.

Nobody knew I was a police detective apart from Mark. This evening that I'd planned so carefully was going as well as I could have hoped for. Why spoil it by getting up and offering assistance when I could stay here and have another drink? I could just not get involved.

'Someone's been stabbed,' the young Surinamer shouted. 'Just here.' He pointed down the side street.

Instead of doing what was sensible, I pushed my chair back. The metal legs screeched a complaint on the paving stones. I got up. 'You stay here,' I said to Mark.

He opened his mouth to object but I held the palm of my hand in his direction and silenced him. I needed to concentrate and Mark would get in the way. If there was still a fight going on, he could get hurt. My walk turned into a jog. I automatically checked my watch whilst running. It was 10.21 p.m.

I would have felt better if I'd had my gun with me.

A half-bald elderly man with large facial features and wearing a yellow T-shirt followed me. Nobody else even thought of interfering, and that was a good thing.

I turned the corner and saw a man lying on the ground. He was on his side. I recognised him: it was the intense man in the white jeans. Blood stained his khaki T-shirt a muddled brown. I scanned the street, but it was dead quiet. Cars were parked on one side, with thin white lines marking out each space, but I couldn't hear any engines running and nothing moved. There was no sign of an attacker. Most flats were dark, with the curtains closed and the lights off. How long ago had this man left the bar? Ten minutes at most.

The elderly man nearly overtook me and I grabbed his arm to stop him.

'I'm a doctor,' he said.

I let him through. 'I'm police.'

The doctor knelt at the man's side, felt his pulse then started CPR. I dialled 112. The man's eyes were closed and he was losing blood fast. It was obvious where the wound was. Wounds. Three cuts in the front of his T-shirt. The young Surinamer stood a few metres away. He had taken off his glasses and kept saying, 'Oh my God, oh my God,' over and over again.

'What's your name?' I said.

'Nathan,' he said. 'Nathan Derez.'

'Come over here and help me,' the doctor shouted. He ripped off his yellow T-shirt, baring a wrinkled torso, and held the garment out.

Nathan didn't move.

'Hold this, Nathan.' Using his name would get him out of his state of paralysis. I handed him my phone, grabbed the T-shirt, knelt down by the young man and pressed the cloth against the wound on his stomach as the doctor indicated. Blood had pooled onto the victim's skin and now flowed thick and warm over my hands where the T-shirt couldn't absorb it all. It congealed between my fingers until I felt I was glued to this man. As I heard Nathan telling the ambulance crew our address, the evening became so thick with the metallic smell of blood that I could taste it. What had been a pleasant warmth was now oppressive.

'We need the police,' I shouted. 'Tell them that we are urgently – extremely urgently,' I corrected myself, 'looking for a woman . . .'

Instead of simply relaying my message, Nathan held my phone to my ear as I kept pressing down with the now blood-soaked T-shirt.

'This is Detective Lotte Meerman,' I said into my mobile. 'We are extremely urgently looking for a young woman. Probably in her twenties. Dark hair tied in a ponytail. Wearing a floral summer dress and a denim jacket. She's wanted in connection with a murder. Potentially armed with a knife.' Out of the corner of my eye I saw Mark standing frozen and staring at me. 'Put it out to all cars.' I moved my head away from the phone and concentrated on the man under my hands again.

More people turned up behind me, probably from the bar. I shouted that they should stay back, to keep the crime scene secure, but I continued to stare at my hands, at the creases in the yellow T-shirt and then at the doctor doing his best to keep the victim's heart going. I tried to keep the man's life inside him, but the amount of blood pumping out told me I might fail. I was so stuck in the moment that even when the ambulance turned up and the paramedics rushed over, it was hard to lift my hands.

One of them, a young woman, took my place. I rested back on my heels, then stood up. The world disappeared into blackness for a second. I steadied myself against a parking payment machine and left a red print behind. I turned around to look for Mark where I'd seen him last, at the end of the street, but he was no longer there.

The ambulance crew examined the man on the ground. 'He's gone,' one of them said.

Chapter Two

A myriad of blue swirling lights destroyed the last vestiges of a pleasant evening and made the quiet street seem a dangerous and threatening place. Two police cars were parked nose to nose as if ready for a fight. Tape closed off the street at either end, locking in the forensic scientists with the body. A van had carried eight more officers to the crime scene and they were now busy taking statements from everybody who'd been in the bar. The fluorescent yellow stripes on their uniforms stood out starkly against the dark blue. The ambulance was still waiting, ready to leave once Forensics had finished with the victim's body. At least a blanket now shrouded him from view.

'I didn't hear anything,' Nathan said. 'I had music on but it wasn't that loud. Shouldn't I have heard something?'

I sat with Nathan Derez and the doctor, Gerard Campert, on the edge of the pavement on the opposite side of the road, the three of us like battle-worn survivors. After my colleagues had spoken to us, we were now left alone. Gerard had described the woman in the floral dress in detail. He'd been inside the bar for most of the evening and had a good look at her. I'd filled in the gaps. Nathan hadn't witnessed anything apart from the aftermath.

His partner, a tall red-haired woman, came over and brought us mugs of sweet tea. She'd also handed me a towel after I'd scrubbed my hands for five minutes at their kitchen sink. I'd even rubbed kitchen roll under the already clean tips of my nails, wanting desperately to wash the thought of blood away. She'd said that we could wait indoors, but until I changed my clothes, I shouldn't sit on someone's sofa.

'There was no shouting? No argument?' I asked.

'No, nothing.'

I hadn't noticed anything out of the ordinary either until I'd heard Nathan's cry for help. 'I saw him and the woman turn into this street about ten minutes before you found him,' I said.

A few police constables rang doorbells along the street. Maybe I should join them, but somehow it was hard to move.

'He'd lost a lot of blood in that time,' Gerard said. 'We could never have saved him.'

'It wasn't until I stepped outside for a cigarette that I saw him. If only I'd heard something, I could have got help sooner.'

Gerard put a hand on Nathan's arm. The doctor was now wearing a red polo shirt that Nathan's partner had given him. It was a tight fit. His blood-soaked yellow T-shirt had been bagged up by Forensics. 'It's not your fault,' he said. 'There's nothing you could have done. With knife wounds like those – one to the lung, two to the stomach – it wouldn't have made a difference. I could tell from the start

14

that . . .' he rubbed his forehead with the knuckle of his thumb, 'that he was most likely going to die.'

The young man nodded, his eyes serious behind his glasses. He leaned back against a birch tree. From where I was sitting, I had a perfect view of the crime scene, the dead body, the forensic team moving about and the parking payment machine with the bloody handprint I'd left behind.

Another car drove up and pulled into the spot next to the ambulance. Detective Ingrid Ries got out. She was very tall and her skinny jeans only accentuated the length of her legs. She sometimes reminded me of a plant that had grown without enough light; her limbs were too long, as if she'd had to reach for the sun all the years of her childhood. She'd been at home when I called her.

She hurried towards me. 'Are you okay?'

I put my hands on my knees and got up from the kerb. Nathan and Gerard also stood, as if I had disturbed our little survivors' tea party. I made the introductions.

Ingrid put an arm around my shoulders. She did it to comfort me, but it was restraining too.

'I just watched someone die.' I said it softly. It would be more precise to say that I felt him die. I'd felt his blood drain out of him. My hands shook with a tremor that originated in my fingertips and I stepped away from Ingrid's hug. I hid my hands in the back pockets of my jeans. Maybe I was in shock because death was so incongruous after the pleasant summer's evening, or maybe I'd just had too much to drink.

The front page of yesterday's newspaper lay in the gutter. Geert Wilders' photo was illuminated by the street lights.

'Muslims should integrate or go home' screamed the fat print of the headline.

I pulled myself together. I'd written down the man's details. We'd identified him from his security card, which had been bagged up by Forensics earlier. 'Piotr Mazur. Polish national.' On the pass, the green emblem of one of Amsterdam's large department stores showed right above a photo of the now-dead Piotr Mazur's smiling face.

'A security guard,' I said.

I'd phoned the store after I'd finished washing my hands. I had spoken to the guard who was on night duty. He told me it was all quiet at their end but he'd call his manager and they might get some more security staff in, just in case the murder had anything to do with them. I didn't see how it could, but they wanted to be extra careful.

A little breeze cut through the still night. 'He was in the bar with a woman in a floral dress.'

'She's our main suspect then.'

I thought about how they had been when they talked. I couldn't remember any animosity, but there had been tension between them. He had been staring at her intensely. Still, I'd only seen them briefly. The barman or another of the men in the yellow T-shirts would have more information. 'Let's say she's someone we urgently need to talk to. They left together. If she's not the murderer, she must have seen something. Witnessed something and didn't call for help. There was no other call to 112, was there?'

'No, just you. Come in the car. Sit down.' She reached out a hand as if to steer me into the vehicle by my shoulder.

I stepped away from the contact. 'I'd rather not. I'll wait here for a bit.'

Forensics were doing their work by the body. One of them was examining the bloody handprint on the parking payment machine. It was hard to recognise them in their white Tyvek suits.

'You don't have to test that one,' I said loudly. My voice wobbled. 'That's mine.' The man correctly ignored me and photographed the machine from all angles. It was evidence of our failure to keep the man alive.

'The woman in the bar probably gave a photo to the victim,' I told Ingrid. That photo was now with Forensics. It was a photo of a small boy. A toddler. He was a cute child, with blonde curls, smiling broadly, holding a blue and red boat out to the camera with both hands. Not much of the background was visible: some grass, a park maybe. The back of the photo was blank. 'I saw her give him something from the pocket of her jacket. We found the photo in his wallet.' The woman had been tense as she'd handed it over and Piotr had suddenly smiled. Their reactions made this photo seem significant to me.

'Are you sure that was what she gave him? You saw him put it in his wallet?'

'No, I didn't.'

'So it was something he could have already had.'

'Yes, but I think I saw her give him a photo and that was the only one he had on him.'

Ingrid stared at me. 'He could have handed it back.'

'Sure. You're right. But she definitely gave him something and he was happy about it.' The thought of how young and boyish Piotr Mazur had looked at that moment made my tongue clumsy in my mouth. Compared to the death of this man, my ruined evening was of course insignificant. 'He was happy,' I said again.

'You should go home,' Ingrid said. 'You've done enough for one night. We've got it from here. Thomas is on his way. We'll contact the next of kin.'

'I asked the department store about his family when I called them. They have no record of a wife or a partner. He'd written down his parents in Poland as next of kin on his employment form.'

'Great. I'll get a translator ready. Just in case. The woman he was with, was she Polish?'

'I don't know. Check with one of those guys in the yellow T-shirts. They were inside the bar. Talk to the doctor. I was sitting outside and only came in to get a drink.'

The Yellow T-shirts were members of a rowing club. I didn't know why they had been in this particular bar, but they made perfect witnesses. Apart from Gerard, the doctor, there was a lawyer, a town councillor and a couple of bankers.

An elderly couple walked by hand in hand. Their steps hastened as they came past the blue lights but their faces turned towards the covered dead body on the pavement. Even though they were worried by the flashing lights on top of the police cars and the tape that identified it as a crime scene, they still looked. You could never stop people from staring at the aftermath.

'I'll come to the station and give you a description of the woman,' I said. 'We need to put that out and find her as soon

18

as possible. She's either a murderer or a key witness. We need to talk to her.'

Ingrid shook her head. 'You need to get out of these clothes.' She gestured at my jeans. 'It's . . .' she swallowed, 'it's too much like last time, isn't it?'

Last time. I knew she meant the time I'd shot a man. Even though he had been a murderer and I'd had no choice, my own actions still appalled me. I had never killed anyone before.

I looked down at my legs. For a few minutes I'd forgotten about the large bloodstains on my trousers. It reminded me of how Piotr's blood had flooded over my hands and I shuddered in sudden revulsion. I wasn't sure how it had got all over my clothes. Maybe I'd mindlessly wiped my palms on my jeans or maybe it had dripped there when I kneeled by the victim's side or soaked up from the pavement while I'd been trying to keep him alive. My hands shook in my jeans pockets, reverberating through my arms and into my shoulders.

'You look terrible,' Ingrid said. 'Go home. We'll talk about this tomorrow. You only saw her for a second. If any of those guys can give a clearer description of the woman, I'll use them.'

'I'll wait here for a bit.' I shivered again, as if the July night was really a winter's evening. 'I'm on my bike.' I didn't trust what my body was doing. That I was cold was probably the down after the adrenaline high. Shock was a possibility too.

Ingrid looked at the officers milling down the street, then back at me as if she was weighing me up. Judging me. 'Don't cycle. I'll give you a lift. Bear with me a couple of minutes.'

19

She briefly talked to one of the police officers. I saw her gesturing towards me, probably to tell the guy that she was taking me home. The man checked something in his notebook and seemed to give Ingrid a brief outline of what had happened. She talked to one of the younger Yellow T-shirts, who nodded to affirm whatever Ingrid was asking him.

She made a phone call, then walked back towards me. 'The young guy got a really good look at the woman. Says he remembers clearly what she looked like. Thomas is coming over to take him to the police station.'

She got in the car and opened the door on my side. I said goodbye to Gerard and Nathan. I'd pick up my bike tomorrow.

Ingrid did a U-turn then drove along the canal towards the bridge. I pulled my seat belt closer around me, as if that would keep me safe. Just as we approached the bridge, the traffic lights started to flash and the barriers came down. This was one of the wider canals, which allowed larger boats through. Ingrid switched off the engine. We could be here a while.

'This must have been hard,' she said. Her voice in the silence was loud. Now that she no longer needed to look at the traffic, her attention was relentlessly on me.

I was jealous of the boat that managed to disappear out of sight, hidden behind the now-vertical part of the bridge. It was a mid-size sailing ship. It had its sails down and used the motor to get it through the canal. When I'd been a child, it had perplexed me that the road surface would come up and the white lines would point to the sky and

I'd wondered if that was what a runway at an airport looked like.

'I'm okay,' I said.

'Did it bring back memories?'

I pulled my eyes away from the bridge and faced her. 'No, it didn't.' I made my voice strong as much to convince myself as her. The only similarity was that a man had died under my hands.

'I haven't forgotten what you did for me,' she said.

I caught my bottom lip between my teeth. 'Can we not talk about that?'

But Ingrid didn't stop. 'It's because you were covered in blood. When I saw you sitting on the kerb . . . I don't know, it immediately brought it all back.'

I didn't reply. What was I going to say? That I hadn't needed anything to bring it back to me as it hadn't been out of my mind? The boat appeared on the other side of the bridge and the road surface lowered again slowly.

'I want to make it up to you,' she said.

I shook my head. 'Please don't say that.' I swallowed something back. Bile tasted like guilt. How could I explain to her that every time she got me a cup of coffee or did a late-night shift in my place, it reminded me of the man I'd shot dead almost three months ago. Every kindness stabbed the knife in deeper.

'How much did you have to drink?' she said.

'I had a couple,' I said, 'maybe three.' It was always harder to keep track when there was waitress service. I realised I hadn't paid. Mark must have picked up the bill.

The barriers opened and Ingrid started the engine.

'Is that why you want to get me home?' I said. I didn't like the thought that she was trying to protect me by getting me away from the murder scene.

'You were slurring your words. I didn't want to say anything before we got in the car. I didn't want anybody else to overhear. And you really don't look too well. Thomas and I have got this. One of the guys had been inside the bar for most of the evening and he's a much better witness than you are.'

I turned my face towards the window and watched Amsterdam go past. The streets were busy with people making the most of the summer's night. Only three more turns and I would be home. We crossed a narrow bridge. A group of people coming from the other side had to walk in single file as the pavement was almost entirely taken up by parked bicycles chained to the bridge's white railings.

We reached my street. My apartment was the top floor of a seventeenth-century canal house. Tomorrow morning the hordes would come past my front door again on the way to the Anne Frank house. Now it was quieter, apart from the sound of laughter that bounced against the houses. On the canal a group of people in a pedal boat saluted the balmy July night with bottles of beer. From this close it was hard to tell that the canal was actually a large semicircle that at one point had protectively embraced the entire centre of Amsterdam. What was now a tourist attraction had centuries ago been the main form of defence.

Ingrid left the car in the middle of the road with the door wide open. She walked me to the front door and made sure that I could get the key in the lock.

'What were you doing in that bar anyway?' she said.

My hands were shaking so much I had to have a couple of goes before the key slid in. A silver-grey Volkswagen pulled up. The street was narrow with the canal on one side and the houses on the other, and Ingrid's car blocked the road. The driver made a hand gesture at Ingrid. She ignored him and kept looking at me.

I finally managed to unlock the door. 'What difference does it make?' I pushed it open.

'Bit out of the way for you, isn't it? It took us what, twenty minutes to drive here. With so many bars within walking distance, why go to the west side?'

'Avoiding the tourists.'

'The waitress told the other officer that you were there with a man.'

I rubbed my hand over my face. 'I met Mark Visser.'

'Really? I didn't know you were in touch again.'

I made a non-committal humming sound. 'I just bumped into him.'

'I didn't see him,' Ingrid said

'No, he'd already left.'

Volkswagen man rolled down his window. 'Are you going to be long?'

'Shut up,' Ingrid said. 'We're nearly done.'

'Some of us have homes to go to.'

I looked Ingrid in the eye. 'I'll get his statement for you.'

She nodded. 'Great. We'll talk tomorrow. Try to get some sleep.' She put a hand on my arm and then got back in her car.

I waited until both cars had driven off and then went through the front door. Get some sleep. As if that was even possible.

The chandelier in the communal hallway was comfortingly familiar, shining as if nothing had happened tonight. I slowly took the stairs up to my floor. My mobile rang when I was nearly at the top. I read his name, hesitated then answered it. 'Hi, Mark.' With my other hand I unlocked my front door. Pippi greeted me with a loud meow. I bent down to scratch the little black-and-white cat behind her ear.

'Lotte, hi. I'm sorry I didn't stay.' Mark's voice was low, with an odd echo to it. 'I know I should have but I saw you covered in blood and it all got too much. I'm really sorry.'

I shook my head. It was just like talking to Ingrid. 'It's okay, I understand.'

'Did the man survive?'

'No, he died.'

'I'm sorry.'

I waited to hear if he was going to say anything else, but he was quiet. 'I need to get your statement at some point,' I said.

'Sure. Okay. But I didn't really see anything.' His voice was abrupt.

Only a few hours ago there had been rapport between us. Even if we wouldn't be lovers again, I'd thought that we could at least be friends. 'It will be brief.'

'I prefer not to come to the police station. I'm sure you understand.'

'Yes.' He didn't want to come there because it would bring back too many bad memories. I preferred not to go

24

to his house because it would bring back too many good ones. 'We can go somewhere else. I'll be in touch.'

'Sure. Let me know.' He ended the call.

I went into the bathroom and turned on the shower. I folded up my clothes and put the bloodstained jeans and T-shirt carefully in a bin bag. Maybe they'd want them for evidence of my proximity at some later point. If Forensics found any fabric fibres on the body, they would want to check them against what I'd worn to rule out that they'd come from me. My DNA would be all over the victim's body.

All this time I avoided looking in the mirror. In the shower, the warm water embraced me as I shampooed my hair three times, as if massaging soap into my skull would also wash away the memories of the dead man. Make me forget how his blood had flowed over my hands. How we hadn't managed to save him. At the thought, I grabbed the shampoo again and washed my hair for a fourth time. I bent my head back and let the water stream over my face like a flood of tears.

I put my fingers on the circular scar on my right shoulder where I'd been shot seven months ago. Now a man had bled out right under my hands. With loofah and soap, I scrubbed every centimetre of my body until my skin felt alive again. I still didn't feel clean, because I couldn't feel clean. I gave my hands one last scour before turning the water off.

When I opened the shower curtain, Pippi was sitting on the bathmat, looking at me as if she understood the insanity of her owner. As I dried myself, her green eyes followed me. She started a meow that was no more than a rumbling in her throat, as if to ask whether Mrs Owner was okay.

'Did I forget to feed you, sweetie? I'm sorry. Would you like some food?'

At the word *food*, Pippi dashed into the kitchen. I followed her. She stared longingly at the cupboard that held the Felix. The Felix cat looked just like Pippi but without my cat's cute black nose. I tore open a packet and emptied it in her food bowl.

Cat fed, I sat in my front room but didn't turn on the lights. In the dark, I stared out over the expanse of the canal, wider than the roads on either side. The houses at the opposite side, with their gabled roofs, were all slightly different, some with curls, others with steps, as if someone could use the gable to climb up the roof. All an illusion, of course, to make the houses seem taller. I liked to imagine that someone on the other side of the canal was looking back at me.

Pippi-puss jumped on my lap. 'You won't believe what happened this evening,' I told her. She meowed softly, as if she wanted to encourage her owner to tell her the whole story. I rubbed her behind her ear. My reward for stroking exactly the right spot was that she gazed at me with a look of undying devotion in her big green eyes.

A sightseeing boat came past, cutting through the water. Earlier in the evening, they would have served dinner and drinks. I'd been on one of those, many years ago. You had to eat quickly or they would dock before you'd finished.

I went to bed, even though there was no chance of sleep with this much going on in my head. The thought of the stabbing kept me afloat in consciousness rather than letting me sink into slumber. I wondered who the child in the photo was. I wondered what had happened to the woman whom Piotr Mazur had been in the bar with. Had she killed him? Had she seen everything? Was she the reason he'd been attacked?

I tossed and turned until even Pippi got off the bed. I checked my alarm clock; it was just after 3 a.m. I was too warm and covered in sweat, even though all my windows were open. I got up and took the duvet out of the cover. I lay on my back, covered only by the sheet, unmoving like the dead.

I could see us in sharp outline as if we were in high defin-ition. I stood with Ingrid and a masked man in a field, the three of us forming a triangle of people in long black coats with guns pointed at each other. The knee-high grass swayed slowly and made an incongruously pastoral setting for the cinematic armed stand-off. The wind made my coat flap against my boots. It was louder than my breathing. Louder than my heartbeat. Even though the man's face was con-cealed, I knew who he was. He wasn't looking at me. He was facing Ingrid. His gun was pointed at her.

But she and I both had the man in our sights. Two against one. I could feel the extreme weight of my gun in my hand. My finger was glued to the trigger and I had to battle not to pull it. Ingrid, please shoot, I thought, please shoot so that I don't have to.

Instead Ingrid lowered her gun and just stared at the man. Did she know something that I didn't? Was she confident that she wasn't going to be harmed? I was sure the man was going to kill her. It was now entirely up to me to save her life. I had to neutralise him. The word seemed right. I looked along the extended barrel of my gun. Only if I killed him would Ingrid live. That was the trade-off. I exhaled and allowed the movement of my finger on the trigger.

It didn't fully register that the masked man had lowered his gun. I didn't even really notice Ingrid's face, relieved that it was over. Instead I was so in the moment that I continued to pull the trigger. The bang was deafeningly loud, like a close thunderclap. The recoil jarred my shoulder. Part of me realised that my gun didn't normally make that sound. That it wasn't normally this heavy. That there was something very wrong. Through a cloud of smoke I saw the masked man slump to the ground.

Ingrid kneeled by his body. I turned away from him and looked into Mark's eyes, staring at me in judgement. Like he had stared at me when I'd held a T-shirt to Piotr Mazur's stomach. I looked down at my body and saw that I was covered in blood splatter.

I woke up with a start. My heart was racing. 'That wasn't what happened,' I said out loud into the dark room to scare the dream away. 'He didn't lower his gun. He was going to kill her. I had no choice.' I tried to laugh at my dream for turning a traumatic work situation into a Tarantino movie. It sounded more like a sob.

At the sound, the cat meowed at me from the bottom of the bed as if she agreed with me.

Ingrid had said that seeing me covered in blood had brought it all back to her. The incident had been declared legal by the official review committee, but it had damaged us both.

I was afraid to go back to sleep and I was relieved when the morning light started to peek over the top of the curtains.

My hair this morning was sticking out in all directions, as if last night had turned me into a hedgehog. If I hadn't had it cut yesterday, I could just have tied it back. Now I had to splash water on my head and dry my hair straight. My eyes were small compared to the dark circles underneath. I had a thumping headache and looked every day of my forty-three years this morning. Every wrinkle was etched deeply into my face. I made some coffee, took a couple of paracetamol tablets and sat at the kitchen table. I should have eaten more than just snacks last night. Or had less to drink. I sipped from my coffee in the hope that it would make the painkillers kick in and chase the hangover away.

I finally got dressed and put on some make-up to brighten my face. I had to remember to pick up my bike at some point. Now I had to walk to work. Tiredness stung my eyes like grit and I put my sunglasses on. I was probably the only one who didn't welcome the morning sunshine. My route along the canal was a slalom course of early-morning tourists. I skirted past a large group of Italian people following a woman carrying a red umbrella, on their way to the Rijksmuseum. I narrowly avoided a man who stepped in front of me to take a photo of a picturesque furniture shop.

The police station came into view, solid and unmovable. I swiped my card through the reader and watched the entry light flash green. Our office was two floors up and I took the steps two at a time. When I came past Chief Inspector Moerdijk's office, his voice sounded out from behind the half-closed door. 'Lotte, have you got a minute?'

Chapter Three

The boss's words weren't a question but a summons. I pushed the door open and stepped inside. He'd torn a ligament in his left knee a few weeks ago and his doctor had prescribed two months without exercise. Not running had put five kilos on him. Now he actually looked healthy. His face had filled out and it suited him. I knew he was counting the days until he could return to his passion.

'You heard what happened last night?' I remained standing, hesitant to take the chair that wasn't offered.

'Yes. A terrible end to a summer evening.'

The muscles around my jaw tightened. I took my sunglasses from my head, where I had been using them to keep my hair out of my face, and shoved them in my handbag.

'Ingrid told me you got a good look at the main suspect?'

'I saw the victim in the bar with a woman and I saw them leave together.'

The boss frowned at my choice of words. 'You don't think she killed him?'

'She could have done. But I don't know where she would have kept the murder weapon. In the pocket of her jacket? And when they were in the bar, they were just talking.' I shrugged. 'Still, we don't have anything to go on apart from this woman. We need to talk to her. I guess we haven't managed to find her?'

'No, no sign of her.' The boss stretched his arms above his head and groaned as if even this little movement was now an effort. 'We got a very good description of her from the barman.' He leaned forward and placed his elbows on his desk. There was a slight smile on his lips and I could almost see the question on his face; he wanted to know why I'd been in that bar, but it wouldn't be appropriate to ask. Luckily whatever was on his computer screen became more interesting than my private life and he turned to his keyboard and started typing.

It was the perfect time to get permission to escape. I knew he would have practically forgotten that I was still there. Ingrid had once said that she was sure the CI spent most of his time on Facebook. He was probably just addicted to email and had to read anything new that turned up in his inbox, regardless of who was nervously waiting in his office. I'd read somewhere that the ping of new email gave people a little boost of endorphins. The boss needed that, now that he didn't get it from running any more.

'Anything else?' I said.

'No, that's it.' His eyes didn't leave the screen. It was amazing to think that my father had retired from the police force before the majority of the work involved computers. Apart from accessing the central database, I wasn't sure what he would have used a computer for. Even now he would send me emails that read like long letters. Only recently had he realised that you were supposed to type above the message you were replying to rather than underneath.

'Thanks, boss.' I took a step back towards the door.

'Oh, just one thing: make sure you take it easy. It's tough to see what you witnessed last night.'

'Sure.' The man died. I hadn't managed to keep him alive. Now all I could do was make sure I caught whoever had done it.

I walked the rest of the blue-carpeted corridor to get to our office.

Ingrid and Thomas were already at their desks. As soon as Ingrid saw me, she got up as if to give me a hug, but then stopped herself. 'Are you okay?' she said.

'I'm fine. Thanks, Ingrid.' I put my handbag on my desk. 'No sign of that woman?'

Thomas shook his head. 'No, none.' With his dark hair slicked back from his pretty-boy face, he looked like a boy-band singer who hadn't aged too badly. He wore a sky-blue shirt. He always wore a blue shirt, as his wife had once told him it brought out the colour of his eyes. He pushed a picture across to me. 'Is that her?'

It was a shot from a security camera. It was grainy but recognisably the woman in the floral dress. 'Yes, that's her,' I said. 'Is this from the bar?'

'Yes. From last night.' Thomas stuck the picture on the whiteboard at the far end of our office. A photo of Piotr Mazur was already on there. It was a copy of the picture on his security pass.

'What did the pathologist say?'

'Three stab wounds. Two in his stomach and one through the left lung,' Ingrid said.

I nodded. That was what the doctor had said last night as well.

'What time did he leave the bar?' Thomas asked.

'It was twenty past ten when I heard Nathan Derez shout for help. That wasn't long after Piotr and the woman left the bar.'

'Okay. Did you see where they went?'

'Yes, they turned left into the Korte de Wittekade.'

'Where he was killed.'

'Yes.'

'You didn't hear anything?'

'To be honest, Thomas, I wasn't really paying attention. But Nathan, the guy who found the victim, said he hadn't heard a thing. No argument, no commotion.' I noticed that one thing was missing from the board. 'Where's the photo of the child?'

'Forensics are testing it,' Ingrid said. 'Because you thought the woman might have given it to him. They're looking for fingerprints. We spoke to his parents last night. They are still in Poland. They told me he doesn't have any children. But then they also said he didn't have a girlfriend and we found this.' She held up Piotr's phone. 'With a whole bunch of texts on it. Look here.'

I read them as she scrolled through them.

I need u now. U want it 2.

Where are u? I'll give u what u want.

'The caller is stored as a Natalie,' Thomas said. 'But

without any other contact details. We're tracing the number. We rang it but it went straight to voicemail.'

'You think this Natalie is the woman in the floral dress?'

Ingrid nodded. 'It could well be, couldn't it? Thomas and I are going to search Piotr Mazur's flat.'

'Fine. Then I'll go to the department store.'

'No, don't worry,' Ingrid said. 'Why don't you stay here, try calling this number again. You need to take it easy,' she clarified.

'I'm not an invalid,' I said. 'I'll go to the department store and talk to some of his colleagues. If I find out anything about this Natalie or if anybody recognises the woman, I'll call you guys straight away.'

As soon as I stepped out of the police station to get my bike, the bright light hit my eyes. It wasn't even ten o'clock yet but it was already warm, and I was extremely grateful for my sunglasses. The sky was Delft blue, only broken by the vapour trail of a plane overhead. I got on the tram to go back to the bar. Two stops later, a middle-aged couple got on. The woman held the man's hand and pulled him through the door. She put first her card against the scanner and then his. The man's grey hair rose up from his forehead. She had a worried expression that seemed prematurely superglued to her face. She pushed the man ahead of her onto an empty seat. I realised that they were not that much older than me. Seeing them made me feel ancient.

During the rest of the twenty-minute tram ride, it seemed I only saw smiling people all around me. In a country where it rained so often, a sunny summer day was like a public holiday. My bike was miraculously still where I'd left it. I unchained it and walked along the canal to where Piotr had been killed last night. I stood by the crime-scene tape, at exactly the same spot as where Mark had been when I'd last seen him. When he'd stared at me. A white line showed where Piotr's body had been. Why hadn't he shouted out when he'd been stabbed? The terrace was far enough away that the sound might not have carried over our conversation or that of the table next to us, but surely Nathan should have heard something. It was such a warm night that everybody had their windows open. Had Piotr not put up a fight? There had only been the three stab wounds, and I couldn't remember any cuts on his hands indicating defence wounds. I would have to check that in the pathologist's report. The killer must have taken him completely unawares and that might point towards the woman in the floral dress. Maybe Piotr hadn't thought she was the type to do this. Or were we looking in the wrong direction?

I got on my bike and cycled to the department store. I had called ahead to Piotr's boss to let him know that I wanted to talk to him.

The building had been newly refurbished and the outside was as glossy as the products they sold. Tourists would come in to buy something small and almost affordable, to get one of the easily recognisable green plastic bags. In the shop windows, between the mirrored glass panels, mannequins wore outfits that would cost me a month's net salary. The glass walls of the large building bounced rays of sun back into the street. The extra light added definition to the tram that rattled past. The pavement in front of the store thronged with people. It was surely too nice a day to go shopping. If I hadn't had to work, I might have gone to the beach.

Piotr Mazur's boss had told me to use the lift at the back of the shop and take it up to the sixth floor. It was clear from its tucked-away position that the store preferred shoppers to use the central escalators instead. That way they would be tempted by the items sold on each of the floors that they passed. The escalators only went as far as the fifth floor.

The lift was small, and luckily nobody else got in. When I reached the sixth floor and the doors opened, I stepped out into a wall of warmth. The heat from all the other floors had risen and the sun was pounding down on the roof. Sweat started to form in my armpits.

Kevin Haanen, the security manager, had his office just to the left. He wiped his hand on his trousers before holding it out to me but it was still moist when I shook it. He wore a dark suit and his tie was the exact green of the shop's plastic bags. It was surely too warm for these clothes. I was glad I wore a T-shirt and linen trousers. If I had to be here for a while, I would melt.

'I won't take much of your time,' I said. 'Can you just tell me' – I held out the photo of the woman in the floral dress – 'if you recognise this woman.'

Kevin held up the photo to the light. 'Never seen her before,' he said. 'Definitely doesn't work here.'

'Never seen her with Piotr?' I asked.

He pursed his lips and shook his head thoughtfully. 'No, but check with the others. I don't do the rounds with them all day, of course, so he might have told them what he never mentioned to me. Just follow me to the control room.'

We walked down a corridor with dark-brown carpet that looked as if it had been on this floor since the seventies. He opened a door to the right. 'Alex,' he said, 'do you have a minute?'

The security guards' office was depressing. There was no other word for it. I wouldn't need to stretch out my arms far to touch the ceiling. The cloth of the nearest chair was covered with stains that I hoped were coffee, very similar in colour to the carpet, and the seat was frayed at the edges. The only thing that was new and shiny in this area was the bank of screens. They seemed to have been transported from a high-tech firm and planted on the sixth floor of the department store. It was what I imagined the flight deck at traffic control at an airport would look like.

The young man dragged himself away from the screen that he had been watching as intently as if it was showing the World Cup final. As he turned round, over his shoulder I could see that the camera showed the outside of a row of changing rooms. 'What's up?'

I showed my ID and said my name.

'Alex van Maren.' Alex was young, early twenties, with short-cropped blonde hair that gave his face a vaguely military hint. Piotr's haircut had been similar and I wondered if they went to the same hairdresser. The security guard's freckled face pulled lines of curiosity. 'Are you the detective who was there last night? When Piotr got stabbed?'

I nodded. I showed my photo again. 'Do you know this woman?'

He took the picture and stared at it. 'Never seen her.'

'Doesn't work here?'

He shook his head. 'Don't think I've seen her on there either.' He gestured with a thumb towards the bank of screens behind him.

'You'd remember everybody?'

'I'd remember if she'd stolen something recently or if she'd met with Piotr.' He turned back to watching the screens with their mosaic of views from the various cameras that captured shoppers milling around. A young girl thumbed through a rack of trousers. A mother was holding a child by one hand and feeling the material of a dress with another. Two schoolgirls were giggling as they held up shirts against themselves. Alex's attitude became more alert. He pulled a walkie-talkie from a pocket, pressed a button and spoke clearly. 'Caz, check the girl in the striped top at the Nicole Farhi area.'

The girl he was talking about was in a corner of the area. I could see her folding a T-shirt and sliding it into the plastic bag she had with her. Caz, the security guard of this area, walked up to the girl and put a calm hand on her shoulder.

'Impressive,' I said. 'You clearly have an eye for it.'

'You get good at it. So much stuff disappears. You see a couple of people steal, you know the behaviour.'

I nodded. 'Anyway, how well did you know Piotr?'

'Not that well at all. I've been here only a few weeks. I was at de Bijenkorf before. But speak to Ronald. He and Piotr were mates, I think.'

'Ronald?'

'My colleague.' He pointed to the leftmost screen. 'Him.'

I leaned forward to have a close look at the man. Even from behind I recognised him. My breakfast jumped around in my stomach. He was watching the exit next to one of the perfume counters. On the screen, he looked like an extra in a cop show. The expendable one. I shuddered.

'I can ask him to come up.' Alex's index finger was poised above a button.

'No, I'll go down.' I was keen to get out of this room. The warmth made my hangover a lot worse. I hadn't known that Ronald worked here.

I went back to the ground floor and skirted between women looking at cosmetics. I walked up to the perfume counter, which was a whole new assault on my senses. It had been over six months ago that I'd seen Ronald de Boer last, when he'd still been a police officer. When we'd worked on a case together. If I ever needed a reminder of what life after the police force could be like, it stood right in front of me: a fifty-something-year-old security guard. Regardless of the smart suit, it screamed of failure. The taste in my mouth was that of vindication.

'Ronald,' I said. 'Can I talk to you for a second?'

He turned around. I'd expected more surprise, but his grey eyes looked steadily into mine. He wore a black shirt under a black suit with a black tie. The security guards' outfit was clearly designed to fit in with the other men here. The only giveaway was a discreet wire that snaked from the top pocket of his jacket to his ear. Alex had probably warned him that I was coming down. 'Lotte,' he said. He stuck his hand out to shake mine.

I didn't take it.

He kept it hanging in the air for a few seconds before scratching the back of his head with it. His face was pale compared to the suntanned tourists. Maybe it was because he patrolled inside the department store and never saw sunlight, or because his colleague had died.

'I was so shocked about Piotr,' he said. 'He was a good guy.'

'Do you know this woman?' I showed him the picture.

He took it and studied it closely. 'Never seen her before.' He handed it back to me.

'Did Piotr have a child?'

Ronald laughed. 'I'd be extremely surprised. Why do you think that?'

'He had a photo of a small child in his wallet. I think this woman' – I pointed at the photo – 'gave it to him.'

'No idea what that could be about.'

'What was he like? Piotr?'

'I liked him. He was easy to work with.'

'Do you know a Natalie?'

'We've got a couple of Natalies working here. Any Natalie in particular?'

'One who swapped texts with Piotr. His girlfriend maybe?'

'Natalie Schuurman probably. But she wasn't his girl-friend.'

'Quite interesting messages from someone who isn't your girlfriend. Quite explicit.'

'She's into fashion. Let's say she's flamboyant. She likes to joke. She . . .' He didn't finish his sentence but turned away to watch people enter the department store again.

'She what?'

Ronald didn't respond.

The air con was turned up high, and every time someone came through the door, I could feel the warmer air streaming in from outside. An Asian woman loaded with plastic bags marked with the department store's logo shot me a glance. She was clearly wondering why I was standing next to the security guard. Probably thought I'd been shoplifting and we were now waiting for the police to turn up. Caught looking, she averted her eyes quickly and hurried out of the store.

'You watch this door all day?' I said.

'It's like a really boring TV programme. And then I walk around a bit. Why do you ask? Are you looking for a job?'

'I've got a job. One of the ones you used to have.'

'This isn't too bad. If a security guard messes up, someone steals something. If the police mess up, someone can get killed.'

The feelings that had been bubbling just underneath my skin flared up. It was a toxic combination of guilt and anger. It wasn't about Piotr but about the man I'd shot. 'I didn't mess up,' I said. Trust Ronald to know those details and hit me with them.

Ronald looked at me silently for a few seconds before turning back to the door. 'Interesting,' he said. 'I was actually talking about myself. Exactly what happened in that bar?'

Last night was a much safer topic of conversation. 'I didn't see anything. He was having drinks with a woman.' I took a step towards the exit. 'So this Natalie, if she wasn't his girlfriend, then what was she to Piotr?'

'She's his neighbour. That's all. I think she got him the job here.'

'Is she working today?'

'She's on the second floor.'

I turned my back on Ronald, got my phone out and called Thomas. He agreed that we should interview Natalie together. He was searching Piotr's flat with Ingrid but he could come over after he'd finished the area that he was checking. I disconnected the call and threw a glance at my watch. I had time for a quick coffee in the store's air-conditioned café.

Chapter Four

They sold chic dresses in bright shades in the part of the department store where Ronald had told me that Natalie Schuurman worked. I could never see myself wearing any of these clothes. As I'd been having my coffee, Thomas had called me back from outside Piotr's flat. He confirmed that Natalie was Piotr's neighbour but said that the sign by the door had read *Natalie & Koen*. It was better to have a chat with Natalie before talking to Koen, and Thomas had left Ingrid by herself to look through Piotr's flat. He should be here soon. In the meantime, I continued to mill around feeling as conspicuous as a moth amongst butterflies.

I touched the sleeve of one of the dresses. The silk flowed through my fingers and felt cool to the touch. It reminded me of a holiday in Rome. I'd still been married and we'd stayed in an opulent hotel where the beds had slinky silk sheets that wicked away heat and sweat during sticky nights. I could have done with sheets like that last night.

The cat wouldn't appreciate them, though. The thought of Pippi sliding on the silk sheets made me smile. I picked up the garment, still on its hanger, and held it in front of me. The bottle green picked out the colour of my eyes and the material was seductive against my skin. Dresses really weren't my style. I should put it back.

'Can I help you?'

I spun round to see a striking woman behind me. Her blonde hair was so pale it was almost white, and it drew attention to her eyes, which were deep blue like sapphires. Her name badge showed that this was Natalie Schuurman. She wore an outfit that probably came from the collection of the same designer: a tight-fitting fuchsia cardigan over a tangerine top with a narrow dark pencil skirt. Her job was to convince shoppers to start buying their autumn clothes, but just the thought of wool on a day like today made my skin itch with heat. Natalie still managed to look like a character out of *Frozen*. The only thing to mar her beauty was a large bruise that hugged her left cheekbone. Even her thick make-up couldn't completely hide the purple edges. The skin underneath her eye had a tinge of yellow. The bruise was a few days old.

'Do you want to try it on?' she said.

'I don't have any occasion to wear it.'

'A special dinner with your ...' Natalie's eyes moved down to my ringless hands, 'boyfriend?' she finished.

No need to tell her that there wasn't a boyfriend and that there hadn't been one for a while. I was relieved to see Thomas come up the escalator. I showed Natalie my badge. 'I'm Detective Lotte Meerman and this is my colleague Detective Thomas Jansen. Can we talk to you somewhere in private?'

The professional smile left her face. 'Of course.' She took the dress from me and put it back on the rail, smoothing it carefully to prevent any creases. 'Come on through. This is about Piotr, isn't it?' She didn't look at me as she said it but concentrated on pushing numbers on a keypad next to a discreetly disguised door, painted black to blend into the wall. Behind it was a hidden storage area with a desk squeezed in. It was much more obvious once you were inside that what had seemed a solid wall was nothing more than plywood painted black. Boxes and metal bars full of clothes in plastic wrappers filled most of the room. There was only one chair, so Thomas and I stayed standing.

'We found texts from a Natalie on Piotr's phone.' I gave the number that the texts had come from. 'Is that yours?'

She leaned back against the desk but in such a way that her tight pencil skirt didn't crease. She rested one hand behind her. Her nails were polished in the exact same shade of pink as her lipstick. I was very aware of the tatty T-shirt that I was wearing. Natalie was beautiful in an immaculate way. It would take her hours in the morning to look this good. She stared at me without emotion.

I read some of the texts out loud. '*I need u now. U want it 2. Where are u?* Any of that ring a bell?'

The look on her face hardly changed, but her eyes flooded with tears that didn't make her mascara run. After a few seconds she managed to control herself.

'Yes, I sent those. Piotr and I had a bit of a fling.' She ran a single finger carefully under the edge of her eyelashes.

'Take your time,' Thomas said. 'I understand you're upset. You were in a relationship with him?' He rummaged through his pockets until he found a handkerchief and held it out to her.

46

She shook her head 'Relationship? No, it wasn't anything serious.' She sniffed at the end of the sentence, the way a bunny rabbit would smell a particularly tasty carrot. 'But it's been so hard ever since I heard that he was murdered. Everybody was talking about his death this morning and I had to pretend that he was only a colleague.'

'He was also your neighbour,' I said.

'Yes, but that's different. It's a relief to finally speak about it. Even if it's only in front of the police.' She shot Thomas a dazzling smile through her tears. 'Nobody knew.'

So Piotr hadn't told Ronald that Natalie was more than just his neighbour. Unless Ronald had lied to me.

Another girl came into the storage area and rummaged through the clothes on the rail. She was a brunette version of Natalie, and equally impeccably groomed, down to her French-manicured nails. She shot Natalie a look and lingered until she noticed I was staring at her, then she quickly took a dress and left.

'You and Piotr saw each other a lot?' Thomas asked when the door had closed again.

'Not really. And only here.'

'Here?' I looked around me at the small storage room. Not the greatest place even for quick sex.

'At work, I mean. Never at home. I'd text him and he'd come down.'

'But you live with Koen,' Thomas said.

'He's my fiancé.' Natalie turned to rearrange the dresses, spreading them out to fill the gap that the removed one had left behind. 'We got engaged last month.' She showed the band on her left hand.

'And he found out about Piotr?' I pointed at the black eye. 'Is that what happened?'

'No, Koen doesn't know.' Natalie held her hand against the bruise. 'This was just an accident. I bumped into a kitchen cupboard.' She straightened the plastic around two dresses. 'Please don't tell him. I love Koen. Piotr . . . well, he was just a security guard.' Finally happy that all the dresses were correctly draped again, she moved back to her position against the desk.

I pushed my fingers against the outside corners of my eyes to stop the sudden throbbing. '*Just* a security guard?'

'It was purely physical. I liked him, we had a good time, but I wasn't in love with him or anything.'

'*I need u now*, you texted him two days ago.' I heard the tension in my own voice and took a deep breath. I caught Thomas watching me. But I remembered Piotr's smile and how it had transformed his intense face, I remembered trying desperately to keep him alive, and now this woman who had been sleeping with him didn't care in the slightest. Sure, she'd shed a couple of tears, but all she was worried about was her fiancé finding out.

Natalie got her handbag from underneath the desk and took out a tissue. 'To be honest, the texting was the best bit. It can get quite boring here.'

I couldn't control an unprofessional surprised laugh at her callousness. 'He was killed last night.' I heard the sarcastic edge in my voice. 'He might just have been a bit of fun for you, and not as important as the fiancé who got you that ring, but this man has died.'

Thomas frowned at me.

'I know,' Natalie said. 'That's why I'm being so honest with you. I would never have left Koen for him. Koen is everything to me. Piotr was cute. I got carried away.' She shook her head. 'If I think about what I was risking, it was stupid. Luckily nobody knows.'

I swallowed down my annoyance. I had to keep my personal issues out of this.

'These things are never easy,' Thomas said. 'Being honest is definitely the best thing right now.'

'That's what I thought. I know it was wrong to . . . well, you know, to have sex with Piotr,' she whispered the last few words as if they were embarrassing to her, 'but he was so funny, and always full of life. He looked at me with his grey eyes and I couldn't help myself. He had this smile and it changed his face. But even when I was with him, I thought of Koen and felt guilty. It only happened a couple of times.'

'How long had this been going on?'

'A few months maybe?'

That didn't sound like 'a couple of times' to me, but I didn't say anything. The texts we'd found from Natalie on his phone were recent. He must have deleted the earlier ones. Maybe he'd deleted messages from other people too. 'Do you know this woman?' I showed her the photo of the girl in the floral dress.

Natalie took it carefully between her perfectly manicured fingers. 'Is this the woman who killed him?'

'How did you hear about that?'

'One of the security guards told me last night, after he'd been called in to do an extra shift. I think you contacted the store?'

I nodded.

'Then I googled it and read that you were looking for a woman in connection with his murder.'

'He was in a bar with her last night.' I pointed at the photo.

'I've never seen her before. Maybe someone else he was shagging.'

The word jarred with her perfect outer persona and made me wonder if maybe she had cared about him more than she showed. Was she putting up a front because last night he had been in a bar with another woman?

'Did Piotr ever mention a child?' Thomas said.

'A child?' The photo dropped from Natalie's fingers. She bent over quickly to pick it up. 'No, never,' she said as she handed it back to me.

'Are you sure?' I said.

'Quite sure.' Her whole posture was back under studied control.

'Do you know anybody who might have wanted to kill him?' I said.

'Nobody.'

'What about Koen?'

'Piotr was our neighbour. Our friend.'

'Where were you between ten and eleven last night?'

'Koen and I were at home. We didn't go out at all. Is that it? I need to get back to work.'

She showed us out. Thomas and I left the area and joined other shoppers on the escalator down.

'Let's go and have an ice cream,' Thomas said. 'You need to cool down.'

'Shouldn't we interview Koen?'

'His fiancée has just given him an alibi. Ingrid can go round to talk to him as part of the normal door-to-door.'

'An ice cream,' I said. 'What are you? A five-year-old?'

'It's hot. I know why you were like that with her.'

'And how was I with her?' I stepped off the escalator and walked towards the exit through the handbags. Not because I wanted to look at them, as Thomas probably suspected, but because I was avoiding the exit by the perfume counter.

'Angry. Judgemental.' He pushed the door open.

'That woman got on my nerves.'

There was an Italian ice-cream shop right opposite the department store. Thomas must have seen it on his way in. It was mid-morning and there were still empty tables outside. With this weather, in an hour the queue would be out the door. We bought our ice creams and sat down. Next to us, two teenage boys were holding hands under their table. They couldn't have been more than sixteen. Had I been into open displays of affection at that age? The boys didn't talk. They sat in silence, licked ice cream with eager tongues and watched the world go by.

Thomas wrapped a napkin around the bottom of his cone to protect his sky-blue shirt against spillage.

'We're skiving in the middle of a murder investigation.' I took a large bite of lemon ice cream and enjoyed the sensation of it melting in my mouth and cooling my head internally.

'No we're not. We're on a break. You needed it. I could see you were getting angry,' Thomas said, 'and I know why.'

There were too many reasons. 'I was with Piotr when he died. I couldn't save his life so yes, I was getting quite annoyed when his girlfriend—'

'Girlfriend?' Thomas interrupted.

'Well, whatever you want to call her. The woman he was sleeping with. His squeeze? That better? She didn't seem to care.'

Thomas bit the edge of his cone. 'It's not about that, though, is it? I know your husband left you. That he cheated on you.'

I smiled and shook my head. Trust Thomas to observe closely. Only this time he'd watched and drawn the wrong conclusion.

'You're even doing it now,' he said. 'Deflecting.'

'I'm not doing anything. I'm having an ice cream. I'm cooling down. This was your suggestion. And you're really wrong.'

A group of teenagers came loud as a storm down the street. They sounded high on the joy of summer. The boys next to me quickly untangled their hands.

'Even though she was cheating on Koen with Piotr,' Thomas said, 'that doesn't mean she doesn't deserve sympathy for her loss.'

It was her lack of loss that had angered me. How callously she'd talked about not caring for him. Her claim that he'd just been a bit of fun. That her fiancé was important and her lover wasn't.

I moved my chair to make space for the kids, but they didn't sit down with the two boys. Instead they waited on the pavement for the pair to get up and be part of the group again. The boy closest to me left quickly, without looking back. He had been absorbed by the huddle before the other kid had even got up. For a moment I saw loss flicker on the kid's face. In his eyes I recognised that desire, that longing, to make the moment last and to be a couple for longer. He dawdled after the group, on the edges, where the other boy was already right in the centre.

'You're married,' I said. 'If you found out your wife was cheating on you, would you hit her?'

'You're thinking about Natalie's black eye.'

'Would you kill the guy? Would you knife him? Shoot him?'

'I hope not.'

I took a bite of my ice cream and the icy sting soothed my brain. Thomas had been right about one thing: I had been angry.

'Seriously,' I said, 'if you found out your wife had had an affair, what would you do?'

'I don't think I'd be violent. I'd be distraught. My marriage gives me stability. I need it.' The biscuit of his cone crunched between his teeth. 'This is going to sound silly, but if it fell apart, I would too.' He looked at me. 'But you know that, because you did, didn't you?'

'Fall apart? Maybe. But mainly I was angry. I could have stabbed him. If I'd had my gun on me, I might have shot him.'

'You wouldn't have.'

'My ex got his secretary pregnant. Trust me, I might have.'

'But you didn't. You didn't even hit him.'

'No, I smashed some things of his. Of ours. After he'd left.'

'Very sensible. What things?' He nibbled the side of his ice cream, which was now down to half its original size.

'A clock.'

'You smashed a clock?'

'His parents had given it to us as a wedding present.'

'How symbolic,' Thomas said.

I laughed. 'Don't mock. It seemed very meaningful at the time.'

'Do you know that in certain parts of Asia, if you give someone a clock, it means that their time is running out?'

'That was probably his parents' view of our marriage from the start. It all seems rather funny now, swiping that clock from the mantelpiece.'

'Waste of a perfectly good clock.'

'Nah, it was an ugly thing. Best use of it possible.' I watched the street for a bit.

'What if Natalie wasn't the only woman Piotr was sleeping with?' Thomas said. 'Maybe the woman in the floral dress was his partner. Maybe that's why she gave him the photo, to remind him of his child.'

'But nobody knows anything about this child.' In fact, Ronald had said he'd be very surprised if Piotr had a kid. But then he also hadn't known that Piotr had been sleeping with Natalie.

'Did you see how Natalie reacted?'

'Maybe he has a family back in Poland,' I said.

'Not according to his parents.'

'No. True. Piotr was happy to see the photo but the woman was nervous. Anxious.' I remembered her tense muscles. 'Have you found anything at the flat so far?'

'He's got a lot of photos but none of them relating to a child or even a relationship. It was rather clean. But I was only there for an hour or so. Maybe Ingrid will find something.'

'That's strange. He didn't have any photos of Natalie?'

'We found a laptop and we'll go through that later. Our only lead is the woman he was in the bar with.'

'Had he been in the country long?'

'Over six years. He must have spoken decent Dutch, as most of his texts are in Dutch. He'd worked at the department store for the last couple of years.'

My mobile beeped. It was a short text from Mark asking when I wanted to take his statement. I shouldn't have felt as happy as I did; this was purely a legal necessity. It wasn't quite *Where are u? I need u now*, but I smiled at the thought that it was the second time in a row that he'd contacted me instead of the other way round.

Chapter Five

Mark and I walked side by side across the white wooden drawbridge that led into the Westerpark. We were perfectly in step and I wouldn't have to reach out far to hold his hand. Even before, we hadn't done that in public. I brushed my fingers against the back of his, and said, 'Sorry.' I moved sideways, closer to the handrail, as if that would prove that touching him really had been accidental. My heart thumped at the base of my throat. The sun was high and bright in the sky and turned life into a holiday.

When I'd returned his text to arrange to take his statement, he'd surprised me by saying that he was going to eat something in the park, close to where he was redeveloping another house, and why didn't I join him there. Now we strolled together past the buildings that had previously been a gas factory. It had been transformed into a cinema specialising in Dutch movies, as well as two restaurants and three bars. A woman with a couple of toddlers in a large pushchair came the other way. It was that time when morning transformed into afternoon, and the mother and children were part of the early shift leaving to have lunch at home. She smiled at me. Mark and I probably looked good together.

We took the path that led to the lake. Mark carried a plastic bag from the nearest supermarket. A baguette stuck out of the top. He could have asked me to come to the house he was working on and given his statement there. It would have taken ten minutes at most. Instead he'd invited me for a picnic.

A change of climate embraced us as soon as we were deeper in the park. It was cooler here than it had been in Amsterdam's centre. A quiet descended. We were surrounded by trees that functioned as a sound barrier to keep traffic noise out and make birdsong audible. The heavy planting of the Westerpark gave it a very different feeling from city parks like the Vondelpark. This space, designed more than a century later, was a nature reserve with room for wildlife as well as humans.

'I don't know why I don't come here more often,' I said.

'It's my favourite place,' he replied.

And he had brought me here. There was tension in my jaw and a tightness over my cheekbones as my muscles prepared themselves for a huge smile, because at any moment now something good could happen.

Tall reeds indicated that, hidden between the plants, way down below, there was a stream. In Amsterdam you were never far away from water, but here there was a pure quality to the air that you didn't get along the canals. Even where we'd sat yesterday evening had had that smell of overripe fish that hot weather often created.

'What did you see last night, Mark?' I said.

'Can we talk about that later?'

'Okay.' I tried not to think about work but to enjoy the surroundings. In the distance I heard the deep rumbling of an industrial lawnmower, and the wind carried with it the green smell of freshly cut grass. Here it was still high and verdant, dusted with buttercups and dandelions. It would be cut down later. A parakeet shrieked from one of the trees with the sound my bicycle brakes made when pressed against a wet wheel rim.

'Why did you leave?' I couldn't stop myself from asking. 'Last night, I mean.'

He put the plastic bag on the ground. 'It wasn't easy for me to see that man lying on the ground and all that blood.'

'It wasn't easy for me either.' Swifts drifted high above us, their black forms like shadows in the sky. They never stopped flying. They slept on the wing. Mated on the wing. I'd read somewhere that their legs withered away. Sometimes I felt like those swifts, unable to stop flying, unable to stop thinking about the violence I saw around me. Had some part of me gone? Did those swifts hate it like I sometimes did? Would they like to rest on the ground or sit in a tree in the same way that I would like to stop seeing crime everywhere?

'I saw him.' Mark's face looked tight. His eyes were intense. 'And you were holding a blood-sodden rag to his stomach.'

I noticed something in his expression that disturbed me and I had to look away from it. I stared down as if I wanted to closely study a ladybird scaling a blade of grass at my feet. 'I tried to keep him alive,' I said.

'Watching you like that,' Mark said, 'it brought everything back. What you do for a living.'

That pulled me up. 'Don't tell me you'd forgotten about that?'

'No. No, maybe not. My head's just in a spin right now. I saw you with that man and all that blood . . . I don't know. You scare me sometimes, Lotte.'

'I scare you?' I pushed my sunglasses onto the top of my head so that I could see him more clearly. I also allowed him to see in my eyes that his words hurt.

'I wanted to talk. I thought it would be good to talk about last night. And about some other things. Now I'm not so sure.'

A heron plunged its head into the slow-moving water and came out having speared a squirming fish. 'Talking always makes things worse.'

He looked down at my hands. 'You were covered in blood.' He shuddered. He actually physically shuddered. 'And it made me feel sick. I rushed around the corner and had to throw up.'

'You thought you'd take me on a picnic to tell me that?' My words felt bitter like bile in my mouth. I didn't want to hear how much I nauseated him. Anger was brought into sharp relief by the preceding moments of happiness. I brought my sunglasses down like shutters. 'Is this some sort of revenge?'

'Lotte, don't—'

'Don't what? You look at me in disgust. You tell me I scare you and you're clearly repulsed by me. Looking at me made you literally sick.'

'I've seen you outside my house, Lotte,' he said.

59

'We should skip the picnic, don't you think?' The laugh I went for almost turned into a sob, but I kept my voice steady. 'I'll come to take your statement later.'

I walked away from him quickly, handbag hoisted high up my shoulder. I didn't look round but I heard he wasn't following me. He didn't call me back. Had I secretly hoped he would? Had I hoped for one of those movie moments when he'd rush after me, grab me by the arm and stop me to say it had all been a mistake? If I'd hoped for it, it definitely didn't come.

I'd been stupid to think that as long as I stayed in my car, he wouldn't notice me.

Chapter Six

Nothing was as great for taking my mind off my fucked-up life as work. I forced myself to think about Piotr Mazur. When I'd seen him in the bar he'd smiled and his face had been transformed. Then someone had stabbed him and I couldn't keep him alive. And Natalie Schuurman, the woman he'd been sleeping with, had said he was 'just a security guard', a fling to get through the boredom of her job. That memory brought up the anger necessary to melt the lump of sadness underneath my breastbone. It still worked.

The murdered man had cared about that child in the photo. Seeing the picture of the smiling toddler had made him happy. His parents didn't know anything about his life. They didn't know about his child. Nobody knew about the child. Nobody seemed to care that much about Piotr's death.

I lifted my face to the sky so that gravity would pull the sadness back into the corners of my eyes. I rubbed the edges of my fingers underneath my lower eyelashes to wipe away any mascara that might have smudged. Putting on extra make-up for the picnic had been a great idea. I went into the police station.

As I walked past the interview rooms, I noticed a woman

in a dark-blue dress come down the corridor with DI Adam Bauer and one of his team. The woman didn't look my way but I recognised her. She carried the orange bag that I had coveted last night at the bar. Against the dark dress it made even more of a statement, and here in the police station it was immediately clear that I couldn't get away with owning something like that. It went perfectly with her dress and would look stupid with my T-shirt and jeans. What was she doing here? Had she seen something last night?

Bauer's stomach wasn't much smaller than that of a thirty-week-pregnant woman. That he ever passed any of the fitness tests was a miracle. He walked with the lumbering gait of a grizzly bear. Still, he and his team had an enviable record for clearing drug cases.

I hesitated only a second and then ducked into the dark of the observation area. It wasn't purely curiosity about what the woman was going to say; the longer I stayed away from my desk, the more of a grip I'd have on myself. God forbid Thomas would want to continue our discussion of failed relationships.

I flipped the switch so I could hear what was being said on the other side of the one-way mirror. The dimness was comforting. I liked watching other people. That had never seemed like a bad thing before. I got my notebook and pencil out of my handbag, then put my bag on the floor and pushed it under the chair. I leaned my elbows on the shelf in front of me, which was made from very similar wood as the tables had been at the bar. It had that classroom-type air to it, as if to remind the observers in the dark that we were here to learn something.

'Thanks for coming in.' Bauer trudged towards the mirror and inspected it as if he knew there was someone sitting here. Had he seen me duck into the observation area, or was he just checking that he looked presentable? Sweat stains showed around his armpits. Carrying around all that extra weight must be hard work on a hot day. Being this close, I could see where his collar had chafed the skin of his neck. He needed a shirt at least one size bigger. He turned round and pulled up a chair. His shirt was plastered against his back. If it hadn't been this warm, maybe he would have worn a jacket that could have hidden all his sweat problems.

'Tell us what happened that evening,' the man next to Bauer said. I'd seen him around, of course, but I didn't know his name. From the back I had a perfect view of his mass of pale-blonde hair that looked remarkably like the bottom of a mop. He sat slumped in his chair like a bored teenager at school.

I drew two circles in my notebook and linked them. They looked just like the large sunglasses that the woman had tucked into the front of her linen shift dress.

'I'm surprised you asked me to come here.' She wrapped her arms around herself, and the microphone picked up the sound that her two large bracelets made as they clinked together.

'You called us to say you knew where your friend got the drugs from,' Bauer said.

'He wasn't really my friend. Should I have a lawyer present?'

'That's entirely up to you. Did you aid him in the purchase?' He moved on quickly with his questions, probably

63

to get her to answer before she could follow through on that thought of a lawyer.

'I didn't get him the drugs.'

'Did you purchase any for yourself?' He had a checklist in front of him and poised a pen just above the paper as if to tick off any statement that she made.

'No.' She sat back as if even the suggestion was an insult.

'And you're certain he was after cocaine.'

'Yes. That's what he was telling us. We tried to shut him up but we couldn't stop him.'

Was she talking about her really annoying friend, the Beard? He had been talking about wanting drugs, I recalled that.

'Tell us from the beginning what happened that evening,' Bauer said.

It was interesting seeing someone else go through this standard investigation technique. Get a willing witness to tell you everything that had happened leading up to an incident and you were much more likely to get the full story. Talking about what had gone on before seemed to make them able to recall details more fully.

'My husband called me to say that a business acquaintance of his was over from Frankfurt and wanted to go out for dinner, and did I want to come? I wasn't doing anything that evening and my sister was at my place and we said: why not? It was a nice evening, it would be pleasant to eat outside, so we decided to go to Groen.'

'Is Groen close to your house?'

'Yes, it's within walking distance and we go there all the

time. But this time we drove – I drove – so we could drop Karl off back at the hotel.'

Karl must be the name of the Beard.

'Had you met him before?'

'No.' She pulled a face. 'If I had, I might not have gone. He was rather obnoxious. Loud to begin with and quickly getting worse as he had more to drink. My sister was starting to feel uncomfortable in his company and I knew she wanted to leave. He kept touching her, as if he thought we'd invited her along for him. I persuaded her to stay for one more drink. I'd get so bored otherwise with the men talking shop. Then Karl began asking about drugs and my husband was mortified. Especially because Karl seemed to assume that we knew where to buy them.'

'And you don't.'

'No, of course we don't. He said he wanted cocaine. Snow, he said, but I knew what he meant.'

Bauer looked down at a piece of paper that I recognised as a pathologist's report. 'He died early this morning of a heroin overdose.'

I stopped doodling. He'd died? No wonder they'd called her in for a formal statement.

'I know. We heard and we talked about whether to come forward or not,' the woman said. 'But there was a police-woman at the table next to us and she overheard him asking about drugs and didn't do anything, so we didn't think we'd done anything illegal.'

Bauer shot a glance at his colleague. 'How did you know the woman at the table next to you was a police officer?

'When that other guy got stabbed, she rushed towards the sound. That was rather odd. You don't expect a woman to get up from a table when you hear some screaming. Certainly I didn't. But she jumped up straight away and told the guy she was with not to get involved. To stay behind.'

My breathing quickened. I leaned in closer to the window, rested my elbows on the shelf in front of me and my chin on my folded hands. I didn't really want to hear what she was going to say, yet I couldn't pull myself away from the window. It was as if I was watching a TV series where you knew something bad was going to happen but you couldn't tear your eyes away from the screen.

'You heard all of this?'

'Yes, the tables outside are quite close together. You can't help but hear every word.'

'So this woman heard Karl talking about buying drugs.'

'At first I'd hoped that she hadn't. I was mortified. And she and the guy she was with . . .' she laughed and touched her sunglasses, 'let's say I thought she was paying more attention to him than to us.'

I shouldn't have been here but I was unable to move away. Listening to a stranger describe us was addictive. On the other side of the mirror they could luckily neither see nor hear me.

'They were talking all evening.' Her smile carried a hint of wistfulness. 'She was really into him. You know, don't you, when you see a couple and one of them leans forward all the time and the other leans back. But when Karl started talking about buying drugs,' the woman continued, 'she looked over at me with this disapproving look, as if she blamed me for having brought him there and spoiling a perfect evening.'

A perfect evening. But Mark had been leaning away from me all the time. He knew I'd shot someone dead three months ago. He had told me that a police officer had been jailed for eighteen months. He'd said he'd seen me outside his house and he probably didn't even know the full extent of it.

And then I remembered that he'd said I scared him.

The top of my throat thickened, right at the back of my tongue, and for a second I couldn't breathe. I hid my face in my hands. He couldn't have meant it.

The door behind me opened.

I had only a second to pull myself together, but it was enough. I pressed my fingers against my eyes and pushed the tears back. I picked up my pencil as if I had been taking notes all the time.

I recognised the guy who came in. In the light from the hallway I could see that he was smartly dressed in a shirt and chinos. One of Bauer's team, Tim Poels. I was truly grateful that it was dim in the observation area.

'I didn't know there was anybody in here,' Tim said. I knew his name because Ingrid had once pointed him out to me. She really liked him, but for all I knew, she'd probably never spoken to him. He was new and had only recently moved into Bauer's team.

'Just listening in,' I said.

'Are you okay?' He wore a pair of small wire-rimmed glasses, which he took off to look at me.

'Hay fever,' I said. 'It's terrible at this time of year.'

'What did I miss?' Tim said. 'I got held up.'

I looked at him in disbelief. 'Other than the whole thing?' That was why Bauer had looked at the mirror. Because he thought that Tim Poels was sitting here.

'You're just upset that we're going to take this case from you.' There was a smile in his voice and the teasing allowed me a chance to give him a watery grimace back that could probably pass for a grin.

'What are you talking about?' I'd watched Piotr Mazur die under my hands the other night. I had to keep working this case.

'Ah, so I haven't missed it yet,' Tim said. 'You'll cover for me, won't you? If anybody asks, I was here all the time.'

'Sure,' I said. 'Have my notes.' I moved my notepad towards him as if I was seriously suggesting that my doodles of sunglasses and the couple of words I'd taken down were useful.

'Did Karl say that he wanted to buy coke specifically?' Bauer was continuing the interview.

'Not then. My husband Paul, he told him to shut up. That we didn't do any of that. Then Karl went into the bar. I thought he just needed to use the bathroom, but he was there a while and he didn't come out and I went after him. Maybe Paul should have done that, I don't know. He was going around those guys wearing yellow T-shirts, asking them one by one if they had any drugs.'

The yellow T-shirts. I'd held one of those T-shirts against Piotr Mazur's stomach as he was bleeding out. I thought of how his blood had covered my hands. I remembered the thick metallic smell in the warm evening. I thought of Natalie calling him *just a security guard*. I picked up my pencil

68

and wrote down: *Talk to the doctor. What did he hear?* Maybe he'd been there when Karl was trying to score drugs. I had his name and I should give that to Bauer.

'Karl was so drunk at that point, I don't think he knew what he was saying. I apologised to the guys, explained that he was off his face and that he really didn't want to imply that any of them looked like dealers. One of them was getting quite annoyed. Not because of the drug thing but because of how Karl was pestering the waitress too. I was going to get my husband to drag him out of there and get him back to the hotel. I tried to talk to Karl but he kept saying, "I just want some snow."'

The woman continued her statement. 'Those guys were nice about it. They could see that I was mortified. I chatted with them for a bit to make amends, but when I turned around, Karl was talking to the guy in the white jeans. And the guy gave him something.'

'What guy?'

'The guy who got stabbed. He was the one who sold him the drugs.'

I stared at the window in disbelief. 'That doesn't make any sense,' I said. We hadn't found any drugs on Piotr's body, and surely Ingrid would have told me if they'd found any at his flat.

'But he didn't use the drugs then. He OD'd this morning,' Bauer said.

'I dragged him out of the bar and asked the waitress to get us more drinks. When that man was stabbed, we immediately left. I drove Karl back to his hotel, and my husband and I made sure he got to his room safely. He was so drunk he could hardly stand up. He fell on the bed and we left him there.'

'So that's why this case will go to us,' Tim said. 'It's a real mess.'

'Piotr Mazur didn't have any drugs on him,' I said.

'We'll have to have another look.'

Annoyance grew. 'Are you saying we didn't do a good job?' I was worried; the CI would be happy enough to assign it to another team. One case fewer for us, one more for the Serious Crime team to work on.

On the other side of the window, the woman started to cry. 'Then my husband called me this morning to say his meeting had been cancelled because Karl had been found dead in his hotel room.' She covered her face with her hands for a second. When she had herself under control again, she opened the orange handbag and got a tissue out.

'Take your time,' Bauer said.

She blew her nose. 'Sorry about that.'

'Are you ready to continue?'

'I feel responsible,' she said. 'I knew he had those drugs on him but I thought it was none of my business. That as soon as I'd dropped him off at the hotel it was no longer my problem. But he died.' She looked directly at Bauer. 'It doesn't matter whether I liked him or not. I let him die.'

I sat back in my chair and stared at the mirror. I bit my lip. I knew exactly how she felt.

The door to the CI's office stood open and I popped my head in. 'What's going on? Why didn't you tell me?' Rows of law books lined the boss's office. He probably kept them here to look more knowledgeable, but they were also indicators of having to do things by the rules.

He sighed as if seeing me here was the most inconvenient thing ever and dragged his eyes away from his computer screen. 'I told Ingrid and Thomas. You weren't there.' At least he didn't pretend not to understand what I was talking about. 'It was decided once this woman came forward. Pauline van der Heuvel. Did you see her?'

'Yes, she had the table right next to me. With that guy who OD'd.' I assumed he was talking about last night. I shouldn't tell him that I'd listened in to the interview. Best to keep that quiet.

'Did you witness him buying the drugs?'

'No, I must have been outside at the time. But he was talking about wanting drugs. Any drugs. Maybe he bought heroin.' When I'd heard him, the Beard hadn't mentioned coke specifically.

The boss shook his head. 'It doesn't matter. We can't take the risk. You know that other case is huge and it's still going on. If someone else is selling contaminated coke, then it could be that dealer was right and it wasn't his fault.'

The 'other case' had been Bauer's main focus over the past twelve months. Six tourists who thought they were buying coke but were given white heroin instead had died. Do a line of that and you could OD pretty quickly. When that was going on, we had boards in the tourist areas of Amsterdam warning people that they should be careful what they were buying and who they were buying it from.

Surprisingly enough, the dealer had come forward after he'd recognised himself from some security footage. He'd always maintained it had been an honest mistake and that he hadn't meant to kill anybody. He was a dealer, not a murderer.

I shook my head. 'We had no idea who he was until he handed himself in, and now it turns out we had the wrong guy?' If we had another case here of a heroin overdose when the victim thought he was buying coke, that would put that conviction in serious doubt.

'We have the right guy. There's no question about that. We've got him on CCTV with one of the victims.' The boss threw a quick glance at his computer screen, but it was still less interesting than talking to me. 'But the guy always claimed it wasn't his fault. That there was nothing anybody could have done because to the naked eye there was no way of telling the drugs apart. Unless he regularly sampled his own wares, of course, which he claims he never did.'

'Not his fault. Right. So this is now a drugs case?'

'If Karl Frankel had only OD'd, I would have wanted you to keep working it. But a woman has come forward to say that he wanted to buy coke. Now this is clearly a continuation of that other case and we need to treat it as that.'

I shook my head in disbelief.

'I heard you were there with Mark Visser,' he said.

My lips pushed together. 'Yes, I was.'

'I know you're old friends, but be careful what you say to him.'

I didn't trust my voice and only nodded.

'This is now a drugs case. Give them whatever information you have.' He looked at me over his reading glasses. 'Is there a problem with that?'

'I watched him die. I was there.' And it was what was keeping my mind busy and away from how I'd behaved with Mark.

'That doesn't matter. Give Bauer everything you've got so far.'

I nodded again.

'Are you okay?' the boss said.

'Hay fever,' I said automatically, the same excuse I'd given Tim Poels.

'It's bad today. My wife suffers too. Are you taking antihistamine?'

'I haven't yet. I should.'

'Now you can have a quiet weekend. Enjoy the nice weather.'

'I might go to the beach,' I lied. 'More sand but less pollen.'

'My wife says that the helm grass in the dunes is a killer. It always makes her sneeze like crazy.'

'For me it's not the sneezing so much; it just makes my eyes swell up.' Nothing like getting excuses in early.

I went to the office upstairs. I didn't have to explain to DI Adam Bauer why I was there. He didn't even ask. I focused on the whiteboard. Six photos were aligned along the top; six people who were no longer alive. 'The guy who's in prison killed all of them?'

'Is responsible for the deaths of all of them,' Bauer rephrased it. 'That's why we're taking over your case. We're not going to let ours fall apart because some petty dealer got stabbed to death.' He pointed at a picture of a man in his early twenties. 'He was the first one. He died fourteen months ago.'

I recognised where the guy had taken the selfie because of the corner of the monument that he'd managed to get into the shot. Evidence to share with his friends that he'd been in Dam Square. He held a glass of beer raised in a salute.

'This was the last photo on his phone before he died. We didn't really look into it much, you know, just thought he'd come over to do heroin. Even when his friend swore he never touched it, we didn't take his testimony seriously.'

'Because if he had, he wasn't going to admit it. He was an Aussie, right?'

'Right, but then there was another one a day later.' A fat finger landed on the second photo. Similar in age to the first victim. Looked Southeast Asian, or maybe Indian or Pakistani. 'So that guy's girlfriend' – Bauer tapped the photo – 'came over to Amsterdam. She told us he only ever snorted coke. Told us is putting it mildly. She screamed. Anyway, we tested his hair. And bingo. She was right. Regular coke use but no traces of heroin. Never used the stuff until he died of it. So Forensics retested the first guy and it was the same thing. Here we had two habitual coke users who OD'd on heroin.'

'Then the two the week after, right? That French couple.'

'Found them in their hotel. At least this time we did all the tests straight away.'

74

'As if we're not in enough trouble with the French over drugs,' I said.

'And finally the two Swedish tourists. The ones that made our man come forward. That was a year ago now. It's taken a while for this to come to court. Anyway, none of these people, or their families, are going to get justice if this case falls apart.' He hitched up his trousers, first at the back then by the belt buckle. 'Another drug dealer swapped coke for heroin: the judge might start to believe our man's claim that this was just a mistake, that it could have happened to any dealer, and call it involuntary manslaughter. That would be a joke. We can't have that happen.'

I handed everything over to Bauer's team. It left me with two days with nothing to do. Not even a case to work on any more. The weather forecast was for relentless sunshine.

Of course I didn't go to the beach on Saturday. In fact, if it hadn't been for Pippi, I might not have got out of bed. Maybe that would have been better.

Chapter Seven

The single sheet was as hot as a winter duvet. The open window brought very little freshness. I moved my upper leg so that my thighs weren't touching and it made me feel marginally cooler. My head was heavy and lifting it from the pillow would be too much effort.

Pippi meowed.

Gunk glued my eyelashes together and that slight obstruction made opening my eyes impossible.

I wasn't going to get up. As long as I lay here, silently, motionlessly, I wouldn't have to deal with anything in the outside world. Not address, accept, confront or acknowledge. As long as I kept my eyes closed, yesterday hadn't happened.

I fell asleep again but woke up with the thought that yesterday wasn't the problem. I had to turn time back one more day, to Thursday, and then all would be fine.

I could have got Nathan Derez to push the yellow T-shirt against Piotr's stomach whilst I held the phone and spoke to the ambulance. If I hadn't been covered in blood, I wouldn't have reminded Mark of what I'd done and then I wouldn't have scared him.

I could have waited and not rushed to Piotr Mazur's

side. I could have stood aside and not got involved. Yeah, right, when did that ever happen? When did I last not get involved?

Maybe now was a good time to start. I could stay in bed and Adam Bauer could sort out the murder. All I was going to do today was move my feet to search for the cool places in the bed and go back to sleep. It would make things go away.

I woke again with a pounding headache. Pippi meowed, louder this time, but I didn't open my eyes. She tapped my nose with a paw. Her nails scratched against my skin.

'Go away, puss.' My voice was croaky.

She tapped my right eye.

I flung out an arm. When it connected with her fur, I didn't swipe her off the bed, as I'd first planned, but scratched her head. I felt her ear, her soft spot. She bumped her head into my hand. When I stopped fussing with her, she tapped my face again. I knew from experience that petting her wasn't enough. This wasn't about love and attention; she needed food. I turned over, towards the wall, and pulled the sheet over my face.

She bumped her body into the back of my head. Against my will, it made me smile. My cat was nothing if not insistent.

I knew she wouldn't stop until I got up, so I gave in.

Was Saturday the most boring day of the week? What was there to do when you were by yourself and had nobody to talk to and no case to work on? It wasn't even 8 a.m. yet, but already it was too hot in my flat. After I'd fed a now contentedly purring Pippi, I sat in my front room wearing shorts and a T-shirt. I was sweating. Even with all the windows open, only a warm breeze entered. If only the wind direction would change and we'd get a fresh westerly that would bring us some sea air.

I opened my laptop. It automatically logged me into Skype and I saw Mark's name with the green dot next to it. So he was awake as well. Was he watching my name too?

I moved the cursor onto his name and clicked. The message box opened up. *Hello, how are you?* I wrote. My heart raced as my hand paused above the enter key. What was I going to achieve by sending it?

I deleted the message.

I'm really sorry about everything, I typed instead.

I didn't send that message either. The last thing I needed to do was to get in touch with him. I closed the Skype window. Better to take a step away from temptation.

I left the house. I'd got up earlier than the street cleaners and the road along the canal was covered with leftover junk; empty cigarette packages and plastic cups littered the area outside the bar on the corner. I got on my bike, followed the canal and turned right. That was already an improvement on turning left to watch Mark Visser's house.

I hadn't meant to go to the department store, of course; I had nothing to do with that investigation any more, but I arrived there as on autopilot. I chained up my bike and walked around the glass-fronted building until I got to the entrance where Ronald had stood the other day. It was still shut and wouldn't open up for another half an hour or so. The reflective windows made it hard to see inside. I rested my head against the glass and put my hand above my eyes to shield me from the sun's glare. Ronald was on the other side of the perfume counter, close to the escalator up. His back was ramrod straight and he was wearing his uniform of dark suit and tie. It fitted him well. He didn't look out of place in the upmarket store at all.

I tapped on the window. He didn't look round. I banged a bit harder and got his attention. I gestured that he should come my way.

He unlocked the door with a metal key and opened it a fraction. His face was as pale as it had been yesterday. He must be the only person in the country who didn't have a tan yet.

'We need to talk,' I said.

'Now there's a threat,' he said.

'I'm serious.'

'Okay, come in. I need to do one final loop before we open up.'

'You have all the excitement.' I'd hoped it would be cool inside, but either the air con wasn't on yet or it wasn't coping well with the unusually high temperatures we were having. It didn't get above 30°C very often in Amsterdam, and a high of 33°C had been forecast for today.

'You can join me on my rounds. You met my boss yesterday, didn't you?' Ronald looked up at one of the security cameras that hung from the ceiling.

'Is he watching us? Want me to hold up my badge?'

'No, we're good. He'll recognise you.' He set off towards the other end of the shop at the speed of a uniformed cop on a leisurely stroll down the high street. 'What's up?'

'You said Natalie Schuurman wasn't Piotr's girlfriend.'

He didn't break his stride but turned left and opened the fire door, which led to stairs down. 'She wasn't.' He didn't make eye contact.

This was another part of the store that I normally didn't see. The concrete steps bounced a damp coolness. I took the bottom edge of my T-shirt and flapped it to treat my skin to some of the colder air.

'She admitted to us that she was sleeping with him,' I said. 'You didn't think to mention that?'

He didn't reply; kept taking the stairs down at a calm speed and only shook his head.

'And your friend was a dealer. A drug dealer.'

'Did Natalie tell you that as well?' There was a hint of sarcasm in his voice. He took out a swipe card from the inside pocket of his jacket.

'No, we have a witness who saw him deal to her friend. That man OD'd yesterday.' I followed him down and stood next to him, waiting for him to open the door.

Instead he paused. 'Your witness is mistaken. Or lying. Piotr wasn't a drug dealer.' His voice was calm, as if he was stating such a well-known fact that he didn't even need to try to persuade me.

With the door still shut, I was standing too close to him. I considered taking one step back up the stairs to increase the distance between us, but that would be a defeat in whatever his game was. Why was a security guard also a drug dealer? Did he have to supplement his income? Maybe his colleagues hadn't known about his other activities. I didn't know what Ingrid got up to after work. So why did I doubt

Ronald? The dark circles under his eyes were almost as grey as his eyes.

'You look like shit,' I said. My voice had a hard edge. I felt a trickle of sweat run down between my shoulder blades.

He leaned against the wall and created more space between us. 'It's not easy to sleep in this heat.'

I put my hand on the wall furthest away from him. The concrete was surprisingly cool and I rested my back against it. 'True. I didn't sleep well last night either.' The hard coldness was pleasant under my spine.

'Try sleeping during the day.'

'You work nights?'

'An hour or so to go before it's the end of my day.' He looked at his watch. 'And I'll have worked for sixteen hours. You just caught me at the end of my shift yesterday morning.'

'You must be exhausted.' No wonder he looked terrible. 'Do you want to have a sit-down?' I pointed towards one of the steps.

'That would probably make me fall asleep.' He held his swipe card against the reader and opened the door to the car park.

He set off towards one of the corners. I followed him. My eyes slowly adapted to the low light levels. Two cars were parked on the far side. Yellow lamps sunk into the walls threw a sickly glow over the white lines that divided the large space into neat rectangles between concrete pillars. The emptiness made it hard to tell what time of day it was. It could have been the middle of the night.

'According to you, Piotr Mazur wasn't a drug dealer, he wasn't sleeping with Natalie and he didn't have a child.' My voice echoed against the bare walls.

'Correct.'

'What's going on here, Ronald?'

He approached the leftmost car of the two, a small red vehicle. I wondered why he was going that way and then I noticed the exhaust fumes coming from the back of it. The engine was running.

'You were a lousy judge of character in the past too,' I said.

He suddenly stopped, right in the centre of the car park. 'I made a mistake. A misjudgement. Are you going to keep throwing that in my face? Why are you really here?' The expression on his face wasn't quite anger, but he had a deep frown between his eyebrows.

I threw up my hands. 'Because I thought you might want to tell me what was going on with your friend.'

'I tell you the truth and you don't believe me. So what's the point?'

'Because if he was a drug dealer, I'll stop investigating.'

'Why? You still need to find his murderer, don't you?'

I shrugged.

'What?' He raised his voice. 'So now you suddenly don't care about his death any more? Are you really that callous?'

I was so angry that it took a couple of breaths before I could speak again. 'Are you dealing drugs too? Just like Piotr?' In the back of my mind, I knew my words were driven by the need to hit out.

'What the fuck? Are you insane? No, of course I'm not. And' – he looked up towards another security camera fixed like a gleaming eye on the ceiling – 'this is neither the time nor the place.' He walked to the stationary red car and knocked on the window. It lowered with a whirr and a gust of cold air came from the car. The woman inside was red-faced. She still had her seat belt on.

'Everything okay here?' Ronald asked her.

'Yes. I'm waiting for the shop to open and I'm just hot. I've got the air conditioning running.' She seemed mortified and closed the window again.

'What a waste of petrol,' he muttered as soon as the woman couldn't hear him any more.

'I'm sorry I came here,' I said. 'I should have known you wouldn't help me.' As I stomped off towards the elevator to take the official route out of the basement car park, I heard him curse behind me.

Chapter Eight

For a Saturday, it was busy on the motorway from Amsterdam to Alkmaar. As I drove north past the Alkmaardermeer, I could see that the water of the lake was covered with white sails. It felt as if the entire country was spending time outdoors. This hot and sunny weekend was tempting many people to the beach and I overtook quite a few cars stuffed to the roof with beach balls and windbreaks. The roads from Alkmaar to the seaside villages of Egmond and Bergen would be jampacked. At least I wasn't going that far.

This motorway reminded me of when I'd first met Ronald de Boer. When my father had still been a police detective, Ronald had been his partner. I'd reopened a case that my father had investigated just before he retired and ended up working closely with Ronald. I'd thought that he was helping me but his actions had landed my father temporarily in jail. Some of my anger against him was probably caused by a feeling of guilt, because I had doubted my father as well.

My thoughts were out of step with the weather. I ought to be thinking how lucky it was that this glorious sunshine was happening at the weekend and that I had two free days. Instead the thoughts tumbling in my head were mainly about death and drugs.

I hit Alkmaar's roundabout and then there were only a few turnings before I was at my father's house. I parked my car behind his BMW. Every time I visited him, I thought that no ex-police detective should live in a house this big. It had at one point made me wonder where he had got his money from, but now I knew it was all my stepmother Maaike's. I rang the doorbell, which made an old-fashioned ringing sound like a bicycle bell.

'Hi, sweetie, this is a surprise,' my father said with a wide smile. 'Didn't know you were coming.' The white stubble of his hair was in sharp contrast to his holiday tan. Maaike also paid for their long trips away. They'd come back from the Seychelles only three weeks ago. What was the point of being the boss, she'd joked, if you couldn't take a long vacation?

'Is now a good time?' I said.

'Every time you're here is a good time.' He opened the door wider. 'Come in, I was just about to have lunch. Maaike's at work. You can join me. Isn't this weather wonderful?'

I pointed at my shoes. 'Do you want me to take them off?'

'Yes please.'

I left my shoes on the doormat and followed my father through the corridor on bare feet. The place was immaculately clean. The carpet was as white as my father's hair. As he had once told me, he had nothing else to do when he was by himself.

'Did you read about that stabbing?' I said.

'Yes, I did. Sit down, sit down.'

I pulled out one of the chairs placed around the large beech-wood table. The chair had an embroidered cushion on it adorned with a picture of two kittens picked out in cross-stitch. 'Sorry, is this Maaike's chair?'

'Doesn't matter.'

The cushion made me too tall for the table. Maaike was quite a bit shorter than either my father or I. I pulled the cushion out from underneath me and put it on another chair. 'So yes, that stabbing. I was there.'

'You were?' my father said from the kitchen. He came out with a tray full of food. 'But it's nowhere near your place.' The tray contained jam, peanut butter, chocolate sprinkles, cumin cheese, salami and ham. He went back to the kitchen to get some plates, knives and forks and a loaf of bread.

'I was escaping the tourist hordes. The dead man and the woman who probably knifed him, they were at the same bar.'

'What can I get you to drink? Water? Juice? Glass of milk?'

'Milk, please.'

'And some fruit? I have bananas and satsumas.'

'I'm fine. This is plenty.' The large French windows at the back of the house were open and it extended the dining room into the garden. But the air that drifted in was hot and energy-sapping. I had some sympathy for the woman who'd been sitting in her car with the air conditioning on.

My father put the glass of milk in front of me and sat down beside me. He reached out a hand and rested it on my arm. 'Are you okay?'

I grimaced and took a slice of bread to avoid his glance. 'Everybody asks me that.'

'Because we care about you.' My father took some bread too and spread it thickly with peanut butter. 'I'm not allowed to have this, of course. I'll tell Maaike that you ate it.'

I laughed. 'Sure, I'll cover for you. You should watch that, though; there's a lot of saturated fat in peanuts.' My father had had a heart attack and was still on a diet and medication. I buttered my bread and put some chocolate sprinkles on top. I never bought them myself. Having lunch somewhere else, with someone else, was an opportunity to have something different on my bread.

'It's a shock seeing somebody die. You never get used to it, do you?' I cut the bread in half and brought it to my mouth without losing too many of the sprinkles. As soon as I bit down on it, I lost that fight and most of the chocolate fell onto my plate.

'You don't want to get used to it.' Somewhere inside the old man was still that young traffic cop whom I'd seen in the photos. My father had been quite dashing in those days, almost fifty years ago now, conducting the traffic and inviting cars to come forward with his white gloves. 'Once you see so much death that it no longer worries you, you're not human any more.'

'I guess so.' I picked up the glass of milk and washed the last of the chocolate sprinkles from between my teeth.

'Did you witness the murder?' He looked at me over his orange juice.

'No, I heard shouting and ran over to the victim. I didn't know that the assailant wasn't there anymore.'

My father nodded. 'I get that. You put yourself in potential danger.'

'That's our job.' I held my glass between both hands. 'Right, Dad? That's what we do.' My hands were shaking so much that I had to put the milk down.

My father awkwardly took one of my hands between his wrinkled ones. His calloused strength was calming, even if it was just that he understood. I'd missed him when he'd been away. Not having anybody to talk to about work was hard.

'What are you upset about?' His face was so close that I could see the patch that he'd missed shaving, right underneath his nose.

That I'd been there with Mark Visser and that the murder had spoiled everything. That I scared him. 'They're taking the case away from me,' I said instead. 'Because the victim was a drug dealer and seems to have sold heroin to a guy who overdosed the next morning. One of that guy's friends came forward and testified that he thought he was buying coke.'

'Isn't there someone in jail for that already?' He raised his eyebrows, which he clipped short because they kept growing into tufts.

'And there we have the problem.' I pulled my hand free. 'The boss is worried that the other dealer is going to use this as evidence that he wasn't guilty after all.' I dipped my index finger in the chocolate sprinkles on my plate and brought the sweetness to my mouth. 'Well, not guilty of anything other than selling drugs. He's going to say that it was an honest mistake and that he obviously isn't the only one who sells the wrong stuff because now Piotr Mazur has too. It's been his defence all along.'

'Do you think he's right?'

'I can understand why the boss is worried. The other dealer killed six people, all tourists, and we can't afford to let that conviction get overturned. But someone died under my hands. Even if he was just a drug dealer, I still feel oddly responsible.'

'But you did all you could.' He took another piece of bread and reached for the jar of peanut butter, but my frown made him pick up the low-fat spreadable cheese instead. 'Had you been drinking?'

'Just a few glasses.' I pushed my plate away. 'There was a doctor on the scene too. It wasn't just me. I feel as if I shouldn't care, but I do.'

'Are you not going to have any more? Have some more.'

'No thanks, Dad, that was plenty for me.'

'How about a satsuma?'

'No thanks, I'm trying to give them up.'

My father didn't laugh at my joke but helped himself to a slice of salami, rolled it up and ate it in one big bite.

'And there's something else,' I said. 'The woman who's the main suspect, I think I saw her give Piotr a photo of a toddler. I can't help but think that this isn't purely about drugs. That this child has something to do with it. Nobody is interested in that angle. So the case got moved to the other team and I'm going to be nowhere near it.'

He got up and carried the tray back to the kitchen. The meat and cheese went back in the fridge, the bread stayed behind on the work surface, then he pushed the rest of the tray in its entirety into one of the kitchen cabinets.

'The other team can take care of it. I'll stop thinking about this dead man.' I cleared the rest of the table. I took my plate and put that and the knife and fork on top of his. 'But I had his blood on my hands. Quite literally.'

'This bothers you.'

'Wouldn't it bother you? It's possible, just possible, that I could have done more. That I'm now responsible for yet another death.'

'Are you thinking about the other man who died? That time you discharged your weapon?'

'Discharged my weapon. It sounds so clean.' I paused. 'Let's just call it what it was, shall we? The man I murdered.'

My father looked at me with a deep frown between his eyebrows. 'Not murder. It wasn't premeditated.'

'Thanks, Dad, that makes a lot of difference.' My voice was sarcastic. I opened the dishwasher. 'Is this dirty?' On his nod, I put everything in.

'If you don't investigate this, you'll still be here next week, next month, wondering if you should have done more.'

I closed the dishwasher door. 'Do you know who I bumped into?' I made it sound like a change of subject. 'Ronald de Boer. He worked with Piotr Mazur. He's a security guard now.'

'I heard he'd moved out of Alkmaar after the inquest.' My father's voice was remarkably unconcerned. I would have been much harder on someone who'd tried to stitch me up.

'That doesn't surprise me,' I said.

'I'm glad you testified at his hearing. I think it made things better for him.'

'I didn't want to help him, but I felt it was only fair to tell the truth about what happened.'

'He did save your life. You were unarmed and he had to shoot someone. You of all people should know how that feels.' My father finished cleaning the sink and put the cloth away.

'If we're keeping score, then yes, on the plus side, I have to admit that he saved my life. On the other hand, it was his misjudgement that put me in danger in the first place.' It was hard to feel any gratitude towards Ronald. Because of him, I'd been shot. My father was right: Ronald had taken the gunman out, thereby making sure I wasn't actually killed, but I would never have been in that situation if it hadn't been for his blindness to what had actually been going on.

'And you've never made mistakes?' my father said, as if he could hear my thoughts. 'You really should forgive him. I have.'

I grimaced. 'After what he did to you? It's not that easy.'

'If I can, then you should,' my father said. 'Anyway, about Piotr Mazur. I know you, Lotte. You're like me: you can't let anything go. For your own sanity, you need to find out who murdered him.'

'How am I going to do that? It's being moved to another group.'

'Ask to be seconded,' my father said after a slight pause. 'Call your boss. You know it's the right thing to do.'

There weren't many people I trusted, but my father was one of them. He knew me and he knew this job. It was too warm to argue about anything anyway, or even to think things through properly.

I got my mobile out of my handbag and dialled the CI's number before I could have second thoughts about it.

That evening I sat in my front room with all the windows open. Ever since I'd made the call, I'd been calm. The curtains hung down limp and no draught came through the flat to give any relief. The only thing drifting in through the windows was buzzing mosquitoes. It was the price I paid for living on a canal. A trickle of sweat ran between my shoulder blades. Even wearing a sleeveless top and linen trousers I was hot. The wooden floorboards were lukewarm under my bare feet. Pippi lay on the floor stretched out as long as possible, but there was nothing she could do about being covered in fur.

I went into the kitchen and held the insides of my wrists under the cold tap for a few minutes. I stared at the water as it ran over my skin and cooled down the blood in the vulnerable blue veins. The boss had been hesitant about accepting my request but he had to admit it made sense. I'd been right there at the bar where everything had happened. That was enough reason to have me help out Adam Bauer and his group.

The doorbell rang. I dried my hands and pressed the button on the intercom. It was Ingrid. I didn't have to ask why she was here. I buzzed her in and waited by the open door until she'd climbed the three flights of stairs.

She hadn't even got over the threshold before she started to speak. 'The boss just called me. Is it because of me?'

'Hi, Ingrid, come in. Do you want a drink?' I still had a

bottle of white wine. I'd put it in the fridge on Thursday, just in case Mark wanted to come back with me. As that clearly hadn't happened, and wasn't going to happen, I might as well open it now. Without waiting for her reply, I walked to the kitchen and got two glasses down.

She pulled the front door closed behind her with a definite click and followed me. 'Lotte, don't avoid me. Let's talk about this.'

'Chablis okay?' I opened the fridge and took the bottle out.

'I feel bad about this,' she said. 'You don't want to work with me any more, do you?'

I stabbed the corkscrew in the top and eased the cork out of the neck with a satisfying pop. I liked the sound. I never bought bottles with screw tops, purely because I didn't get the same pleasure from opening them.

'I knew that murder had brought it all back,' she said.

I poured the wine and handed her a glass. 'Cheers.' I held my own glass against my neck. It was wonderfully cool and I sighed from pure bliss.

'I'll request to be moved instead. You can stay working with Thomas.'

'Come through. Sit down.'

'I've been trying to make it up to you. I know it was my mistake.'

'Ingrid . . .' I wanted to say that this had nothing to do with her, but that would be too harsh. 'It's not you, it's me.' Next I'd say we should remain friends. 'I was there when Piotr Mazur bled out. I saw the guy who OD'd. He had the table next to me. I was right in the middle of all of this.'

'You can give Adam Bauer your statement.'

'I feel responsible. You understand that, don't you?' My voice was languid. It was too warm for anger or annoyance. I was tempted to hold the cold glass against the soles of my feet but thought better of it. I'd do that once Ingrid had left.

'I don't believe you. Piotr Mazur was a small-time drug dealer. It's not the kind of case you normally get obsessed with.'

I drank some of my Chablis. It really was rather good. Mark would have liked it. 'It's great how you can use "obsess" and "normally" in the same sentence while talking about me.' I put the glass back against the veins in my neck.

She frowned. 'I'm trying to have a serious conversation here.'

'It will just be for a few weeks. Only a little while.'

'You're sure it's not about me? You're sure you don't just need some space? Because, you know . . .' she took a sip of her wine, 'I would hate for the team to split up. I would hate to lose my mentor.'

I could feel my face pulling into a grimace and put my glass to my lips to hide it. I held the cold wine on my tongue and only swallowed when it had warmed up to the same temperature as my mouth. 'It won't be for long. But when I get back,' I said, 'please stop treating me like you owe me something.'

'I have nightmares about it.' She held her glass between both hands. 'I see that guy again, his gun pointed at me, I see his finger twitch on the trigger and I'm frozen to the spot. I know that I need to do something but I'm paralysed. In my dream, you're not there and I die.'

'In my nightmares,' I said, 'he puts the gun down but I still shoot him.'

She shook her head. 'No, he would have done it. He would have killed me.'

I topped up my glass. Ingrid had hardly touched hers.

'But oddly enough, it's not about that,' she continued. 'It was my responsibility. I should have taken the shot and I didn't. It's made me question if I'm actually any good at this job.'

'I've fired my gun fewer than ten times in the twenty years that I've been a police officer. It's not what makes you a good detective.'

'But it's about being able to do it when you have to. What if he'd threatened someone else? What if he'd threatened you and I couldn't take the shot? What then?'

'That didn't happen. It's all fine.'

She leaned forward. 'I know it's on your conscience, this death, and I know it should have been on mine. That's what I feel awful about. That's what I feel I owe you for. Not for my life, but that you've spared me the guilt and are carrying it with you instead.'

Chapter Nine

I paused on the threshold of what would be my home for the next few weeks. None of the three men in the room looked in my direction. Their eyes were glued to the whiteboard at the far end of the office. DI Adam Bauer's broad back concealed the contents from view. Should I knock? Say hello? The longer I stood there, the more awkward it was. Maybe it was best if I just joined them. I took a step forward and my handbag bounced against the door frame.

Bauer turned round at the sound. 'There she is! Our temporary team member.' He said it with a jollity I could imagine him using with his favourite snitch. 'Come in. Meet the rest of the group. We've cleared space for you.' He pointed towards a spare desk opposite Tim Poels. 'You should have seen what we found once we started emptying it out. I think Tim's entire wardrobe was in there.'

Tim reached over to extend a hand across both desks. His handshake was almost too firm. He didn't show that we'd met before. We both wanted to keep that quiet. 'The woman who worked so hard to save a drug dealer's life. We're honoured.' His voice had a teasing edge.

'I knew what I had to do, because I heard you had to have

balls to be allowed in here.' Something made me say the words before my brain could question the wisdom of them. Not nerves. Something else. A second of silence, then a surprised guffaw from Bauer. Whatever I was known for, I was sure it wasn't my sharp repartee. The total attention felt like stepping into a hot bath, uncomfortable at first, then very soothing. 'Thanks for letting me join you.'

The third man didn't bother to get up. He just acknowledged me with a raised hand and said, 'Maarten Wynia.' Knowing what these guys did, he'd probably worked through the night and was just at the end of his shift. 'We even removed a pair of Tim's underpants,' he said. 'We didn't think you'd like to work with that in your drawers.'

I couldn't think of anything funny to say to that comment and decided to ignore it.

I dropped my handbag on the floor and pulled the chair back. 'What can I do?' My father had been right to tell me to come here. The sun was shining, the sky was blue and here was an important case to keep my mind occupied. It felt like a holiday.

'We should use you for what you're good at,' Bauer said.

What was I good at? The answers flashed through my mind. Watching people. But also pulling the trigger. Killing a man. My muscles tensed.

Bauer must have read the look on my face. 'I know you're great at looking at older stuff.'

'I guess so.' Some of the tightness the memories had brought drained from my shoulders.

'After we locked our dealer up, Tim has been monitoring the ODs. It was just to make sure there was nothing the defence team could use as ammunition. Let's look at them all again. We'd like to think that this Karl was a one-off, but if any other heroin ODs look dodgy, we need to check.'

I nodded. I could do what Bauer wanted me to do and still find out who'd killed Piotr Mazur. 'I overheard that guy Karl talking about drugs. Maybe he scored heroin on purpose.'

'No, we spoke to a couple of the guys from inside the bar. The ones in the yellow T-shirts. They said he definitely hassled them for coke.'

It seemed that everybody was a better witness to the events of that evening than me. No wonder nobody had contacted me yesterday to take my statement.

'You'll work with Tim. Is that okay?' There was something dismissive in Bauer's tone.

'Of course it is.'

'Maarten and I are going to have a chat with a few more dealers to get info on Mazur, just in case anybody has heard any rumours.'

Maarten looked at his watch. 'Not much point,' he said. 'Too early for any of them.'

'We still haven't found the woman?' I asked. 'The one in the floral dress who was with Piotr Mazur?'

'No, no sign of her.'

It was then that I realised there wasn't anything on the whiteboard about Piotr. Not his photo, not the photo of the woman nor the photo of the child. That must still be with Ingrid and Thomas downstairs. I could pick it up later.

'We should search Piotr's flat again,' I said. 'Ingrid didn't find any drugs.'

'Sure,' Bauer said. 'Do that, then check the old ODs.' He headed out with Maarten.

I started up the computer. As I typed in my password, I noticed Tim looking at me over his screen.

'This is going to sound stupid,' he said, 'and I don't want to offend you.' He took off his glasses, as if that would allow him to see me more sharply. 'But were you scared?'

I took my hands from the keyboard. 'When?' A strand of hair fell into my eyes and I tucked it back behind my ear.

'When you shot that guy. He had his gun pointed at Ingrid.'

I rubbed my forehead with the base of my hand. 'You've done your homework.'

'Everybody talked about it. I've never shot anybody. I've never been shot at.' He sounded as young as he looked.

'You want it to stay that way. I'm not particularly proud of it.'

'Sure,' he said.

But in his eyes I could see admiration.

A quick count of the doorbells at the block of flats where Piotr Mazur had lived indicated ten floors of apartments. The place definitely wasn't luxurious but it didn't scream crime either. Still, the sweet, flowery smell of dope was hanging in the elevator as we went up to the fourth floor. Just the kind of odour to get me prepared for searching a drug dealer's flat.

The corridor leading to Mazur's flat was open to the elements on the right, and I took a step closer to the wall so that the drop didn't beckon quite so much. Number 41 was at the far end. The open balustrade allowed a perfect view of the perfect sky. The railings had been painted an identical blue, as if inspired by summer weather.

Tim opened the door with the key that Thomas and Ingrid had used three days ago when they searched the place the first time. They hadn't found anything. I followed him into the flat.

'Wow,' he said.

I was assaulted by images of Amsterdam. The walls of the living room were covered with hundreds of framed black-and-white photographs, hanging side by side to form alternative wallpaper. They were all A4 size and the result was intense and overwhelming. These weren't tourist snaps but artful close-ups, blown up to expose details that normally stayed hidden.

'Not what I'm used to seeing,' Tim said. 'Murdered dealers normally live rather differently.'

There was a subtle pattern in the way the photos were placed. From left to right they zoomed in ever-closer on details. The row at eye level started with the spire of the Westerkerk and finished with the skull that adorned the church's east door to remind those entering that death was close and you'd better repent while you could. The row on the far wall began with a canal house and finished with the decaying grouting around a lone brick. I scanned the room. There wasn't a single person in any of the photos.

'Where do you want to start?' Tim said.

I could have stayed looking at these images for hours, to figure out where each shot was taken. 'We're going to have to take these off the wall.' As the patterns were still intact, I doubted that Thomas and Ingrid had done that, and if we were trying to find something that they'd missed, it could well be here.

'That sounds like you're volunteering. I'll take the bedroom. Who knows what kind of photos I'm going to find there.' He disappeared before I could even say that I could do with some help in here.

I puffed the hair away from my face. With my hands on my hips, I stared at the photos. I should take them down row by row and wall by wall. That way I wouldn't miss any and I would keep them in order. Somehow it mattered to keep Mazur's installation intact.

I pulled the sofa forward and saw that the photos continued right to the floor. If he had hidden a couple of hits behind each one, that would have kept him in business for a while. The bottom row featured the Vondelpark from the gates at the front to a close-up of a parakeet. I lifted that line of prints from the wall one by one and put them face down on the floor. Then I took the first one and undid the metal clips on the back. I lifted the cardboard underside, expecting to find a small plastic bag.

There was nothing. Only the blank reverse of the photograph.

I sat back on my heels. I'd been so convinced that this was where Piotr had hidden his stash that I could feel the disappointment into my stomach. Maybe this one had contained the hit he'd sold to the Beard, I told myself.

I worked my way around the room, checking twenty-three photos in quick succession. I got into a calming rhythm of taking the backs off, finding nothing and returning them.

I was on my fourth row and lifting a photo of de Bijenkorf when I heard the voice. It came from behind the wall. Right where I was standing.

'Don't you leave. Don't you dare leave.' It was a woman's voice.

I stopped with the photo in my hand.

What had they made these walls out of? Cardboard? The words were so clear that I could recognise the pain in the woman's voice. I listened in anguished fascination.

The man's response was too low for me to catch.

'I love you,' she said.

'You have an odd way of showing that.' The man must have moved closer to the wall.

I hugged the photo to my chest. It was as if I was listening to a radio play.

'You know I love you. Don't you love me any more?' the woman said.

I pressed my ear against the wall to find out what he was going to say. Why did his answer mean so much to me?

'I still love you,' she said. 'I'd do anything for you.'

There was a silence. 'And maybe that's the problem,' the man said. It sounded final.

'You can't do this,' the woman sobbed. 'You can't leave me.' Then I heard a scream and something crashed loudly against the wall.

The sound made me jump. I dropped the photo on the sofa and was out of the flat before I could even think about it.

These neighbours weren't strangers.

That woman was Natalie Schuurman, and she was arguing with her partner Koen. Did he say she had an odd way of showing her love because he knew about her relationship with Piotr Mazur? Piotr who'd been stabbed to death?

I had my hand on the gun on my hip. Domestic violence wasn't easy. It was delicate to decide when to intervene. In the past, one of my colleagues had been attacked by the girl he'd been trying to protect. I rang the doorbell.

The door opened a fraction. A man looked through the gap. His right hand held the edge of the door tight. 'Yes?' He was in his late twenties, with dark hair and a tight-fitting white T-shirt. He wore a ring around his middle finger. The rest of his body was hidden by the door. He was extremely attractive. He and Natalie would be the kind of couple who turned heads in the street.

'Is everything okay in here?' I tried to look over his shoulder to check if I could see her.

'Who are you?'

'Police. Can I come in?' I showed my badge.

He didn't open the door any further. 'What's this about?'

'I want to ask you a couple of questions about Piotr Mazur.'

Koen scratched his forehead with his left hand. A ring around his thumb glinted. It was a plain golden band. The other hand never left the door. 'I spoke to someone on Friday already.'

'We're just following up. There's some new information since then.'

'I really don't know anything.' He wasn't going to move from the door.

'What about your girlfriend?' I threw a glance at the names by the door to pretend I needed to check. 'Natalie.'

'What about her?'

'I'd really like to speak to her.'

'Oh man.' He pulled his hair back and smiled a bashful smile at me. 'You heard, didn't you? We were just having an argument. Some stuff got broken.'

Maybe if you woke up next to someone this good-looking every morning, it would get boring. Otherwise I couldn't imagine what Natalie had been doing with Piotr. 'I'd like to make sure she's okay,' I said.

'Sure.' He turned round. 'Natalie,' he said loudly, 'the police are here.' He seemed calm.

I didn't like that I still couldn't look into the flat. 'You don't have to let me in if you don't want to.' I spoke evenly, because domestics tended to escalate quickly. 'But then all your neighbours can hear exactly what we're talking about.' I directed the last words down the corridor, where another door had crept open. It was now pulled shut again but I thought I saw the letter box move.

'We have no secrets from each other here.'

'So what had Piotr been up to?' It was taking too long for Natalie to come to the door. Even though I kept my voice steady, I could feel my heart rate speeding up and adrenaline starting to pump through my veins.

'Nothing much. He was a nice guy. Pretty quiet.'

The longer that front door was only slightly ajar, the more I felt there was something inside that flat I wasn't supposed to see. Something to do with Natalie's black eye the other day, perhaps. My body was getting itself ready for action. I would have to push Koen out of the way and make sure he had no chance to shut that door on me. I wondered where Tim was. 'Natalie, are you okay?' I said loudly.

Koen threw a glance at me. 'Natalie, hurry up.'

'I'm coming,' I heard from inside the flat.

Footsteps came to the door. Koen opened it further and Natalie arrived at his side. 'Sorry,' she said. 'It's a bit of a mess in there.'

'Are you okay?' I repeated. 'I heard the noise.'

'Yes, I'm fine.'

'You sure?'

'Yes, absolutely.'

I scanned her face. No sign of new bruising. She was wearing a strappy summer dress. There were no marks on her arms either. I nodded. I had to take her word for it.

We talked for a few minutes in the corridor. They confirmed that they'd been at home on Thursday night, that they hadn't heard anything that might throw new light on Piotr's death and that they didn't know anybody who would have wanted to kill him. I had no choice but to let them go back into their flat.

Over the next couple of hours Tim and I continued to turn Piotr's flat upside down. I heard no more noise from next door and we didn't find any drugs. The place was clean.

We returned to the police station and Tim left to go for a run. That seemed a stupid thing to do in the heat of the day.

I popped down to the canteen to have a quick bite to eat. As I was eating my sandwich, I paged through the pathologist's report on Piotr Mazur's murder. Unsurprisingly, there had been cocaine in his blood, but only traces, so he hadn't used any on the evening he died. There had been no defence wounds on his hands or arms. I thought about his flat. Where did he keep the drugs? He must have had another place somewhere. I made a note: maybe he'd lived with the woman in the floral dress. Did she now have his stash? We needed to find her. Forensics had lifted a clear fingerprint from the photo in his wallet. It wasn't in our database, but once we found the woman, we would be able to tell if she had handled that picture or not.

None of the photos in Piotr's apartment had shown any people. We didn't even find a snap of his parents. It had been immaculate, almost as if the flat was purely there to display the photographs.

I went back to the office to do what Bauer actually wanted me to do and looked through all the people who had overdosed on heroin. I'd just pulled up the list from the central database when Tim came back.

'Where shall we start?' I said. 'Last twelve months? Is that too long?'

'I've got the list right here. I've been looking at these. Twenty-eight ODs on heroin across the country. Eight in Amsterdam. Can we rule out other drugs? Like the student who died taking contaminated MDMA?'

'Yeah, that doesn't seem to fit.' Eight. Not too bad in the scheme of things. I rolled my chair over to Tim's desk to look over his shoulder at the list he'd pulled up. He moved his coffee mug out of the way to make space for my notepad. I had to lean in to read the names on the screen.

First on the list was a sixty-five-year-old man. A long-term user. They'd found him with the needle still in his arm. Old school. 'That's not a candidate,' I said.

'And neither is his wife. Same age. Also injected. Died the same day. Maybe a suicide pact?' A drop of sweat rolled from the edge of his short-cut hair down his neck. 'Either way, doesn't seem to fit the pattern. Not with the needles.' He wiped his forehead. His shirt was glued to his back. I could see the shape of his muscles through the damp fabric.

He caught my eye. 'Sorry, I should have had a longer shower.' He picked up his mug and drank, as if that would rehydrate him. 'It was so warm outside.'

If testosterone had a smell, it would surely be this mixture of coffee and shampoo, with a hint of deodorant.

'Right. Here's a young guy of Moroccan descent. I remember him.' Tim pulled up the details. 'Maarten and I spoke to the parents. They swore he'd never used heroin before. Too religious to do drugs of any kind.'

Parents were always the last to know their children's secrets.

'He was found dead in a gay bar,' Tim continued. 'They didn't accept that either. But there really wasn't anything suspicious about his overdose.'

'Habitual use?'

'The boyfriend came forward and said they'd taken it together on occasion. Amongst other things. Mephedrone, if I remember rightly. The parents didn't want to believe it, of course. The father got aggressive and tried to hit Maarten.'

107

He shook his head. 'Gay and a drug user. Ruined every memory the parents had of their beloved only son.'

The next four were men who'd all had a long history of arrests and drug use. 'Those first two used methadone for a while. Didn't help.'

That left us with one more. A young woman, Sylvie Bruyneel. 'Such a waste. Only twenty-four.' Tim pulled up a picture. 'Cute.'

Not that cute, I wanted to say, but it would have been a lie. 'Very pretty.' I looked at the details. 'She'd had counselling.'

'Oh shit.' His voice lowered. The sweat drops down his neck multiplied. 'Her counsellor came in. I talked to her. She claimed it couldn't be right as they'd tested the girl numerous times in the clinic and found no signs of H use.' He wiped his forehead. 'We dismissed it at the time. She'd been out of the clinic for a couple of years when she OD'd. Who knows what drugs she'd been doing since?'

I rolled my chair back to my desk.

'We should meet with the counsellor, shouldn't we?' Tim said.

'It's what Bauer wants. Let me call her. Name?'

'Petra Maasland.' Tim read out the number and I dialled.

'She's not going to be happy to see me,' Tim said.

'Why not?' The phone was ringing at the other end and I kept my hand over the mouthpiece in case it was suddenly answered.

'I told her things she didn't want to hear.'

The call went to voicemail.

Chapter Ten

Sylvie's parents, Mabel and Harald Bruyneel, sat side by side on a large sofa with a bold blue stripe pattern. The curtains, made from the same material, were closed, either to keep the heat out or to keep the sofa and the carpet from fading in the bright sunlight. For the parents it was too late; they'd lost their colour years ago. They sat close together, their arms linked to harness themselves against the bad news that a visit by the police often proved to be for the families of drug addicts. Even six months after their daughter's death they automatically assumed this parental bracing position. They matched like a salt-and-pepper set. Their identical haircut was slightly long for a man but brutally short for a woman. Their hair was that in-between colour that would look blonde in sunshine but washed-out brown inside the house. They both wore grey shorts that ended just above the knee, and polo shirts. The dog, fast asleep in a large wicker basket to the side of the sofa, completed the circle.

Tim and I had driven here after the counsellor, Petra Maasland, had returned my call and told me that she could only see us in the evening as she had clients all day. If we could come to the hospital where she had her clinic, she'd have time to talk to us after six o'clock. We could of course have insisted on seeing her straight away, but there was no point in antagonising a woman we needed information from.

Instead we were talking to parents who had not found their daughter's death suspicious. It was equally important to interview people who didn't suspect foul play.

They lived in a small house in one of the newer streets in Zaandam. The town was just on the other side of the Noordzee Kanaal from Amsterdam. Houses were a lot cheaper here. You'd be in Amsterdam in ten minutes by train. During rush hour it took much longer by car, as all the commuters from the north had to be funnelled through three tunnels under the wide canal, causing daily traffic jams.

Sweat glued my T-shirt to my back. It was stifling in the room and the closed curtains locked us in with the heat. I was dying to get up and open the back door to let some air in. I could also really do with a glass of water, but they hadn't offered us anything. We were on their side but they probably thought otherwise.

'You weren't surprised when Sylvie died,' I said.

Mabel sat so close to Harald that their legs were touching. He wore white socks. She had bare feet in her sandals. 'Not in the slightest,' she said. 'We'd been expecting that call for years.' Her voice was soft.

'When did you see her last?' Tim asked.

'When she came for money.' Mabel's voice sounded resigned. Quiet. 'That was the only reason she'd talk to us. But we told her no because we knew what she did with it. Allowing her to buy more drugs isn't helping, is it? We, as

110

parents, had to draw a line.' If she had been angry at any point, that had been worn away by years of disappointment.

I'd seen it often enough with the parents of drug addicts. There came a point when the continued lying and drug-taking had eroded all the love. Some parents stuck with their children to the bitter end, through rehab and rebound, hoping that this time they would beat their addiction. And sometimes they did.

But some parents couldn't or wouldn't. It was often the ones with other children to care for who made the hard choices. I'd read in Sylvie's file that there was a sister called Katja. Maybe it was to protect her that the parents had washed their hands of Sylvie.

'When was this?'

'It was years ago, when she still lived at her sister's place. She was used to having a certain type of life. Katja wasn't earning much, she was only temping, and Sylvie didn't have a job at all. She kept coming to us for clothes, for a new bike, help with her phone bill.' She turned to look at Harald. 'But we realised that wasn't what she used the money for.'

'How old was she then?' I asked.

'What do you think, Harald? Twenty-one? Twenty-two?'

'Something like that.' The words came out slowly, as if they took all the energy he could summon. He slouched on the sofa, his back rounded.

'She left home when she was seventeen. Sometimes you have to do what's right for yourself,' Mabel said, as if she was defending herself against an accusation I wasn't making. 'Even before that we couldn't cope with her any more. She stole from us, was flouting all our rules. We drew some boundaries and gave her one last chance. But when she came home at five in the morning, completely off her face on whatever, we had no choice but to show her the door. She packed her things and moved to Amsterdam to live with her sister.'

'So her sister had already moved out as well?'

'Yes, Katja's the eldest. She moved to Amsterdam as soon as she was able to afford it. She always wanted to live there. Things went well for her for a while. Now she's decided she doesn't want anything to do with us any more. She told us she wished there was such a thing as divorce for children.'

I winced. That had been a cruel thing to say, but Mabel was oddly matter-of-fact about it.

It struck me that there were no photos in the living room at all. Maybe it was the contrast with Piotr Mazur's flat. No pictures of either of the daughters, or of the family together. The wall opposite the TV was dominated by a large painting of husband and wife with their dog.

'We did our best with those two but it seems our best wasn't good enough. With Katja it was hard from the beginning. Sylvie was much easier, until she hit puberty.'

'What do you know about the drugs that Sylvie did?'

'When she still lived here, she partied and went to nightclubs. We think she was using cocaine and amphetamines at that time.' Mabel talked about the drugs in a slow and precise voice, as if she was speaking in a foreign language. 'She would come home at four, five o'clock in the morning on a buzz. And she was only fifteen.'

Was she hiding her guilt by showing no emotion whatsoever? Did she think she could have done more to stop her daughter?

'They let her in at that age?' Tim said.

'She always was very pretty,' Harald said. 'Could twist anybody around her little finger. She looked just like her mother.'

Mabel didn't smile at the compliment.

I kept my face still. Beauty was clearly in the eye of the beholder. From the photos that Tim and I had seen, Sylvie had looked nothing like the washed-out mother. Tim definitely wouldn't call Mabel 'cute'. Maybe she had been when she was young, or maybe her husband thought she was attractive because looking at her must be much like looking in the mirror.

'The drugs,' Tim started again after a short silence. 'Do you know what else she was using?'

'She died of a heroin overdose, so she must have moved on to that,' Mabel said. 'Probably when her sister kicked her out. Sylvie was stealing from her too, until even Katja had had enough. We had a meeting here, at the house, to discuss what we were going to do. We refused to pay Sylvie any more money and I think Katja was at the end of her tether. We told her that clearly it wasn't as easy to deal with Sylvie as she'd imagined, so she should cut us some slack.'

'We told Katja that she was going to end up just like her mother,' Harald said. 'We warned her, but she wouldn't listen.'

It suddenly dawned on me that when he talked about the girls' mother, he didn't meant Mabel at all. Were they his daughters from a previous marriage? Had he left a pretty wife for this female version of himself? Had his first wife been a drug addict too? It would explain Mabel's coldness towards the daughters, especially the pretty one who looked so much like her mother.

'We told Katja time and time again to be careful, but she wasn't,' Mabel said. 'And now, when all my worries have come true, she doesn't want to see us any more.'

'When did Sylvie leave Katja's place?'

'Oh, I'd say three years ago. Katja wanted to get her into rehab. We said that she should do what she thought was best.' Mabel exchanged a look with her husband. 'We'd washed our hands of both girls at that stage. Too much had happened. But Sylvie refused and Katja kicked her out.'

Tim looked down at his notes. 'But she did go to rehab.'

'That was later, and not voluntarily. She was caught stealing from her work – we hadn't even known she had a job – and it was part of her sentence. This was about a year after her sister kicked her out.'

I made a small drawing in my notebook to work out Sylvie's timeline from the mother's disjointed answers. She'd moved in with her sister at seventeen and lived with her until she was twenty-one. A year later, she was arrested for theft and went into rehab. Then we knew nothing about her for the next few years until she OD'd six months ago aged twenty-four. 'Do you know where she lived for the last few years?' I asked.

'Probably in a squat or a gutter somewhere. Or found some guy to take her in. There were always plenty of them around. From a very early age.'

114

'So when she died of a heroin overdose . . .' I said.

'We weren't surprised, no.' Mabel finished my sentence. 'You hear it all the time.'

'She'd been clean for a while.' That was what the pathologist's report had said. He'd tested her hair and there had been no cocaine or heroin use until the hit that killed her.

'Yes, and then she probably got down about something, maybe man trouble, and took heroin. Isn't it typical for people to overdose then? We read that somewhere, didn't we, Harald? That addicts go back to the same amount of drugs they used before, only their bodies are no longer accustomed to it.'

Tim nodded. 'Yes, that can happen.'

'It's such a shame it didn't work out. It's painful, of course, to know that you've failed, but you can't save them all. There are always high levels of drug use amongst them. Higher than with the general public. We were disappointed that she'd moved on to heroin, weren't we, Harald, but we weren't surprised. We had expected it.'

'What about Katja?'

'All those years, we really tried,' Mabel said. 'At the time, our friends told us we were crazy taking those two girls on, but we thought it was worth trying. They looked right, you see. But I guess they were always going to end up like that.'

'What do you mean,' I said, 'you took them on?'

'Katja was five and Sylvie three when we adopted them. Their mother had died young and the father wasn't around any more. We looked after them for almost fifteen years. I don't think they ever loved us.'

115

Harald put his hand on his wife's knee. 'Two children with their background, I think we just took on too much.'

I looked at the painting again of the couple with their dog. Was their life better now, without the girls? With one dead and the other no longer speaking to them? I finally understood the 'divorce' comment that Katja had made.

'I know,' Mabel said, 'that you never can tell. But there was no obvious damage and their hair' – she reached out and touched her husband's head – 'it was the same colour as ours.'

I was happy to leave that house.

'We'd better talk to the sister, don't you think?' Tim said once we were outside.

I called the police station and got the address. During the drive back to Amsterdam, I could only think of two little girls who had been selected for their hair colour.

We went to Katja's flat, but there was nobody home.

Chapter Eleven

The rattan couch was covered with thickly stuffed magenta chintz cushions with a pattern of roses. I sank so deeply into the sofa that I was worried I might never be able to get up. Tim had wisely chosen one of the firmer chairs. He'd probably been a victim of the sofa last time he was here. He fiddled with his pen, taking the cap off and putting it back on. A small fan whirred in the corner and blasted tepid air around the room.

Petra Maasland had decorated this space in her own image. Anybody giving her a hug would probably disappear in her flesh; her hair was grey and downy like dandelion fluff and her face as puce as the chintz. Only her jeans and T-shirt clashed with the floral interior. I guessed she was in her early fifties. She sat down on the other sofa with a small grunt, then shuffled from one bum cheek to the other to create a comfortable hollow in the cushions. 'You wanted to talk about Sylvie Bruyneel?' she said. Her blue eyes were sharp. She had openly ignored Tim when he came in, I assumed because he'd disregarded her concerns around Sylvie's death six months ago.

The surroundings were more suited to a boudoir than a counsellor's room in a clinic. Tim was too angular in this oasis of femininity. Maybe the female informality inspired confessions of a different type than he would extract in our interrogation rooms. Words that came from a sense of security instead of a fear of force. Whether those revelations would be more honest depended on whether you were more likely to lie to a friend or an enemy.

'You knew Sylvie well?' I said. Tim was still fully concentrating on playing with his pen. If he'd been within reach, I might have snatched it from his hands.

'I did a lot of work with her. She seemed to be one of the ones I'd reached. One of those rare success stories.' Petra met my eyes with sincerity. Counsellors tried to change people's lives.

And then we dealt with the aftermath if they failed. 'But she overdosed.'

Petra's grey hair bounced as she shook her head sharply. 'That's why I thought it didn't make sense.' She paused. 'Even though I know these things happen. I'm not that naïve.'

'You flagged it up to us. Why didn't this one make sense?'

'I don't know.' Petra shuffled forwards on the sofa. 'What are the police doing to stop heroin from being sold?' Her eyes flashed from me to Tim. 'Or don't you actually care when people die?'

He paled a little but didn't challenge her words. Beforehand, we'd agreed that I'd run the questioning, but that didn't mean he needed to stay silent. He took the pen's blue top and put force on the end with his thumb until the plastic snapped.

Petra blinked a couple of times at the sound.

'Tell me why you thought you'd reached her.' I kept my voice even, didn't linger on the word 'thought' as I'd wanted to.

'The month before she died, I told my husband that it was young women like Sylvie who made this job worthwhile. So when I heard the news, I was in shock.' She bit her lower lip as if she was trying to keep something inside. What was it? Tears? An explanation?

'She died from a more serious drug than she came in here for.'

Petra frowned. 'When she first arrived here, she told me that doing a line every now and then was all the rage. She didn't think she was doing anything wrong. Understanding her dependency was a big step on her road to recovery.' She pushed her lips together as if she suddenly understood what she had said. Because Sylvie hadn't really recovered.

'Coming here was part of her sentence?'

'Yes, the theft was her first offence. She got community service plus a period here in the clinic to go through a programme.'

'She was only using coke at that point?'

'And alcohol, of course. They often go together.' She looked at Tim.

The posters on the wall were a mixture of framed art reproductions and public-health notices. Use clean needles. Call us if you're thinking about using again.

'You don't think she used heroin before she came here?' I said.

'And she didn't use it while she was here either. She said she'd never used anything other than coke and some party drugs. MDMA mainly. She didn't lie.' Petra shrugged each shoulder in turn like a boxer getting ready for a fight. 'We know that because when our clients join us, we test them. On a voluntary basis only.'

I'd looked through the pathology report on Sylvie's death back in the office and had paid special attention to the toxicology section. 'There was heroin and cocaine in her body. No other drugs.'

'That's why I thought it must have been wrong. I came to check – but you know this, of course.' These last words were directed at Tim.

He nodded but didn't say anything.

'You were the one who questioned it,' I said. 'Not her family.'

'They lost contact,' Petra replied. 'Anyway, why is our dead addict of interest to you now, almost six months after she died?'

'There might have been another death where someone bought coke but most likely got white heroin,' Tim said.

'Those tourists.' Petra pushed herself further forward on her chintz sofa. It needed the help of both hands to overcome the suck of the cushions. 'Of course, I read about them. But there's someone in jail for that. And Sylvie was a local.'

'We're worried that it's started again.' I slipped into an official tone at her more confrontational stance. 'Another foreigner has died. A German. We're concerned that local deaths are hidden in the statistics or that they might have got to hospital on time.'

'Yes, I see. The police are investigating now that another visitor to Amsterdam has died.' She spat out the words. 'That's bad publicity and you need to sort it out. Poor Sylvie, you never really cared about her death.'

'Did *you*?'

'Of course. I liked her, I really did. You still only see her as a number.' She pulled a hand through her thick grey curls. 'All you want is to make it safe for tourists to come here and snort coke. Are the tourist board paying your salary?' Her eyes swung back to Tim. 'When it was only a local girl, you never investigated.'

'At that time—' Tim began.

'You just wrote her off.' Petra calmly cut off his words. 'You thought: here's another dead addict who choked on her own vomit. For us, she was a girl who shouldn't have died. I was angry for a while and then I thought that . . . that . . .' She shook her head. 'Never mind.'

'No, tell me,' I said. 'What did you think?'

'That she'd used too much by accident.' It came out too quickly, the words spilling from her mouth. She picked up her iPad. 'But you only care about your tourists. Look at her. Look closely.' She shoved the tablet under my nose. 'Does she look like an addict to you? And still she died and you didn't care. You get labelled as an addict and nobody cares about you. You're a cost centre.'

I took the iPad and looked at the photo as Petra Maasland had asked me to do. It was a photo of a smiling young woman in a field somewhere, her arms stretched out to the sky. It could be any girl. Blonde, healthy, happy.

'That's how I remember her,' Petra said. 'She sent me this two days before her death.' She grabbed the iPad back as if she'd made a decision. There were tears in her blue eyes. 'We should never have let her go.'

'What do you know about her social life? Or her sister?'

'Forget about her. She's completely unreliable.' She looked at her watch. 'Is there anything else? I have to go now.'

Tim and I left the clinic and walked back to the office. Tim was still very quiet.

'You okay?' I said.

'I missed it, didn't I?' He stared straight ahead.

'I don't know.' But at this stage it was a possibility.

'This is really going to bug me.'

Bug? Not the word I would have chosen. It seemed too light. The lowering evening sun picked out the golden strands in his short hair, but a pair of aviator sunglasses hindered my ability to read his expression. It surely must bother him more than he was showing.

'She could just have moved on to heroin,' I said.

'The boss will be furious.' He was dismissive of my attempt to make him feel better.

'That's never been something that worried me.'

'Easy for you to say. You have all this success behind you. For me, it won't look so good.'

There was no wind to speak of, but the heat of the day had finally abated to something more pleasant and bearable. 'It could well be nothing. Don't get yourself worked up.' I would happily walk a detour and stay outside a bit longer.

'You're right.'

'The parents didn't question the toxicology report.' On the Keizersgracht we stopped at a red light on the crossing. The queue of tourists wanting to visit the Anne Frank house still curled along the canal and around the Westerkerk. A long rainbow banner ran down the length of the church's tower. 'Look, Sylvie left the clinic almost two years ago. God knows what she got up to in the meantime. We need to talk to the sister; maybe she'd seen her more recently.' The blue in the rainbow flag precisely matched the blue of the top of the tower. It suited the church to be adorned with this multicoloured streamer.

'If I missed it,' Tim said, 'Bauer will go nuts. I can just hear him: "You only had to do one thing . . ."'

'We're going for a drink,' Tim said an hour or so later. 'Do you want to come?' He'd got changed and was wearing a T-shirt that was tight around his arms. A tattoo peeked out below the sleeve. A circular interwoven band. I didn't normally like tattoos, but this one suited him perfectly.

It was a Monday night. An automatic refusal was already on my lips. That I said 'sure' instead surprised me, and probably Tim as well. 'I could do with a drink. And the last time I was in a bar, someone got killed. I don't want to develop a phobia.'

'We'll keep you safe.' He flexed his biceps. The tattoo stretched. 'We're strong around here.'

He was young. I really shouldn't stare.

Whatever Bauer had against Tim, it didn't stop him from coming out for drinks with us, even though two hours later he was the first to leave. He was the only one who had a home to go to. The evening was balmy and we sat outside at a bar not that far from the police station. I recognised quite a few of the faces around me.

Mosquitoes were annoyingly attracted to the light in the middle of the picnic table. I squashed one on my arm. No blood, so I hadn't been bitten yet. Maarten made a joke that I laughed at too loudly. My head was woozy. Why hadn't I done this before, gone to a bar with my colleagues and just had fun? It was good to let off steam. Not be so serious all the time.

Maarten offered to get another round. I shook my head. I really had had too much to drink. My stomach felt loose. No more alcohol for me. 'I'm only halfway down this one.'

'Wuss,' he said, and got up to get the drinks in. I stayed behind with Tim.

He rested his arms on the picnic table between us. 'What was your best arrest? That guy who'd killed his daughter?'

I caught myself staring at his muscles and looked back into his dark eyes. 'Maybe.'

He smiled an appreciative smile. 'The one that made you famous and there's still a better one out there? You're amazing.'

'I do my best.' It sounded like I was boastfully under-playing my accomplishments rather than just telling the truth. I liked how the words felt on my lips. I liked the admiration in his eyes even more.

Maarten came back with two beers and a girl. She was young. Maybe the age Sylvie Bruyneel had been when she died. Tim's age. I should leave. What was I doing here with them? I took hold of my handbag and got ready to stand up.

'Scoot over,' Maarten said to Tim. He grabbed his beer. I looked at the girl so that I wouldn't stare at Tim as he swung his leg over the picnic bench and sat down next to me. I could immediately feel his closeness in my stomach.

'This is Miranda,' Maarten said. 'Tim you know. Meet Lotte.'

I raised my hand to acknowledge her then folded it around my half-empty beer glass. It was still just about cold enough to cool me down.

Maarten was soon deep in conversation with the girl and Tim gave me a grin. The crinkles around his eyes pulled a smile to my lips too. I couldn't think of anything to say. I felt myself moving towards him and pulled myself upright. Too much alcohol made me sway. A moth came down to the lamp in the middle. It was throwing itself against the glass. Luckily it wasn't an open candle. I looked in front of me. Better to be in a conversation with four people. Safer.

Miranda noticed my glance. 'We were just talking about what I should wear to this party.'

'And I said: something sexy,' Maarten said.

'What kind of party is it?' I asked.

'It's a work do.'

I shook my head, but that made the world spin; I felt as if my brain was moving separately within my skull. 'Better play it safe where work's concerned.'

Miranda nodded, as if I had provided her with some very sensible advice.

Tim was busy with his phone. I glanced down at what he was doing. *Coming out for beers?* someone had texted him. *Can't bro, on a hot date*, he replied. He put the phone back in his pocket. A hot date?

I hadn't been anybody's hot date for at least a decade. There was something attractive about being desired. Unlike being with Mark, who'd said I scared him. We'd been lovers and now I scared him?

More drinks turned up. This time one for me as well. I'd always had a rule about people at work. Everybody would know within a day. There were no secrets here. Maybe it had just been a joke. I stared at the foam on top of my beer. Maybe he wanted to sound interesting to someone. He couldn't possibly see drinks with me as a hot date. Or could he? I looked sideways and saw that he was staring at me. Our eyes locked and I had to hold on to my beer to stop my hand from reaching out and touching him. Desire washed over my body. This would be a really stupid thing to do.

I took a gulp of my beer and was instantly saved from myself. I was so nauseous that I had to stop drinking or I would throw up. 'I've gotta go home.' Being sick would definitely not make a good impression. The words were hard to form in my mouth. I could feel by the way my tongue moved that I was slurring them. I stood up, lifting my leg carefully high enough to get it over the bench. If I fell over now, I would never live it down. I used to be able to drink a lot more, but now I could only ever handle a certain amount of alcohol, and my stomach was telling me that my limit had been reached a couple of beers ago.

'Are you sure?' Tim said. 'We've got people joining us,' he looked at his watch, 'in ten minutes or so.'

'No, I've really got to go home.'

'Well, it is a school night.' Maarten's comment told me I hadn't been fooling anybody.

I shrugged. 'I'm on lates tomorrow.'

Maarten smiled. 'Sorry we couldn't get you any fireworks tonight. I know you're expecting that these days.'

I looked down at Tim. Fireworks enough. Maybe he would offer to walk me home. Walk me home, as if we were teenagers or something. I had to leave right now. I said my goodbyes again. Muttered something about a nice evening and seeing them tomorrow.

I walked back through the warm night. It reminded me of being young and on holiday in Spain or Italy with a bunch of friends. Partying all night, sleeping all day. Picking up some guy in between.

I got home, fed Pippi and started to send Tim a text. I thought about that one line for twenty minutes, wanted to let him know that I had enjoyed myself but not write something so stupid that he would show it to Maarten and make me the laughing stock of the office for the next month or so. In the end I went for *Thanks for the drinks. That was fun. Nobody died!* Using proper punctuation probably showed my age.

I brushed my teeth and managed not to be sick, then drank two large glasses of water, as if that would make tomorrow's hangover less severe. Luckily I didn't have to be at work until midday. I opened Skype. The dot next to Mark's name was green. *Went for drinks with my new colleague. Think he fancies me.* I hit send and felt really good about that. It would remind him that other people didn't think I was scary. He might even Skype me back.

Chapter Twelve

Of course I had a vicious headache the next morning. What had I expected? I wasn't a great drinker, and the older I got, the worse my hangovers were. It felt as if the alcohol had shrunk my head so that my skull was now crushing my brain. The numbers on the alarm clock indicated that it was not even 5 a.m., but it was already another sunny day. I started to hate summer. I stumbled into the bathroom with my eyes half closed to self-medicate with a couple of para-cetamol tablets. I swallowed the pills with a glug of water and my stomach heaved immediately. The sudden taste of bile in my mouth tipped my nausea over the edge and I only just made it to the toilet bowl in time. Both tablets floated undissolved in swirls of yellow-green. I rested my forehead on the rim.

Pippi headbutted my bare foot and meowed.

'Silly puss,' I said. 'It's too early for food.' I petted her, then rinsed my mouth under the cold tap and sat down on the floor. The tiles were actually pleasantly cool under my bare legs. Pippi dropped down next to me and showed me her white stomach. She purred.

Maybe I should just stay here and sleep sitting like this. I was never going to drink again. Ever.

I woke up again when my head tipped back and hit the hard edge of the bathtub. My left leg had gone to sleep. I stretched it and grimaced at the pins and needles shooting down it. Not so comfortable any more. I pushed myself to standing, grabbed a clean washcloth and held it under the tap until it was soaked. I swallowed two new paracetamol tablets. Pippi did her best to trip me up as I dragged my body back into the bedroom. I explained to her that if I fell and broke my neck, there would be nobody here to feed her. I didn't think she got it.

I collapsed onto the bed and put the wet cloth over my face. I was still too warm. I rubbed the insides of my wrists on the cloth. Finally the paracetamol took the edge off the pain so that I could get the only cure for a hangover: sleep.

Two hours later, I had another go at getting up. I swung my legs out of bed and sat on the edge. Being upright was really hard work. My head was still fragile and my throat hurt from throwing up. If it hadn't been so hot, I might have slept longer, but I was thirsty and uncomfortable. A cold shower, that was what I needed, and a cup of coffee to drive the last shards of the headache away. Try not to be sick again.

Probably tempted by my bare feet, Pippi tapped my leg with an outstretched paw. She meowed. Had I fed her last night? I couldn't remember. Maybe that was why she'd been so insistent at an insanely early hour. From some point, the evening was a blur. I couldn't even recall getting home. Dressed only in underwear and a T-shirt, I shuffled into the kitchen. There was some food left in her bowl so I must have given her something to eat before I went to bed. Autopilot seemed to have functioned. I fed her again, then picked up my phone to Skype Mark about anything at all. Maybe I could make a joke about how much I had been drinking. My muddled brain reminded me that I really shouldn't, and I was extremely good and didn't even open Skype to see if there was a green dot by his name.

A cold shower would take more energy than I had right now. I put some bread in the toaster. My stomach lurched at the thought of cheese, so I spread just enough butter on to lubricate the toast to the point where I could actually swallow it.

Piece of toast in one hand, cup of coffee in the other, I sat down at the table and stared out over the canal. The caffeine expanded the veins in my brain and the headache slowly drained away until my eyes were capable of focusing again. I had that shower and spent longer than usual doing my hair and make-up. Yesterday's sun had thrown some colour on my face but this morning's hangover had wiped it away. This halfway length of my hair looked good once I'd dried it properly. I put on my favourite blue T-shirt and my new white jeans. Not too bad for a forty-three-year-old who felt like shit.

Then my mobile rang and the call ruined whatever hadn't been bad yet that morning.

As soon as I opened the communal door downstairs, I was assaulted by the heat. Even though driving would come with the guaranteed cold of the air con, I was worried that I was still over the limit. So instead I unlocked my bike and hoped that cycling would blow some cool wind over my face. The air was filled with the smell of stagnant water and dying fish.

The streets were busy. It was just before 10 a.m., and the tourists were out in force. A group of Asian people were walking three abreast down my road. I rang my bell. Nobody moved out of the way. There was something about being in a group that made people think they didn't have to pay attention to anybody else. Or pay attention at all. I rang my bell again. I shouted, 'Get out of the way.' There was a gap just big enough between a woman holding an umbrella as a parasol and one of Amsterdam's red-brown bollards to get my bike through. That umbrella didn't seem such a stupid idea. Just as I was skirting past, the woman at the front brought the group to a halt to tell them something historical about the canal. A man stepped back and I almost clipped him with my bike. If my head hadn't been so delicate I would have shaken it vigorously to show him what an idiot he was. Instead I was just grateful not to have hit him, because I could have tumbled into the canal. Though at least that would have been cool.

Once I was out of the canal ring, the cycling got easier, with fewer tourists seeking their death – or more likely a small scratch – beneath my bike tyres. Two more turnings and the department store loomed large. Light bounced off the glass front and pierced through my sunglasses.

Ronald de Boer was waiting for me next to the perfume counter, just like last time. 'Come with me on my round,' he said. 'I need to talk to you.'

Yes, I'd guessed that, otherwise you wouldn't have called me, I thought, but I couldn't be bothered to say it. Instead I nodded and followed him to the lifts at the back. We stepped in and Ronald pressed the button for the garage floor.

A sign in the elevator said the maximum load was ten people, but it felt as if there wasn't even enough room for two. I had never suffered from claustrophobia, but this was what it must feel like, being in a small space and desperate to get out.

Ronald stared at the lift door and it gave me the chance to look at his greying hair cut very short at the back. 'I told my father about meeting with you,' I said to break the tension that only I was probably feeling.

The lift stopped. 'How is Piet?' Ronald looked intently at the doors, as if that would make them open more quickly.

'He's very well.'

He held an arm into the beam of the doors to make sure they weren't going to close, and let me step out first. 'I need to tell you something. I don't want anybody watching or overhearing us.' The car park was half full. He stopped at a very specific spot. 'Just keep a pace to the left,' he said.

I followed his command without really wondering why. 'So what's up?' I said.

Ronald pointed to two corners. 'There are security cameras there and there. They cover most of the area but not where we're standing now. They did a lousy job with their security system; there's loads of these black spots where you can stand without being seen or overheard. Especially here in the car park.'

I waited. I didn't want to ask him again what he'd called me here to talk about, or what his problem was. He seemed deep in thought and stared at the nearest car as if it was giving him an answer to the question about the meaning of life.

'Piotr,' he finally said. 'There was something going on. It throws a new light on . . . well maybe on his death.'

I frowned. Someone came out of the second elevator and I stayed silent as a woman loaded with stacks of parcels made her way to her car. Only after she'd put everything in the boot did I say softly to Ronald, 'And what lies are you going to tell me this time?'

He turned around suddenly and walked back to the elevator. 'Just come up to the sixth floor and watch something.' He called the lift and held the door open.

I got in because I didn't have the energy to walk up the stairs, but I pressed the button for the ground floor. 'No, I'm leaving. I don't know why I came in the first place.' Was it because I'd felt too awful to think straight? Or was it because my father had told me that I needed to forgive Ronald? That was easy enough to say in theory but really hard in practice. Maybe I wasn't the forgiving kind.

When the doors opened again, I stepped forward to get out, but Ronald stopped me by grabbing my wrist. 'It won't take long.' He held me back just long enough for a stream of people to enter. A woman pushed her pram in, effectively blocking me, and I had to withdraw to the corner. With the maximum number of people now in the lift, I was pushed close to Ronald. We stopped at the second floor and the open doors showed a glimpse of four mannequins wearing sequinned jeans and nothing else. The woman with the pram got out. This was the moment when I could have got out as well, but I stayed where I was and watched the numbers count further up. We arrived at the sixth floor with a cheerful ping that belied my dark doubts.

'Hey, Alex.' Ronald flicked some imaginary hairs from his shoulder. 'Could you show her what we were looking at earlier?'

'Are you sure?' Alex's lips threatened to break out in a smile. He was only barely controlling the muscles around his mouth.

'Yes please.' Ronald sat down.

Alex's blue eyes narrowed but he switched the display on one of the monitors. 'We were looking at some old footage of Piotr.'

'Show me.'

He clicked play and the image of Piotr, seen from the back, jumped onto the screen. Behind him, you could just see a row of changing rooms. Piotr was wearing the dark suit that was the security guards' uniform. He greeted a woman in a tight-fitting white dress, long-sleeved, with a belt around her waist. Even on the grainy footage Natalie looked beautiful. She walked into view, a huge smile on her face. They didn't touch when they greeted each other, probably in case anyone was watching. She looked around, then pulled him behind her into one of the changing rooms. The door closed. It was as if nobody had ever been there, now that they were in the privacy of the small cubicle.

For the next minute, nobody came in or out of the area. The door behind which Piotr and Natalie had disappeared stayed shut. Only if you had seen all the footage would you know there were two people in one of the changing rooms. Then they both re-emerged.

'You know, he didn't stay in there long,' Alex said.

Natalie tried to look serious but a delighted grin kept appearing around her lips. She looked radiantly happy as she touched Piotr's arm. He said something, then turned back to continue his round.

'Sorry, I shouldn't have said that now that he's dead.'

They both disappeared from view again, going in their separate directions.

'When was this?'

'Three weeks ago,' Alex muttered to the screen in front of him.

'It was on a Monday evening, half an hour before closing time. It's always quiet then. Nobody in the changing rooms,' Ronald said. His mobile rang. He swore, then picked up the call. I only caught a hint of the voice on the other end of the line, but the little I could hear sounded more and more angry. A male voice. He talked for longer than the footage of Piotr and Natalie had lasted.

Ronald slumped on his chair and rubbed his forehead. 'There must have been a mistake,' he said. 'Don't do this, please don't do this.'

It sounded as if the man was shouting, and then there was silence.

'Hello?' Ronald said. 'Hello, Mr van Buren?' He looked at his phone. 'The asshole has hung up. Fuck!' He made a gesture as if he was going to throw the phone at the wall but restrained himself. Instead he stomped towards the security manager's office. 'Kevin, what's going on? Did we not get paid this morning?'

'Don't you ever read your emails? There's been a little delay; you'll get paid tomorrow.'

'You bastards. I work all hours and you don't give me my money?'

Alex and I exchanged a look. 'There's some problem with our overtime schedule,' he whispered.

Ronald came back into the room. He looked sick. 'Alex, can you give me a hand?'

'I'm sorry, I'm stuck here for another four hours.'

Ronald grimaced and looked at me. 'Do you have a car? I think all my stuff is stacked on the pavement.'

I shook my head. 'You're kidding, right?'

'Please?' He paused. 'You know you owe me.'

I would have refused if my hangover hadn't been so bad. Right now I couldn't summon up the energy to argue. It was just easier to cycle back with Ronald to my flat to pick up my car.

I parked on a grubby street. The houses might have been nice at one point, but there were so many bells by every door that they must have been split up into bedsits. More people always equated to more garbage. Also, the people in this road seemed unable to figure out the not particularly complicated system of which bin to put out which week. There was a mixture of green and grey ones on the roadside, as if that would maximise the chances of getting the rubbish collected. The grey ones hadn't been emptied, of course, and now, two days after collection day, one of them had been kicked over and the garbage was spread over the pavement. Milk cartons, a chicken carcass and plastic bags tied around indescribable waste had started to stink in the incessant heat. I stepped out into the road to avoid an apple core. That should have gone in the green bin anyway.

I took a long look at the house that Ronald had indicated. The paint was flaking around the windows. A pile of black bin bags was stacked on the pavement. 'This is where you live?'

'Lived.'

'It's a shithole.'

'I'm on the waiting list for some better housing.' He shrugged. 'In the meantime, this was the best I could afford.'

'How much longer?'

'A friend of mine promised to speed it up. He said it will be two weeks at most.'

'Where are you going to live until then?'

'I'll find something. Once we get paid, I'll stay in a hotel or something.'

He grabbed two of the bin bags, and only then did I realise that they contained his possessions. He carried them to the boot of my car.

'They can't just kick you out.' I took another of the bags. It was lighter than I'd expected. 'You have rights.'

'Not here, and not if you don't pay your rent.'

'What? Why didn't you?'

He stopped suddenly, bin bags in hand. 'Why do you think?' he snapped.

'I'm sorry . . .'

'If the store had paid me on time, I would have been fine. Just.' He swung the first bag into the boot.

I carefully positioned the one I was carrying next to it. It was pathetic how little space his stuff took up in my car. I remembered times when my ex-husband and I had packed more than this for a two-week holiday. But it also reminded me of how few of my possessions I'd taken with me when I'd left him. When I'd moved out of our house because he'd cheated on me. It had been soul-destroyingly traumatic.

But at least I'd had money. Because I'd given my ex-husband seed capital for his company, he'd had to buy me out after our divorce. It had left me very well off. Money doesn't make you happy but it's remarkably useful when your life falls apart. It allows you to buy a lovely apartment on one of Amsterdam's canals so that even if everything else is wrong, at least you have a roof over your head.

It seemed that Ronald didn't even have that. 'I'll drive to mine,' I said. 'You can leave your stuff there and just take what you need.'

He glared at me and I thought he was going to refuse. Then he nodded his thanks. I guessed he had no choice, nobody else to help him.

We got in the car.

'You have no idea how much it cost me,' he said softly after he'd fastened his seat belt, 'when I saved your life.'

'How much it cost you?' My hand automatically went to my right shoulder. 'You were the one who put me in danger in the first place.'

'Thanks for testifying at my hearing,' he said.

'You still got fired.'

'But at least I didn't go to jail.'

My father told me I owed Ronald my life. Some of the anger I'd felt towards him ebbed away. 'That security footage of Piotr,' I said. 'Why were you showing me that?'

'You couldn't tell?'

'Tell what? They had sex in the changing rooms. We knew that anyway. Well, I didn't know they did it in the changing room, so that was very helpful information, thank you.' I couldn't keep the sarcasm out of my voice. 'But it doesn't shine any new light on this case.'

Ronald didn't respond. I parked the car along the canal, not too far from my front door, then grabbed a bin bag and carried it up the stairs to my apartment. This was not what I needed with a sore head. I opened the door to the spare room. 'Just drop your stuff in there.'

I went back down for another bag. What hadn't looked like much stuff standing on the pavement was an awful lot when you had to lug it up to the top floor.

'Can I get you a coffee, or some water?' I offered it on autopilot as if he was a welcome guest. Also, if I was making coffee I didn't have to go up and down those stairs again. Doing exercise with a hangover really wasn't great.

'Thanks. I'd love a coffee.'

I looked at my watch. I had to be at work in an hour. I did my best to ignore the sound of Ronald putting his things in my spare bedroom. He went down the stairs again. I put a fresh filter in the machine and added two scoops of ground coffee, then an extra scoop. I needed it. I filled the water tank and switched the machine on. What had I seen on that footage? Two people going into a changing room. Alex had laughed and said that they had been really quick.

Ronald came back into the flat after his final trip up and down the stairs and closed the front door.

The coffee machine hissed and I watched the black liquid drip into the glass jug. I thought about the security tape again. Had that footage really only been a minute? I'd been watching a closed door and time always seemed to go more slowly when nothing moved. But Natalie had come out looking immaculate sixty seconds after Piotr had closed the door behind her. Not a hair out of place. Her white dress – if I'd remembered it correctly – had been exactly as it had been when they went in. What was it she'd said? That sending messages was the best part? The coffee finished dripping. Maybe they'd just kissed. Still, sixty seconds . . . I needed to see that footage again.

'Do you want milk or sugar?' I said.

There was no response. I poured and took both cups into the front room. Ronald was fast asleep on the sofa. I looked down at him for a moment. I couldn't escape the thought that this could so easily have been me. Ingrid had testified at my hearing, just like I had done at Ronald's. I knew that if I hadn't had CCTV to back everything up, I could have lost my job. I could be the one working all hours as a security guard.

I put the coffee down and shook his shoulder until he opened his eyes. 'Drink this,' I said.

'Sorry.' He sat up.

I took a seat on the other sofa. 'I can give my father a call,' I said. 'I know he'll put you up for a week or so.'

He looked at me with bleary eyes. 'He would?'

'He seems to have forgiven you.'

Ronald rested his head in his hands for a second, then looked back at me. If possible, he seemed even more tired than when he was asleep. 'Alkmaar isn't a great place for me to be any more. It isn't big enough to hide.'

'Hide?'

'Well, get some anonymity. Everybody knows what happened. Everybody has an opinion.' He took a cigarette out of a half-empty pack.

'You can't smoke in here.'

He put the cigarette back in the packet. 'What did you tell them when you testified? I'm truly curious. That I shot a man to save your life?'

'Something like that.' I sat with my cup of coffee tight between both hands.

'You didn't tell them that you thought I'd shot to kill him? That I pulled the trigger on purpose? That I murdered him?'

I hated that those were the exact words that I had used with my father. This was so close to how I saw myself. 'You had to shoot. To protect me.'

He laughed. It sounded harsh and ended in a cough 'Oh that's good. I'm surprised they didn't keep me in the force.'

'You put my life in danger.' My voice rose and I sat forward on the sofa. 'That was reason enough to fire you.' I stood up. 'I was stupid to help you out. Don't worry, I'll let you leave your stuff here. But only because I can't bear having to carry it down the stairs again.'

'You put me in a position where I had no choice but to kill a man. I was fired from the police force and am now working as a security guard at a department store. No pension, no permanent contract.' His voice wasn't even angry. He sounded calm, as if he was just stating the facts. 'This is how it turned out. Yes, I'm glad you testified, otherwise I would have ended up in jail. But this is me now.'

I fought the hangover nausea. I fought the sense that my life was just as fucked up as his was. Whatever feeling of superiority I might have had, it was draining away. There was only a thin line between my position and his. 'You know,' I finally said, 'we've got something in common, you and me.'

'We do? What's that?' He kept looking at his coffee cup.

'We've both taken a life. We both killed a man.'

He put the cup back on the table. 'We've both saved a life.' He grabbed his backpack and started to get up. 'A colleague's life.'

Even though it was factually correct, that was not something I could accept yet.

Because I was working so hard not to throw up, I lost the fight not to feel sorry for him. 'I know you've got no money for a hotel tonight. If I kick you out, you'd have to sleep on a park bench somewhere. I can't do it. My father would be so pissed off with me. You can stay here.'

He looked at me with a grimace and shook his head.

I was relieved. I'd done the right thing; had offered and got away with it.

He wrapped his arms around himself. 'It will only be for a week or so,' he said. 'I sleep during the day, work at night.

143

You won't even see me.' He sounded as if he was convincing himself just as much as me.

Oh, he was accepting it after all. However much I wanted to, I couldn't go back on my offer. I dug the spare keys out of the cupboard and threw them on the table. 'I've got to go to work.'

I cycled to the police station, where the multicoloured rainbow flag flew to celebrate the fact that it was the Gay Pride parade next Saturday. Oddly enough, I felt good about having helped someone I didn't like. That's true altruism for you. Even the people at my mother's church would be impressed.

Tim looked pointedly at his watch with a smile as I came into the office. 'Hello, part-timer. I'd arranged to interview one of the witnesses but I had to call him to say we were going to be late because I was still waiting for you.'

'Sorry, something came up.'

'Something like a hangover?'

'Something I had to take care of. But I'm ready to go now.' I didn't think my stomach was up to handling lunch anyway.

Tim drove us. We were heading west. We crossed the bridge where Ingrid and I had been kept waiting for the sailboat to cross on the night that Piotr died. We turned off the bridge to drive along the canal and I pushed my lips together, because suddenly I knew where we were going.

Chapter Thirteen

'Why are we here?' I said. I didn't get out of the car but stared straight ahead. I didn't even want to look at the house. Like any addict, I should stay far from temptation.

'We need to take Mark Visser's statement,' Tim said.

'And you couldn't have done that without me?' There was a hard edge around my voice. 'You had the entire morning.' I felt as if I was a prisoner locked up inside this metal box and dragged here against my wishes.

'I waited for you.' He had a puzzled look on his face. 'I thought you would want to come. Aren't you seeing him?'

'No.' I shook my head. 'Very much not.' I was trying my hardest not to see him and now Tim had brought me right to his doorstep.

'Someone told me last night that you were.' He looked at me with a sheepish smile. 'And I thought it would be fun.'

'Fun.' I was starting to see why Bauer didn't like him. 'Who told you that?'

'Never mind.' Was he blushing? 'But you're friends, aren't you? You were having a drink together.'

'We *were* friends.' I emphasised the past tense. 'And we were having drinks because I was trying to make amends, and that didn't work out too well.'

'I called him to say we're on our way. It will only take five minutes.'

'I should wait outside.'

He frowned. 'Did something happen between you?'

'I thought you'd done your homework on me.' I sank down against my seat and wrapped my arms protectively around myself. Because I had to admit that I had made it far worse by being so obsessed. I'd been stalking him. What had I even wanted from him? Absolution? Forgiveness?

I was only slowly starting to understand my own messed-up reasoning. I had made some kind of bargain with myself that if he could love me again like I still loved him, and desire me again, then I wasn't really a killer. I'd wanted him – no, needed him – to confirm what the Bureau of Internal Investigation had decided. Because even though they'd ruled I'd been completely justified in discharging my weapon, it still didn't feel like that.

In my dreams, Mark was always watching. Judging me. As if his opinion was the one that counted, not the ruling of the BII.

How fucked up was that?

'I don't want to taint his statement,' I said. 'I don't want him to feel uncomfortable about saying certain things.'

'You can't sit outside his house in the car. That's ridiculous.'

I nodded. 'Agreed.' It was.

Even though an extra ten minutes would make no difference compared to the hours I'd already spent here, in
exactly the same spot but in a different car, I didn't want to
add to my transgression. 'I'll leave,' I said. 'I'll pick you up in
about half an hour.'

'That's crazy. If we were at the station, you could have
observed. Just come in.'

It was ironic that Tim had parked at the ideal spot from
which to watch Mark Visser's movements. That was how I'd
figured out at what time Mark was going to walk past the
bar last Thursday. He was a creature of habit who left work
every day at the same time, went to the gym then walked
to the tram stop to go home. Came past that bar at ten
minutes to eight almost every Thursday.

I decided it would be weirder to stay here than to come
in. 'Okay,' I said. 'Fine. But I'm not going to ask any questions. You can lead this interview.'

'I'll be brief.'

I nodded and got out of the car.

Mark opened the door before Tim had even rung the bell.
He must have been waiting for us to arrive. He looked at
me and sighed.

It was the first time I'd seen him since he'd said I scared
him. I'd hoped to apologise, but instead I was here on
official police business. He probably thought I was trying to
intimidate him.

'Sorry we're late,' Tim said.

Mark looked at me. 'Is this your new colleague?'

'I moved teams to investigate Piotr Mazur's murder.'

He looked Tim up and down. 'I see.'

'This won't take long,' Tim said.

'Come in.' Mark led us through to the kitchen. 'Have a seat.'

We sat around the table like the world's most uncomfortable dinner party.

'What did you notice that evening?' Tim asked.

'Nothing special,' Mark said.

'Tell us about the people at the table next to you.'

'There were four of them and the guy with the beard was rather obnoxious. He got drunk and started talking about drugs.' Mark went through the events of that evening, told Tim what he'd seen. How often he thought Karl had gone into the bar. What else he'd heard them talking about. As he spoke, he avoided looking at me. I could tell I was making him nervous.

'Did you see this woman?' Tim showed him the photo of the woman in the floral dress.

'Yes, I saw her inside the bar, when I had to go to the toilet. She was on her mobile.'

'Did you catch what she was saying?'

'Something like "I can't do this." But I didn't really listen in.'

'"I can't do this"?'

'Something like that. I'm not exactly sure. Sorry, I don't pay as much attention as you guys always do. But she was standing next to the men's room. That's why I remember her. She looked quite nervous.'

'What time was this?'

Mark threw me a worried glance, as if this was an exam question he couldn't afford to get wrong.

148

'Approximately,' Tim said. 'Just to get our timeline right.'

'After Lotte had got the next round of drinks in. Maybe half an hour before the guy was stabbed? Something like that.'

'So a little before ten?'

'I'm really not sure. Sorry.'

'But she was by herself, this woman? Piotr Mazur wasn't with her when she made the call?'

'No, just her. That's why I noticed her, because she was alone outside the men's toilets. It was odd.'

'Did you see them leave?'

'No, I was facing the other way.'

'Well, thank you.' Tim handed Mark his card. 'If anything else comes to mind, please let me know.'

'Of course.' Mark got up. He squared his shoulders and looked me in the eye. 'You really shouldn't send people messages when you're drunk, Lotte.'

I frowned. 'Sorry?'

Tim laughed. 'I got one too.'

'I bet you did,' Mark said.

'Mine was punctuated and everything.'

I had no recollection of sending either of them a text. I got my phone out, opened Skype and clicked on Mark's name to read what I'd written. Oh fuck. I clasped the phone against my chest as if hiding the text would make it go away.

'I'm sorry.' I looked at him. 'I'm so sorry. About everything.'

'Don't worry,' Mark said. 'I've deleted it. Are we done?'

'Yes,' I said. 'Yes, we're done.' It felt like a break-up all over again.

Chapter Fourteen

I got in the car and closed the door, to shut myself in with the blessed coolness of the air con. It was artificial, but who cared about that? I took my phone from my bag and opened Skype. I tapped the three dots and chose 'Remove Contact'. I had to go cold turkey. *Are you sure you want to remove mvisser from your contacts?* the phone unhelpfully asked. Yes, I told it. Yes, I'm sure. Already I felt withdrawal. I'd enjoyed that kinship when I could see that we were both online. Or, late in the evening, watching the green dot by his name turn yellow and knowing that he'd gone to bed. I had to stop making a note of what time that happened each night.

For two months now, observing Mark had been my drug of choice. It didn't make me feel good about myself especially. Once I could think again, I knew I'd hate that I had been following him round. I'd hate that I'd watched him and that just seeing him had made me happy. Sometimes my two-hour vigil would be rewarded with a sighting of his tall frame at the window. The delight of this glimpse gave me an even more intense high because it was tainted by the worry that he would see me. I'd simultaneously dread and hope that he would look my way.

Fear and desire made a particularly toxic blend.

'We should see Katja Bruyneel,' Tim said.

'Sure.'

He drove me away from Mark's house, but I could close my eyes and still be there.

'If you're going to puke,' Tim said, 'let me know and I'll stop the car.'

'I'm fine,' I said. I only felt sick with self-loathing.

From my handbag I took a copy of the photo that Piotr had carried in his wallet. The original was bagged up to preserve the fingerprints. How old was this toddler? Eighteen months, two years maybe. The little boy held a sailboat in his chubby hands, stretched out towards the camera, a broad smile on his face. That grin showed either pride in his toy or love for the person behind the camera. I completely understood why the picture had made Piotr smile.

My own daughter hadn't lived to this age. I'd found her lifeless in her bed. She'd looked asleep but would not wake up again. Cot death.

If I was ever brave enough to trace back the start of this spiral of guilt and my destructive behaviour, I would have to admit that it was when my child died. Dangerous relationships, obsessive desire, unsuitable men. And still none of it had filled the huge crater that the loss of Poppy had blown inside me.

I'd thought I had a chance with Mark and then I had screwed that up.

It was only because the sun was shining brightly that I even dared to think of these things. Soul-searching after dark was too dangerous.

We pulled up outside Katja's house and for the second day in a row there was no response when we rang her doorbell. These flats had been purpose-built around the turn of the nineteenth century. At the end of the street, a group of small children had spilled out of a primary school and were playing football around a fountain. Not surprisingly in this heat, they were more interested in the water than in their ball.

Katja lived at number 83II, so she was on the second floor. I took a couple of steps back into the road and looked along the brown brick building to what would be her window. The roads in this quarter were named after Dutch statesmen, and maybe they had insisted that the apartment blocks built here were straight and tall. I couldn't really see much of Katja's flat apart from a few plants in the window. The sun beat down on my back and created dark pools under my armpits.

'We should check with the neighbours,' Tim said. I'd expected him to joke about the conversation with Mark Visser or drunken texting as we were driving here, but luckily he'd kept his mouth shut and left me to my thoughts. 'We could keep coming back here every day and never find her at home.'

I nodded and rang the bell for 83hs. There were two front doors next to each other for each house: the leftmost one served the ground floor only and the right one was used by floors one through to three. An elderly woman with a purple rinse glanced from between thick net curtains. Here the pavement ran right along the window. Unless you had these opaque nets, every passer-by could look straight into your front room. The curtain fell closed again. I could hear from where I was standing that *Goede Tijden, Slechte Tijden* was on TV. They must be on episode five thousand of that series by now. I wasn't sure if the woman didn't open because she didn't want to have her programme interrupted, or whether she hadn't even heard the doorbell.

I knocked on the window. 'Police, open up,' I said loudly.

The woman appeared at the window again. She had a deeply lined face, and a cigarette hung from one corner of her mouth.

I showed my badge and pointed at the door. My sign language seemed to work. The woman reluctantly nodded. When she finally opened her front door a fraction, we were assaulted by the sound of the TV.

'God, what a noise,' Tim muttered behind me.

I ignored him. 'Do you know where your neighbour Katja Bruyneel is?' I said loudly.

She fiddled with her hearing aid and looked at me blankly.

'Turn the sound down!' Tim said.

She shuffled back inside.

The noise of the TV disappeared and I could hear myself think. 'We're here about your neighbour,' I said.

'Did they complain again?' She spoke with the cigarette dangling from the corner of her mouth. 'It's only because the programme's in Dutch.'

'We're looking for Katja Bruyneel. Your neighbour on the second floor.'

'Oh, her.' She took the cigarette from her mouth. Two teeth were missing. 'She's such a nice girl. She never complains about the noise and helps me with my shopping. But I haven't seen her for a while.'

'Is she on holiday?'

'How do I know? Young people these days, they go on long holidays and work trips. I can't keep up with where they are. Haven't seen her in months.'

'Do you have the key to her flat?'

'No, why would I? We don't even share the same front door.'

'Who has?'

'The complaining ones.' She pointed at the ceiling. 'They have her key.'

'Are they at home?'

The woman sighed. 'Otherwise they wouldn't have complained, would they?'

I didn't bother correcting her again.

Tim rang the doorbell of 83I and the door to the right opened.

We were halfway up the narrow stairs when the TV volume went up again. I could follow the dialogue through the wall of the stairwell.

The neighbour on the first floor opened her door. She was a slim woman who seemed all stomach. Seven or eight months pregnant, I guessed. Her long hair hung limp around her face. I remembered that stage of pregnancy. It was hard work; you were tired all the time and you couldn't sleep properly. In this heat it must be impossibly energy-sapping. At least I had been eight months pregnant in winter. My ex-husband had said that I was like a big pink hot-water bottle. It had been a happy time.

'Thanks for coming round,' the pregnant woman said after I'd shown my badge. 'Who complained about her this time?'

'We're not here about your downstairs neighbour.'

'We've stopped trying to get her to turn it down. It's easier to just watch the same TV programme.' The woman shrugged. 'It's only *GTST*. As soon as that's over, she turns the sound down.' She patted her belly. 'Once the little one is born, we'll be making a lot of noise too. See how she likes that.'

'We'd like to speak to Katja Bruyneel,' I said. 'Have you seen her recently?'

'No, not for a bit. Isn't she on holiday?'

'When is she back?'

'She normally asks me to look after her plants, but she didn't this time.' She rubbed her belly. 'She's been really down recently. Her sister's death hit her hard, and then she lost her job.'

'When did you see her last?'

'It was May. Or April maybe.' She rubbed her belly again. 'Time has gone so fast.'

'That's more than two months ago.' I knew her parents hadn't seen her either. They'd told us as much yesterday. I didn't have a good feeling about this.

The woman rested her hand on the door frame as if for

155

support. 'I can't believe it's been that long. I never checked. I know she hasn't been home because I normally hear her walking around.' She tucked the limp hair behind her ears. 'You've got me worried now.' She looked at the stairs leading up, as if that would miraculously produce Katja. 'Can we make sure she's okay?'

'Do you have her keys?'

'Yes, hold on a moment.' When she came out with the keys, she put her shoes on. 'I'll have a quick look around. See if there's anything to show where she is.'

'Don't.' I shook my head and exchanged a glance with Tim. 'Let us. You stay here. We don't know what we'll find.' Katja Bruyneel had severed her relationship with her parents, her sister had died and she'd lost her job. Nobody would have reported her missing.

The woman put her hand to her mouth. 'I know she was depressed after her sister died. Do you think . . .' She paused, then took a resolute step outside. 'I should have checked on her.'

Tim put a restraining hand on her arm. 'You need to stay here,' he said. 'You really do.'

The woman paled as it sank in what we were suggesting we might find behind Katja's door. She gave me the keys with an outstretched arm, as if she wanted to be as far away from Katja's flat as she could be. I didn't blame her. In my early days as a police officer, I'd been the first person in a flat where someone had been dead for two weeks. That had been in the summer as well, and it had been just as hot. Even the memory of the stench made me gag. I hoped we weren't going to find anything like that now. I hoped I would never find anything like that again.

We went up the second set of dark-carpeted stairs. This stairwell was shared by the flats on the second and third floor. Washing hung on a foldable rack suspended in the stairwell. A couple of T-shirts, a pair of knickers and three sets of socks dangled above our heads. On a ledge were two bicycle pumps, probably one for each flat. I had the keys in my hand and walked up to Katja's front door. Tim had to wait for me below as there wasn't enough room for both of us on the small landing.

I knocked once on the door but didn't really expect any reply. The key turned easily. The door wasn't locked from the inside. I caught a hint of the smell of empty flats: that mixture of sour milk and stagnant water sitting in unused drains. But the good news was that it didn't smell of a decaying corpse.

'Katja? Katja?' I called. Dust covered all the surfaces and gave the dark-wood floorboards a grey patina. The place looked as if it had been abandoned for longer than a couple of months. Nobody had been here in a while. A large rubber plant was dead in a terracotta pot, its thick leaves scattered on the floor. The plants in the window were only green because they were plastic.

I always carried a pair of nitrile gloves in my handbag and I put them on before stepping over the threshold. Not that this was definitely a crime scene, but it was better to be safe than sorry. There was something impersonal about the apartment. The beige walls and white doors reminded me of going to the dentist. Only the smell wasn't antiseptic; rather the musky smell of a place that had been empty for a while. A hint of rotten food and dust. The sofa had a pale wooden frame filled with white cushions and perfectly matched the shelving unit.

I carefully opened the door to the bathroom. It was empty. There were two doors leading off the hallway. I tried the first one. It turned out to be a broom cupboard. That left just the bedroom at the end. My footsteps showed on the floor. I didn't like that the door was closed. It looked surprisingly ominous.

I took a breath in. It should be fine, I told myself; I would have smelled it otherwise. There was no point in delaying.

Tim looked in the bathroom. 'These apartments are such a pain,' he said. 'When they were built, people didn't need showers. They used the bath houses.'

I pushed the door to the bedroom open.

It was empty. The bed was made. Not disturbed. We didn't know where Katja was, but at least she wasn't dead of a drug overdose in her flat. My shoulders dropped as the tension left my body.

'A friend of mine had to put a shower in a cupboard.'

I turned round in relief at not having found a corpse. 'So there's no space for a bath?'

'God, no. They've done an okay job with this one.' He sounded as if he was a bathroom specialist. 'They must have broken out another closet at one point.' He came out of the bathroom. 'Have a look,' he said.

It didn't feel quite right to be nosing around in the flat of a girl who might just have gone on a cruise around the world. 'Let's leave; there's nothing here,' I said.

158

'Could you cope with a bathroom this tiny?' Tim pointed to the little room. 'Have a look inside.'

I did so, just to humour him. There was a toilet and a shower but no sink. How odd. Where would you brush your teeth? Where would you wash your hands? Surely not under the shower. I stepped over the threshold of the small bathroom. As soon as I was in, Tim pushed the door shut from the outside.

'That's not funny!' I wasn't that keen on small spaces and there was no room in here, unless I sat on the toilet or stood under the shower. It was pitch dark because there weren't any windows. 'Open up.' I banged on the door. 'Let me out.' The thin stream of light coming from underneath the door was enough to let me spot a pulley string just to the left. I tugged it, maybe a little harder than necessary, and the light came on.

The entire inside of the bathroom door was covered in photos. I hadn't noticed them when I came in, but as soon as I looked at them, my breath caught.

'What's it worth to you?' Tim joked from outside the door. 'To let you out?'

I recognised Sylvie from the pictures that the counsellor had shown us. But more importantly, I recognised the other woman too.

'Lotte?'

I was still staring at the central photo when Tim opened the door.

'Sorry, you went very quiet suddenly. Are you okay? I was just kidding.'

I could only point. The woman in the picture was wearing a black dress and high heels. Unlike the last time I'd seen her.

Because then she'd been wearing a floral dress and carrying a denim jacket.

Chapter Fifteen

I called the prosecutor's office and got a search warrant. I looked around me. Did the place seem different now that it was no longer the flat of a potential suicide but that of a potential murderer? What did it mean that the woman who might have killed Piotr Mazur was the sister of a woman who had died of a heroin overdose?

'I'd better tell the pregnant neighbour that we haven't found a dead body,' Tim said.

'Sure.'

He left the flat, leaving the door open.

A few posters adorned the wall. One was of an icy wasteland; another was a set of intertwined letters forming no words that I could decipher. Then there was that row of plastic pot plants. Had they been placed there to make the flat look inhabited from the outside? Who would care about that? I heard Tim knock on the downstairs neighbour's door. A car went past. Otherwise there was silence and my footsteps were loud on the wooden floor as I paced the length of the flat.

I opened the bathroom door again and examined the inside. It was entirely covered by photos of all sizes. What they initially screamed at me was that there was no gap. If Katja had given Piotr a photo of a child, it hadn't come from this door.

There was something significant about these photos. The effect of the mosaic of dozens of pictures was intense. As I studied them, I heard Tim talking to the neighbour. He asked her if she knew where Katja could possibly have gone. Did she have any friends who could have put her up? The neighbour answered that she couldn't think of anybody. Was there a boyfriend? Not that she knew. Nobody steady.

There were no men in any of the pictures. No boyfriends. No photo of Katja and her sister with their parents. I wasn't too surprised about that. The photos weren't in chrono-logical order. The one in the centre seemed to be the most recent one of Katja and Sylvie. It could be a few years old. I started to recognise Sylvie in other photos.

I sat down on the toilet, turned on the light and pulled the door closed. The photos filled my entire field of vision.

Sylvie was everywhere: on a donkey, on a bicycle, in the forest, with a couple of other girls, in a primary school por-trait. The topmost photo on the left-hand side showed two teenagers on the beach. They were close in age but didn't resemble each other. Sylvie was tall, pretty, with sun-kissed hair and a willowy body. She was the kind of girl who would turn heads in the street. She was smiling broadly, laughing at the camera. Katja was smiling too; not at the camera but at her sister. Katja's hair had darkened since childhood. She was stocky. The girls' arms were around each other. They'd been fifteen and seventeen maybe? According to her parents, it was around this time that Sylvie had first started using cocaine and speed.

I took a quick snap on my iPhone of the mosaic. Then I opened the door again and took a close-up of each picture individually.

What effect would it have had on Katja to see these photos every day? Looking at the inside of that door was intense. Overwhelming. I would not have felt good having to see a door covered with photos of my dead sister several times a day.

I realised that the door was a shrine.

Was it a penance because Katja had kicked her sister out of her flat, as her parents had told us? A visual reminder that for the last three years they hadn't been in touch at all?

Katja had been in a bar with a security guard who was also a drug dealer. A man who had sold that German businessman the hit of coke that turned out to be white heroin. Katja's sister had also died of a heroin overdose.

Had these photos fuelled Katja Bruyneel's anger until it was intense enough to make her kill someone? But how many women killed in rage?

When I had killed, it had been to protect someone. At that thought, I could almost feel the gun in my hand again. I remembered pulling the trigger. I was certain that he'd wanted me to do it, but that didn't make me feel less guilty. It didn't make it easier. In fact, in an odd way maybe it made it harder. I could have made a better decision. I could have not given him that way out.

What had made Katja want to murder Piotr Mazur? When I'd seen them in the bar, he hadn't been threatening towards her. The witnesses from that evening had said that their conversation had been calm throughout. Things could have changed afterwards, of course, in the street for example, as they were walking away.

Were her sister's death and Piotr's murder linked?

It seemed the obvious answer but that didn't make it the right one. There were other aspects to consider. Maybe Katja hadn't been the one who killed Piotr Mazur. What if she'd been a witness to the stabbing and was now in danger? On the run, not from the police but from the murderer?

And she hadn't been in her flat for months. She'd left here well before Piotr's death. Where had she been living?

I walked to the window, moved the net curtains sideways and looked past the row of plastic plants. A car with a fridge in the back came past, the white rectangle too large for the boot to shut properly. Instead it was held closed by a piece of string. A woman cycled by on an old-fashioned bike. On the front she carried two small children in matching sunshine-yellow outfits. Nothing else moved in the street.

Tim came back up the stairs. He called Bauer to tell him that there'd been a breakthrough. He said we'd be back at the police station as soon as we finished our search.

Why would someone have plastic plants? I'd seen them in hospitals, restaurants and reception areas but not often in someone's home. An extravagant fake peace lily stood next to a pretend azalea. They would never die but always stay green. They had looked convincing from the outside. It showed forethought. Katja had planned to be away for a while but hadn't wanted the neighbours to be suspicious. I opened a drawer and found nothing but a few old copies of

Libelle and a stack of credit-card statements. The cards had been paid off monthly. The most recent statement was from three months ago.

A cupboard hid nothing more interesting than a set of pans and Tupperware boxes. There were books on a single shelf: a few Baantjers, two books by Harry Mulisch and a childhood throwback by Thea Beckman. Nothing really modern. The drawer underneath the coffee table held four different remote controls, all neatly laid out.

I entered the bedroom and opened the wardrobe. There were only suits in various bland colours: a couple of greys, one blue; a bank of ironed shirts. A professional woman's wardrobe. These were the clothes she had left behind. There were no casual clothes. No tops. No underwear. She must have taken all of those with her.

Tim joined me. He opened a cupboard. 'Look at this,' he said. I turned round. It contained the washbasin that I'd expected in the bathroom, as well as the boiler. 'A sink in your bedroom. These flats really are weird.'

I checked the pockets of all the suits but didn't find anything. Empty hangers clicked together where some garments were missing. In the drawer of the bedside table I found a box of condoms. Underneath them a stack of papers. I pulled them out and sat down on the bed to look through them. More magazines.

'I'm sorry,' Tim said. 'I should have gone to Mark Visser with someone else. I shouldn't have forced you to come.'

'It's fine.' Between copies of *Cosmo* and *Libelle* I found a newspaper. It was six months old.

'I had the wrong idea. I'd heard you'd been seeing him since that previous case. The one with the dead builder.'

I looked through the newspaper for any articles that could have something to do with Piotr Mazur or drugs. There wasn't anything obvious.

'He seemed really annoyed that you'd Skyped him last night.'

I closed the paper with a loud rustle. I folded it up but kept it with me. It was hard to concentrate with Tim talking. I might have missed something.

I opened the door to the balcony. Two chairs stood side by side, a small table in between. Apart from that, it was empty.

I leaned on the railing and looked at the back of the adjacent block of apartments. I'd found nothing connecting Katja with Piotr. There wasn't a single bit of paper with his name on it. And apart from the photos, I hadn't seen anything that mentioned Sylvie.

If Ronald had a rummage around my flat while I was at work, he would find out more about me by just opening a single drawer.

'Are you pissed off with me?' Tim had followed me onto the balcony and stood next to me. 'For shutting you in the bathroom?' He rested his arm on the balustrade and the sleeve of his T-shirt rode up high enough to display the tattooed band around his biceps. 'I was just messing with you. It was a bit of fun.' He tipped his head sideways like a contrite puppy.

Fun. That was what he'd said about going to see Mark.

But like with cute puppies, it wasn't easy to stay annoyed with him. 'Are you a tidy person?' I said.

'What?'

'Does this place feel too clean to you?'

'No, it's very dusty.'

'I meant too empty of personal things?' I was hot, and fanned myself with the old newspaper. At some point this weather was going to break with a massive thunderstorm. 'I think Katja Bruyneel cleared out before she left.'

Chapter Sixteen

I pulled the cap off the marker pen and wrote Katja Bruyneel's name on the whiteboard. I wrote Sylvie's name next to it. This afternoon I loved the smell of pen on whiteboard. I even liked the way the pen squeaked when I drew the connecting line between the two girls' names. I admired the straightness of that line. I'd been vindicated in my decision to move to this team. We'd finally had a major breakthrough in figuring out who killed Piotr Mazur, and it wouldn't have happened if we hadn't looked at old ODs. I stuck Piotr Mazur's photo right in the centre. I'd wanted to do that ever since I'd moved into this office. This was the case we should be working on.

'It could just be a coincidence,' Maarten said.

I stopped drawing the arrow between Piotr and Katja and turned to look at him.

He raked his hand through his mop of blonde hair. He'd been here when Tim and I got back to the office. Bauer was still in a meeting. 'Okay,' he grimaced, 'I admit it, I would really like it to be a coincidence. We don't have anything that links Piotr Mazur to Sylvie Bruyneel apart from the sister. Right? We don't know for sure that he was Sylvie's dealer.'

'No, that's true. The only connection is the sister.'

'You saw the sister in the bar with Mazur.'

'Right.' I stopped writing and leaned against the edge of Bauer's desk, which was the one closest to the whiteboard.

'And she gave him something and he smiled.'

'Yes,' I said. 'This photo.' I took my copy from my handbag and stuck it on the whiteboard between Piotr and Katja's names.

'Are you sure that's what you saw? Could she have given him something else?'

'I didn't get a really good look at it. She could have given him another photo.'

'Could she have given him drugs?'

'Drugs? No.' The answer came immediately and instinctively. But then I played that scene back in my mind. She'd handed him something across the table. He'd smiled. I'd thought it was a photo but what was it that had actually made me think that? 'She gave him a piece of paper. I watched her get it from her pocket. It was the shape of a photo.'

The door opened and Bauer came in. I quickly pushed myself away from his desk and put the marker pen back on the edge of the whiteboard. He lumbered towards his seat and I moved back towards mine. We had to do some awkward side-stepping in the centre aisle of the office to pass each other without touching.

He glanced at my drawing and sighed heavily as he sat

down. 'I've just come from a meeting with your boss. I'm already regretting accepting you here.'

'I think I've been helpful.' I tried to keep my tone light. Would Tim have recognised the woman in that centre photo from the image from the security camera? It had been easier for me to identify her because I'd seen her in person.

'That's not the issue.' He grinned with the same level of joy as if he had a toothache. 'Whenever anybody talks about reorganisation, they always mean finding ways of doing the same job with fewer people. They talk about finding efficiencies but they really mean finding who we can get rid of. Having you here,' he gestured towards me with his chin, 'means I've got an extra resource, and it's damaging my negotiating position with Moerdijk.'

'We had a breakthrough,' Tim said.

'I'm not sure if that has made things better or worse,' Bauer said. 'We now have two heroin ODs and a potential connection between the two. I don't like it. Tim, I told Moerdijk he could have you. Oddly enough, he wasn't interested.' He laughed as if it had been a joke.

'It's not certain there's a link.' Tim ploughed ahead as if talking about the case would stop any threat of him being moved to another team.

'No, I get that.' Bauer cut him short. 'But the defence lawyer is going to find this very useful.'

'According to the parents,' Tim said, 'the two girls were no longer on speaking terms. They also said something about the girl being just like her mother. At that point I thought they were talking about Sylvie, but maybe they meant Katja. Maybe she was using drugs too.'

'We found no drugs in her flat,' I said.

'Those girls were adopted?' Bauer asked.

I'd told him this already yesterday, but only now did he show any interest. 'Yes. At three and five years old.'

'Sylvie seems to have been using from her mid-teens,' Tim said. 'She lived with the sister until three years ago, when Katja kicked her out. A year later, she was arrested for theft. That was about two years ago. Went into rehab. No contact with the police since. Also no contact with the parents.'

'I bet the parents know where the sister is,' Bauer said. 'Did they seem nervous when you talked to them?'

I looked at Tim.

'Not really,' he said, 'but we weren't asking about Katja.'

'Talk to them again. Get them to come here. Make them uncomfortable. They know something. So, Tim, you were supposed to monitor any suspicious ODs and you completely missed this one.'

'Six months ago, this didn't look suspicious,' I said. 'Everything has changed because the sister is the main suspect in Piotr Mazur's killing.'

'I'm sure Tim can explain himself, Lotte. No need for you to get involved.'

'The only reason we identified the woman who is still our main suspect,' I said, 'is because we were checking these old ODs.'

'But you haven't actually found her,' Bauer said. 'And

whatever work you two have been doing, you're destroying my previous case.'

'We're investigating Piotr Mazur's death.'

'I don't care about his death.' He wheeled round on his chair, reached out to the whiteboard and tore Mazur's photo down. He threw it towards me. 'I want to make sure that the guy who killed all these people' – he tapped a knuckle on each of the photos of the drug victims in turn – 'gets locked away for a long time. I want their families to get justice.'

'But if someone else is also swapping drugs—'

'Then I don't want to know about it!' Bauer bellowed the words. His face turned puce. I wanted to say that he should calm down or he'd give himself a heart attack, but experience had taught me that this kind of useful comment only ever fanned the flames.

Tim slunk away towards his desk. I was in the eye of the storm. I picked the photo of Piotr up off the floor. 'This man,' I held it up, 'was stabbed to death.' Sweat was running down between my shoulder blades but I kept my voice steady. 'If you'd like me to take this case back downstairs and bring your resource numbers down, I'm happy to do that. I'm sure CI Moerdijk would allow it.' I would have loved to rush out of the office, but I fought that impulse and kept eye contact with Bauer. I wasn't going to back down on this. 'Do you think a Polish immigrant doesn't deserve justice but those tourists who'd come to Amsterdam to score drugs do?'

'Don't give me the hard-working-immigrant spiel. It doesn't work so well when the guy's a dealer.'

'You can't blame us for doing our job just because you don't like the answers,' I said.

'Maybe not you, but I expected better from Tim.' Bauer slicked his hair back from his face. At least he was calming down. 'Oh no, actually I didn't.'

'We'll trace Katja Bruyneel,' I said. 'We'll find out why she was with Piotr Mazur in that bar.'

'As long as Mazur wasn't the sister's dealer, we're still okay.' Bauer looked at his watch. 'I'll see you guys tomorrow.' He got up and left the office.

I took a deep breath in.

'We normally just shut up,' Maarten said. 'It's a better strategy than arguing with him. He's always like this when he comes out of an internal meeting.'

'I'll check his calendar and make sure I'm out of the office after the next one.' I sat down at my desk. My hands were shaking and I hid them by rummaging in my handbag.

'I'll give the parents a call,' Tim said, 'and get them to come in here.'

'I've got nothing on Mazur,' Maarten said to me as soon as Tim was talking on the phone. 'None of my informants know him. Nobody knew he was dealing. He must have been very careful.'

'And where was he keeping his stash? I'd thought it could have been at Katja's, before I knew she was Sylvie's sister, but her flat was clean. No sign of drugs.'

I thought back to Katja's parents telling us that Katja had thrown her sister out three years ago. That flat wasn't big enough to live in with a sister who stole from you. That reminded me that Petra had told us that Sylvie had been in rehab as part of her sentence. I pulled her criminal record. 'Look at this,' I said to Maarten. I shook my head at my own stupidity: I should have done this earlier. Two years ago, Sylvie had been caught stealing dresses from the department store where Piotr Mazur had worked. I spotted Natalie Schuurman's name. It was Natalie who had reported Sylvie Bruyneel to the police. 'There's another link.' It was odd that she'd contacted the police and hadn't just called security.

He read over my shoulder. 'It could be a coincidence. But Bauer's going to go spare.'

Maarten left and Tim finished his phone call. 'The parents are in Maastricht. It's after five o'clock now so it would be late before they could get here. I told them to turn up first thing tomorrow.'

'Okay. That's fine.'

'Lotte, thanks for standing up for me. You didn't have to, and I appreciate it.' He looked at me across the desks. 'I actually deserved the bollocking this time.'

I shook my head. 'You couldn't have known. I wasn't really standing up for you; I meant what I said to Bauer: there was nothing suspicious about Sylvie's death until now. Until Piotr Mazur was murdered.'

'Still. Thanks. Let me buy you dinner.'

I was on lates, so I would be here for another couple of hours before I could go home. I wanted to study the file on Sylvie Bruyneel's death more closely. I wanted to check where she had been working and where her body had been found. 'I'm going to stay here for a bit.'

'You need to eat something. Just something quick.' He was insistent.

I was reminded of the message I'd sent Mark last night: that I thought Tim fancied me. He'd called our drinks a 'hot date'. 'Thanks, but I'm just going to grab something in the canteen.'

'You got shouted at by Bauer on my behalf. The least I can do is make sure you get something to eat outside of the office.'

'You must have better things to do than having dinner with me.' With someone as old as me. I could convince myself I wasn't really fishing for a compliment.

'Well, yes, actually I was going to get a bite to eat with someone else, but she won't mind if you come along.'

So he hadn't been offering dinner with just the two of us. I needed to adjust what I'd been thinking. 'Anyone I know?'

'Hold on, let me just WhatsApp her.' He got his phone out and started typing. 'Yes, she says let's all meet downstairs in five minutes.'

'Downstairs in five minutes?' I tipped my head sideways and faked a smile. 'So a colleague is joining us? This gets more and more mysterious by the minute.'

He blushed.

I narrowed my eyes. He'd blushed earlier today when I'd asked him how he knew about Mark Visser and me. He'd replied that someone had told him last night. Many things about last night were a blur, but I remembered that he'd asked me to hang around for another ten minutes because more people were joining them for drinks. Someone had arrived after I'd left. She had been his 'hot date' and she had told him about Mark. There weren't many people who knew.

He knew I'd saved a colleague's life. The admiration in his eyes hadn't been for my bravery but out of gratitude for the person who was still alive because of me. Because I'd done what she couldn't. I closed my eyes and rubbed my fingers over the wrinkles on my forehead as if that would erase them.

'How long have you and Ingrid been seeing each other?' I even managed to sound happy about it. Thank God I hadn't made a fool of myself last night.

Ingrid and Tim looked good together, I had to admit that. We were in the Indonesian restaurant down one of the side streets just a short walk from the police station. If I were seeing a colleague, I would have gone somewhere else, but maybe they weren't concerned about who knew, or maybe bringing me along was the perfect disguise. I felt like an ageing chaperone or the maiden aunt. The thing I liked about this restaurant right now was that they had been quick to bring our food. I'd ordered without looking at the menu because I had the same thing every time I came here: babi panggang with steamed rice.

'I didn't even have to tell her I was seeing you,' Tim told Ingrid. 'She figured it out.' He said it with pride in his voice, as if he was talking about a smart dog that had managed to perform a particularly difficult trick. 'And she had a go at Bauer.' He broke the large prawn cracker that had come with his nasi rames in two and passed half to Ingrid.

'Is he still on your case?'

'He's not going to stop that any time soon,' he said.

They swapped skewers of beef and chicken satay without asking. He grabbed her hand and licked sauce from her thumb.

A lurid picture of a golden dragon flying against a red background hung on the wall to my right. I took a large bite of my food and tried to concentrate on how the sourness of the pickled vegetables that accompanied the meat bit the inside of my mouth. A flow of guppies drifted in a fish tank strategically placed to provide privacy that I could do without. The sooner I finished my dinner, the sooner I could leave.

'What's Bauer's problem?' Ingrid said.

'He just doesn't think I'm any good.'

'But you are. Don't you agree, Lotte?'

The fact that I had my mouth full gave me time to phrase a suitable reply. I swallowed. 'Well, we've identified our suspect.'

'Thanks to Tim?'

I might not have recognised Katja if he hadn't thought that it was really funny to shut me in a bathroom. Oh well, why not make him look good in front of his new girlfriend. 'Yeah, thanks to Tim,' I said.

'You should tell Bauer that.'

'She did. That's why I'm buying her dinner.'

I looked at my watch. 'Guys, I need to get back to work soon. Do you want to finish the rest of my babi panggang? You're paying for it anyway.'

'Don't go yet,' Ingrid said. 'I want to know how the case is going.'

'It's going,' I said. 'I've come to realise that Bauer and I want very different things. I seem to be the only one who's interested in finding out who stabbed the Polish guy.'

'What about his girlfriend? Isn't she putting pressure on you at all?'

'What girlfriend?' Tim said.

I massaged the wrinkle between my eyebrows. 'Natalie Schuurman,' I said. 'His neighbour.' It was possible that nobody in Bauer's team had read our initial files. That disturbed me. I turned back to Ingrid. 'Natalie isn't going to say anything because her fiancé doesn't know.'

'Are they the two next door that you were talking to yesterday?' Tim said.

'Yes, I could hear them arguing. Those walls are really thin. He's so good-looking. I don't know what she saw in Piotr Mazur.'

'Relieving the boredom at work.' Ingrid grinned at Tim. 'I get that.'

I took a large spoonful of food. I had almost cleared my plate.

'How do you know she was seeing him?' Tim asked.

'They were sexting. I don't remember the exact words, but it was something like *Where are u, I need it.* That kind of thing.'

Tim laughed. 'Doesn't sound terribly explicit to me. Not like . . .' He blushed.

I could fill in the details of what he was going to say. I pushed my plate away. 'I really ought to get back to work.'

'It sounds more as if they were setting up a delivery,' Tim said. 'A deal.'

I thought of all the texts she'd sent him. I remembered the security footage that had only taken a minute, and Natalie's delighted grin when she'd come out of the changing rooms. I finally understood what Ronald had been trying to show me. I looked at my watch. If I hurried, I could swing by the department store before it closed. 'I'm off,' I said. 'I won't crash your dinner any longer.'

Chapter Seventeen

When I arrived at the department store, Ronald wasn't in his usual place by the entrance. He was probably in the security guards' offices on the sixth floor. It didn't matter; I'd speak to him later. I took the escalator up to the fashion section where Natalie worked, but I couldn't see her. Maybe she was on a break, or helping a customer.

The green dress I'd admired last time was still there. The silky material was as cool and soft as I remembered. I walked up to a full-length mirror with the garment and held it against me. It was no surprise that one of the sales women immediately approached me. I recognised her; she had come into the storage area when Thomas and I were interviewing Natalie last Friday. She was called Alice Fransen, her name badge revealed. 'Do you want to try it on?' she asked.

'Can I?' I had to admit that I was curious what the changing rooms were like. It would also give me an opportunity to ask Alice a few casual questions.

'Of course, follow me.'

I checked the ceiling for the shining metal eye of a security camera. I spotted the one in the centre aisle that had captured the footage Ronald had showed me. I could see no others in this area.

If you were going to snort drugs in a changing room, these had more space than most. I got undressed. The efficient air con was on so high that the cold air drew goose bumps on my naked skin. At least it was cool enough that I didn't have to worry about sweating on an expensive dress. I put it over my head and let the green silk flow over my body. I shimmied in it until the cloth hugged my every curve. It was beautiful and I felt beautiful wearing it.

The light here was soft and flattering, perfect for the older women who could afford these clothes. Other stores catered for the younger crowd and seemed to frown when someone over the age of twenty dared to try on one of their pairs of jeans. They tried to scare us away with loud music, and used sharp light that highlighted every wrinkle in our faces and every grey hair.

A discreet knock on the door announced Alice. 'How are you getting on?' she said.

I opened the door. 'It's lovely,' I said.

'That really suits you.' She sounded surprised.

I stepped out into the corridor and looked at myself in the large mirror at one end. I turned this way and that. The dress looked as if it was made for me and brought out the green in my eyes that my ex had described as the colour of the North Sea after a storm. He hadn't meant it as a compliment but I rather liked the description. That had annoyed him.

'You were here the other day, weren't you?' Alice said. 'To interview Natalie.'

'Yes, and I saw this dress then. But I couldn't really try it on, not while I was working.'

'We have had a few other women try it. One of them might come back for it tomorrow.'

'How's Natalie holding up anyway? She seemed very upset.' It was now clear to me what had been going on between Piotr and Natalie, but I was interested in hearing what her colleagues knew.

'Well, yes, upset to—' She cut off her words.

I tried to meet her eyes in the mirror but she looked away. 'Upset to what?'

'Never mind.' She rearranged the skirt that already fitted so well over my hips, tidying up a fold at the back. 'Would you like to try some shoes with that? Then you could see how the skirt hangs with high heels.'

'No, it's fine.' I'd learned how important it was to stay away from temptation.

'Natalie is enjoying her moment in the spotlight. She was never so keen on Piotr as now that he's dead. Sorry, I shouldn't have said that.' This time she met my eyes in the mirror. That hadn't been an accidental slip of the tongue. 'Shall I help you undo the zip on the back?'

'Sure.' I stepped back into the changing room. Alice had clearly decided that I'd worn their expensive dress for long enough. She undid the hooks on the top of the zip. 'How long have you worked here?' I said.

'I've been here for five years. Why?'

'Do you remember Sylvie Bruyneel?' I was sure stuff disappeared from the department store often enough, but someone walking out with a number of designer dresses must have been a memorable event.

'Sylvie?' She paused with the zip halfway undone. 'She worked here a long time ago. Two years ago, I'd guess.'

'She worked here?'

She finished unzipping me. 'For about twelve months. I didn't know her that well. We didn't socialise. You should talk to Natalie, she was her friend.' Her mouth twitched as if she was still annoyed about not being included. 'They shared a flat until they had a massive falling-out.'

'Did they? I didn't know that.' Now at least I knew where Sylvie had lived after her sister had kicked her out. I was slowly piecing her life together.

'The two of them would go partying,' Alice said. 'But it wasn't my scene, you know.'

I could fill in what she wasn't saying: party together, do cocaine together. 'Probably for the best. Do you know what they fell out over?'

'Maybe they were too alike. They were both used to getting all the attention,' Alice said. 'And when Sylvie was caught stealing from here, it was the final straw.'

'I can imagine,' I said. 'And Natalie was the one who noticed the theft? Not the security guards?'

Alice glanced sideways. 'Let me know if you need any help getting changed.' She stepped out and closed the door to the changing room. I had no choice but to turn back from someone glamorous into someone with a day job.

I shimmied out of the dress. I checked the discreet card that was attached to the inside by a minuscule safety pin. In fine handwritten numbers it was penned that the dress cost nearly a month's after-tax salary. I put it back on its hanger with renewed deference. I should count myself lucky that I hadn't torn it getting in or out. I had a better understanding now of why Alice's eyes had kept following the dress as if it had a magnetic force field. How tempting that must have been for someone with a drug habit, especially if you could lift them to order. If you worked here, you could easily take the security tag off and walk out.

I opened the door of the changing room. Alice was hovering right outside.

'Thanks for letting me try it on,' I said. 'It's beautiful, but I would never wear it.' Over her shoulder I caught a glimpse of a woman with blonde hair approaching us.

'I can put it aside for you until tomorrow,' Alice said, 'to give you time to think about it. Otherwise, if someone else wants it . . . we don't have that many in this size.'

'I've got it from here, Alice,' Natalie interrupted her.

Alice nodded and moved on to talk to two Asian women, possibly Chinese, who were looking at the short jackets in primary colours. I wished I could wear those, but I would only look ill in yellow. In contrast, bottle green was a great shade for me.

'That dress. You couldn't resist it, could you?' Natalie held it up again and spread the material wide with the hanger still attached.

'Actually, I came here to talk to you. About Piotr. I know you weren't having a relationship with him.' I lowered my voice. 'You didn't meet here to have sex. You met to snort coke, didn't you?'

Even through her thick make-up, I could tell that Natalie suddenly grew pale. 'I didn't do anything.' It sounded very much like a four-year-old's refusal to accept responsibility for a broken vase, and it was equally believable.

'It's time to start telling the truth.'

She gripped my arm and pulled me away from the racks. 'Not here. I'll lose my job.' She walked towards the discreet door and typed in the security code.

'Yes, I'm sure your employer doesn't want you doing drugs in the dressing rooms. They can ask security for the tapes as soon as I tell them.'

Natalie laughed bitterly as she opened the door. 'Security. That's a joke.'

I followed her in. 'It's very clear to see on a security camera.' We were alone with the railings full of dresses wrapped in plastic and the piles of boxes that formed a second wall.

She shut the door behind us. 'They're the ones selling in the first place.'

'They're all in on it?' Somehow I couldn't believe that Ronald was, whatever I might have said to him in anger the other day, but I couldn't help but wonder, for a second, what was in some of the bin bags that were now in my flat.

'No, just Piotr Mazur. I'm surprised you ever believed I had an affair with that Polish drug pusher.'

'You were the only one sending him text messages.'

Natalie sighed. 'He wanted more money and I gave in. Told him I'd give him what he wanted. Using those words . . . it was just a bit of a laugh, you know? Getting him to speed up his rounds.'

'Who was his supplier?'

'I don't know.'

'Was it someone else here?'

Natalie was silent for a bit. She straightened out a dress and pushed it back between the other garments, as if the physical activity of tidying up made it easier for her to think. 'It can't have been, can it?' She looked back at me. 'Because then someone else would have taken over.'

'Thanks, Natalie, you've been very helpful.'

'Will you tell the police?'

'Did you forget I *am* the police?'

'You know what I mean. Will I lose my job?'

'We'll see. Maybe we can arrange something.'

'I can't give you the dress.' Natalie sounded even more like a petulant schoolgirl.

'I hope you're not suggesting I was asking for a bribe. Help me find out who Piotr's supplier was.'

Natalie looked at me. 'This would be a good time for me to stop, wouldn't it?'

'A very good time. Tell me if someone tries to sell to you and we'll forget all about it.'

She nodded, her face as serious as if she was taking an oath. 'I'll do that.'

'Do you remember Sylvie Bruyneel?'

'Why are you asking about Sylvie?' Natalie said. 'She's dead.'

'Yes, I know. She worked here, didn't she?'

'She stole from us. The stupid bitch.' The word was in-congruous out of the pink mouth under the tearful eyes. 'She put all our jobs in danger.'

'And she was also taking drugs?' I said.

'Snorting coke all the time. It's all her fault.'

'What about heroin?'

'Not then. She must have moved on to that later.' She straightened another dress. This was clearly what she did when she needed time to think.

'She was your friend. Did you ever talk to her after she left here?'

'No, of course not. She was a thief.' She turned back to me. 'She was really angry with me when I contacted the police. She said I'd stitched her up.'

'Why did you call us? Why didn't you leave it to security?'

'I didn't want them to let her go with a warning. And they might have done, you know. She could be very charming when she wanted to.' I could tell that Natalie was getting angrier as she was talking. 'She deserved to be punished. She'd been stealing from me all the time. She would take money from my wallet or stuff from my room and sell it.'

'You shared a flat?'

'And a great success that was. When I kicked her out, that's when she moved on to taking stuff from here.'

'Where was she living then?'

'I don't know. Then she was in that rehab centre. And who knows what she got into there with all those addicts together.'

I thanked her again for her help and reminded her to contact me as soon as anybody else tried to sell her drugs.

There was fifteen minutes before the shop would close, and Ronald had returned to his spot by the exit. He had his back towards me and stared at the door. Next to him stood a good-looking Moroccan guy in a sharp suit. I came closer but didn't want to interrupt their conversation in case this had anything to do with Ronald's work. The guy could be the manager of the store for all I knew. Then I caught part of the conversation.

'It was a young woman,' Ronald said. 'White. Dutch apparently.'

'Okay. If you're sure.' The Moroccan man nodded slowly. 'I'll make it worth your while. That place you're living, it seems you can do with some help.' He laughed. 'I can at least help you with the housing. I'll call you.' He left the shop through the revolving doors.

'Hey, Ronald,' I said.

He turned around sharply.

'I'm not happy with your housing situation either.'

'I fed your cat, by the way.'

'Couldn't you have told me that Piotr wasn't sleeping with Natalie?' I said.

'I did, remember, but you wouldn't believe me.'

'Something blatant like "they're not having sex, they're snorting coke" would have been useful.'

'I told you they weren't having sex. As you didn't take my word for it, I thought you would want something more concrete, so I tried to give you evidence.'

'Was that what that security footage was all about? That one-minute sequence?'

'Exactly. But there are no cameras actually inside the changing rooms.'

'The next time be more obvious. Less cryptic.'

'Will you believe me next time?'

I didn't answer him but left the department store to go back to the office.

The evening was turning into night and a hint of coolness had appeared in the air by the time I left the police station. It was pleasant to be out on my bike. Instead of turning right down my canal, I took a left. I kept pumping my legs. The movement was almost effortless and allowed me to think as I cycled along canals and down little streets in the dark for half an hour. Why I'd ever thought that Tim fancied me I could no longer understand. I'd completely misread those signals. He and Ingrid made a nice couple. Mark Visser deserved to be left alone and I should just live by myself with my cat.

As if my thoughts of loneliness had carried me there, I took one more turning and came to my mother's flat. I looked up to her floor and saw that the light was still on.

She opened the door with a flushed face. 'Hi, Lotte.' She looked surprisingly well. Her white hair was immaculate, as if she'd taken time to comb it properly. I even thought she might have put on a little bit of weight since I'd seen her last. She had been getting too skinny. 'What brings you here so late?'

'Were you going to bed?' I checked my watch. It was just after ten o'clock. I kissed her on the cheek.

'No, no, come in.' She looked over my shoulder into the hallway. For a second I wondered if she'd been expecting someone else.

'I thought I'd see how you were.'

She wore a red scarf in the neck of her white blouse. Even though the material was thin, it was surely too hot for it. I knew she hated it when her wrinkly chest, as she called it, was on display, but why bother if she was here by herself? 'I was going to do the same,' she said. 'You beat me to it.' She poured me a glass of water.

I sat down at the table, at my usual place. My mother had lived in this flat for over forty years now, ever since she divorced my father. She still had some of the furniture we'd had then.

'Your father called me. He asked if I could see you. He sounded worried.'

'Since when are you guys talking again?' All the windows were open and the lights were on, and it attracted the mosquitoes. I could see a number of them drifting into the flat, slowly, inconspicuously, as if they had no intention of sucking our blood. A particularly large one landed on my arm, casually, as if it was just taking a little rest there. I knew what it had in mind and squashed it under my palm. Lotte 1, Mosquitoes 0.

'We only ever talk about you.' Her cheeks were bright red. She could of course have been in the sun too long, but she was also smiling too much. 'He said you seemed down.' And then there was that scarf.

'Things haven't been great. I was having drinks with Mark Visser—'

'Are you still chasing after that man?'

'Mom!' Another mosquito flew past me and I caught it and crushed it in my hand. Lotte 2, Mosquitoes 0.

'Well, I did my best for you.'

'I know, I screwed it up. You should get some curtains,' I said. 'To keep the mosquitoes out.'

'They never go for me,' my mother said. 'I know they bite you all the time but I don't think my blood is sweet enough.' She ignored one that flew right past her face. I found it hard to think when they buzzed past me, but my mother seemed completely capable of tuning them out. 'I think Mark really liked you at one point. It was great to see him after all those years.'

'Mom, please.' I drained my glass of water, only now realising how thirsty I had been.

'Just saying. There's hope for you, just not with him.'

'I was hoping we could be friends.' I went into the kitchen to fill the glass up again. I drank it all with the tap still running.

'Your father said you witnessed a stabbing?' She hadn't moved from her seat at the table, but that was no reason not to keep the conversation going.

'Yeah, well, that comes with the job.' I said it softly, so it was probably camouflaged by the sound of the running tap.

Two empty wineglasses stood on the work surface. 'Mark was with me,' I said. Why hadn't she washed those up yet? She was normally so diligent that it was a surprise to see any dirty crockery out at all. I picked up one of the glasses and turned it round. My mother never wore make-up, but her friend might have done. No lipstick markings. Not on the other glass either.

'And did you do something sensible, like ask for his help?'

'Mum, I'm a police officer, remember?' And I'm now investigating this evidence of you entertaining someone. Who was it? I looked in the recycling bin. There was an empty wine bottle. I checked the label. It was a nasty sweet white. Not my kind of thing at all.

'Men want to be useful sometimes.'

I put the bottle back in the recycling, softly so that it didn't make a noise. 'You're so last century.' My mother kept herbs in tins on the windowsill of her kitchen. They looked a bit droopy. I felt the soil and they were bone-dry. I watered them from my glass.

'You're doing everything by yourself. So independent, so self-sufficient. No wonder he didn't feel needed.'

'So that's what I should have done? Asked him for help with something that is my job?'

'I despair of you sometimes. You think you're so smart but you're acting all stupid.'

I filled my glass one more time and sat back down at the table. 'And you're what? Sensible?'

'No,' my mother said, 'but I've met someone.'

'Was he here tonight?' The two wineglasses. The red scarf. It was so incongruous that I hadn't been able to piece the evidence together. I realised that I must have just missed him. When I'd rung the doorbell, she'd probably thought he'd come back. No wonder she'd been surprised to see me.

'We met at church,' she said with a small smile that could only be described as smug.

I hadn't known this was a competition. 'That's nice,' was all I could come out with. And I knew that in an hour or so, I really would think it was nice that she wasn't alone at seventy-four. She hadn't introduced me to anybody in the last forty years. She must have had flings and just not told me about it. Or maybe she'd been so bitter about the divorce from my father that she hadn't been able to move on. It was only now that she was talking to my father again that she'd met someone new. One of the self-help books on my shelves at home would say that this situation was proof of the need for closure before you could move on. I knew all the theory; it just didn't help me much in real life.

'I asked him to carry my shopping when I'd broken my wrist.'

'*I* did your shopping!' And I'd picked her up from the hospital and let her stay in my flat for five very long weeks. I scratched my arm. A bite was already showing red on the skin. Lotte 2, Mosquitoes 1.

'Well, so did he. So you see, I needed him and wasn't afraid to tell him that.'

'So I should just show Mark that I need him and he'll come running?' Another bite started to itch on my back where a little bit of bare skin showed between the waistband of my trousers and the bottom of my T-shirt. It was going to be a draw after all.

'No,' my mother said with finality in her voice. 'It's too late for that. I just meant that asking for help is fine some-times. It's not a failing. You don't have to do everything by yourself. You don't have to be superwoman.'

Superwoman. It made me laugh. All I managed to do was keep my head above water.

When I opened the front door, my cat didn't meow to greet me.

'Puss, puss,' I called down the empty corridor, 'where are you?' My skin itched like crazy. I had four bites on my arm and three on my back. Lotte 2, Mosquitoes 7. You never beat the mozzies.

Mrs Cat didn't turn up. Having someone else in the flat had probably scared her. She'd come and say hello later. I dropped my bag on the sofa and went into my study. I'd bought the flat from an interior designer and I kept everything exactly as she'd had it. I hadn't thought the big architect's table in the study would be useful, but I've come to love drawing my thoughts on whatever case I'm working on. I hadn't made any drawings on Piotr Mazur's murder. Had I not taken his death seriously enough? Had I been too busy thinking about how I'd messed up with Mark?

Bauer wasn't interested in Piotr Mazur's death, but I had moved teams because I'd wanted to catch whoever had killed him. Bauer had only allowed me in to make sure his previous case didn't get damaged. I'd probably already known that in the back of my mind, but his outburst today had brought it out in the open. That actually made things easier, because once you knew what the issues were, you could deal with them.

I ran the palm of my hand over the sheet of paper pinned to the architect's table. I took out a blue marker pen. I wrote

194

'Piotr Mazur' in the centre of the sheet. I drew a square box around his name. At the top I wrote down the names of the two people whom Piotr had definitely supplied with drugs: Karl the Beard and Natalie Schuurman. I drew red arrows between Piotr's name and the two boxes. 'Dealer' I wrote by the arrows. At the bottom of the page I wrote the names of the two sisters: Katja and Sylvie Bruyneel. By Sylvie's name I wrote: 'OD'. I also wrote that by Karl's name. I drew an arrow from Katja to Piotr and wrote 'together in bar'. I drew a dashed line between Sylvie and Natalie and wrote 'worked together'. When had Piotr Mazur started working at the department store? Sylvie had been caught stealing from there two years ago. Had he already been a security guard then? Ronald had mentioned to me that Natalie had got Piotr his job.

I pulled up Piotr's employment records. He'd started work at the department store eighteen months ago. That was after Sylvie had been convicted of theft. So who had her dealer been? Natalie had said that it was always the security guards dealing drugs.

Only the manager, Kevin Haanen, had already been there when Sylvie was arrested. I should talk to him tomorrow. Tim had scheduled the meeting with Katja and Sylvie's adoptive parents for 9 a.m. I could go back to the department store after that.

I stared at my drawing a bit longer. I took a step back. It was already a mess, a spider's web of tenuous connections that could be coincidences. I remembered hearing the argument between Natalie and her handsome fiancé Koen Westerfaalt. At the time I'd thought it was about her affair with Piotr, but now I knew there hadn't been one. So what had they been arguing about? Her drug use? Or was it only a normal row like every couple has every now and then?

I took another step back.

There was only one thing missing. I wrote: 'Who's the little boy?' and surrounded the words with question marks.

Chapter Eighteen

The parents arrived at 9 a.m. on the dot. I took them to Interrogation Room 1. I opened the door and was hit by how warm it was inside. The air conditioning in the police station seemed to have given up its attempt to cool things down. It was like stepping into a sauna.

Tim was already in his seat. A few drops of sweat showed on his forehead. I took my place next to him and indicated the chairs opposite us. Harald was wearing a suit and tie, as if that was the right attire for a visit to the police station regardless of the heat. Mabel wore a summer dress, and a golden cross showed in the small V of the demure neckline. She carried a thick leather folder. They pulled back their metal chairs in tandem. I looked at my phone; the temperature gauge indicated that it was 25°C in the room. It was best to keep this brief.

If they had helped Katja out of the country, or if they were hiding her, they were in serious trouble. I was reminded of their house, the lounge without any photos of either daughter. Was that because they'd been trying to conceal Katja's identity? At the time I'd thought it was a sign that they'd cut off all ties with her, but what if it had been the opposite?

I pressed the button on the recording equipment and stated our names and the time.

The parents hadn't brought a lawyer.

'Where's Katja?' Tim asked. 'We need to speak to her in connection to a murder.'

'A murder?' Mabel said. 'You said you were looking for her but you didn't mention a murder.'

'We think she may have been involved in the murder of a drug dealer,' Tim said. 'Was she using drugs?'

'We're concerned that she witnessed something,' I said to soften the edges of Tim's blunt words. 'She was in the bar with the victim.'

Mabel's head started to nod a little with a tremor like one of those toy dogs that people have in the back of their car. 'Why would she have been in a bar with a drug dealer?' I could see that Harald was taking her hand under the table.

'That's what we would like to find out.' Tim looked down at his notes.

'We're no longer in touch with Katja,' Harald said in his slow and precise voice. 'We don't know where she is.'

'When was this man killed?' Mabel clasped the golden cross around her throat.

'A week ago,' I said. Sweat was trickling down the back of my neck. I rubbed it away and then wiped my hand on my trousers. 'She hasn't been seen since. We're extremely concerned about her well-being.'

'We thought . . .' Mabel looked at the leather folder. 'We thought you had more questions about Sylvie.'

'Do you know where Katja is?' Tim said.

'No,' Harald said. 'As I told you, we're not in touch with her any more.'

'And you?' I looked at Mabel. 'Are you not in touch with her either? If she's scared and in hiding, we can help.'

'I haven't seen her,' Mabel said.

'Have you spoken to her?'

'I talked to her four months ago and haven't heard from her since.' Mabel started to cry softly. 'I tried to call her but she isn't answering her phone.'

'Did you help her leave the country? You know we'll find out,' Tim said.

Harald and Mabel shared a bewildered look. 'We really haven't seen her,' Mabel said. Her head was shaking violently. Harald enclosed her hand firmly with both of his.

'Did you know what she'd done? Is that why you have no photos of her in your front room?' Tim said. 'So that we wouldn't find out her identity?' It was the same thought I'd had.

'No,' Mabel said. 'No, it's not that at all.'

The couple looked shocked by the bombardment of questions. Surely they would have been better prepared for this if they'd helped Katja.

'Let's take a step back,' I said, to calm things down. Tim shot me an annoyed glance, but I ignored him. 'You mentioned something last time we spoke,' I said, 'about your daughter being just like her mother and not being careful. Were you talking about Katja or Sylvie?'

'Katja.' Mabel put her hand on the leather folder. 'We're so angry with her.'

199

Harald wrapped his arm around his wife's shoulder. His suit jacket rode up from his waist. He should undo the button. 'You did your best,' he said to her. 'You tried.'

'What happened?'

'She's refusing all treatment. Just like her mother.'

'Treatment for what? Drug addiction?'

Mabel shook her head.

'Take your time,' I said. 'What's in the folder?'

'The adoption papers.'

I gestured that I wanted to see them. It would be quicker for me to read what had happened to the mother than to wait for Mabel to tell me this in a muddle. The papers mentioned two girls: Karin and Sonja. Mother: Tanja Aak.

'You changed their names?' I said.

'Yes. But we kept the initials.'

It really was as if they had got two dogs out of a rescue centre. What would that have been like if you were five years old?

'I was surprised when Katja called us out of the blue,' Mabel said. 'We hadn't been talking for a while. When she told me about the cancer, I said it was stupid of her. Sylvie overdosing was one thing, but this was unnecessary. Katja got angry with us. That's when she said it about the divorce for children.'

I scanned the documents. Mother's cause of death: cancer. Father's cause of death: suicide. 'Their mother died of cancer at age twenty-nine?' I realised that all my assumptions had been wrong.

'Yes. Breast cancer. Katja was always very likely to have inherited that gene. We asked her to get tested for it, but she said she didn't want to know, and that if she was going to die young that was okay.'

'That's why you said she wasn't careful.'

'When she called us four months ago,' Mabel's voice was suddenly full of anger, 'it had already spread all over her body and to her lymph nodes and she'd decided not to have chemo.'

'This wasn't long after her sister died.'

'A couple of months after. She'd been stupid. If she'd checked herself regularly, she would have had a chance. Now she said she was only going to the hospital to get her pain meds and to receive palliative care. Nothing else. No chemo, no surgery.' Mabel's voice rose. 'It was too late for that, she said. She wasn't interested in twelve months of a horrible life if she could have four months of a good one.'

'Mabel was so upset, weren't you?' Harald said. 'We tried to do anything we could to get her to change her mind. We went to her place and wanted to drag her to the hospital, but she flat-out refused. I asked her to do it for her mother's sake, to give us peace of mind that we'd done all we could for her, but she couldn't care less about us.'

'So that was the last time you saw her? When you went to her flat?'

'Yes, we tried again a week later, but she wasn't there. She stopped answering her phone as well.'

'Where is she being treated? Which hospital?'

'I don't know,' Mabel said. 'She wouldn't tell me. I'm sure we'll hear at some point that she's died.' She pushed the folder across to me. 'Keep this. Was that all?'

'So Katja never used drugs.'

'No, never.'

'And do you know anything about a child? This child?' I showed them the photo of the little boy with the boat.

'I've no idea who that is.'

'Okay.' At least I now understood why Katja had left her flat. It was to escape her parents. That didn't tell me where she was now, of course.

'If you hear from Katja, please contact us,' Tim said. He accompanied Harald and Mabel out of the room.

Unless she was self-medicating with heroin, Katja would have to go to the hospital for her pain meds. She would be keeping those appointments.

I called the oncology departments of all Amsterdam's hospitals to ask if they had a Katja Bruyneel on their patient list. It only took half an hour before I had the right one.

Chapter Nineteen

Tim's car with the air con on at full blast was blessedly cool. He had frowned when I suggested we drive to the hospital, but I needed a substantial drop in temperature and it was either this or a bag full of ice cubes on my head.

'You could have asked your questions over the phone,' he said.

'Didn't you want to get out of the station? I felt like a tomato in a glasshouse.'

I remembered when weather like this meant driving with your elbow out of the window. I'd done that when I had my first car and had thought it was the coolest thing ever. Now we kept all the windows shut to create this cool box on wheels.

'I'm not going to complain about the sun. Two whole weeks of summer doesn't happen too often.' Still, from the way he was driving, it was clear that he was happy to be inside the car as well. A traffic light went from green to amber and Tim slowed down instead of speeding up. The short delay of a red light was a blessing on the quick drive to the hospital.

'The doctor might let something slip that he'd be reluctant to tell us over the phone,' I said.

'Do you think Katja will still turn up for her appointments?'

'She'll need her meds unless she bought heroin from Piotr Mazur to keep the pain at bay.'

'That would make the boss happy.' He put his indicator light on to pull in to the hospital car park. 'It would make me happy too.'

'Happier than if we arrested her?' I was lucky to be secure in my job, but I still had a hard time prioritising Bauer's opinion over getting some answers. Then I remembered cases that I had worked on where I'd done anything I could to get a conviction. If they had fallen apart in court, I would have been devastated.

'Well, if Mazur was dealing heroin,' Tim said, 'maybe he just gave that German the wrong stuff.'

I reluctantly got out of the car. I wasn't keen on hospitals. Just the smell of antiseptic and cleaning products brought back too many painful memories. This hospital was in Amsterdam's outskirts, close to the ring road and therefore easy to get to. I delayed going inside by having a scan around. To my left, next to the car park, was the day-care centre for the children of patients and medical staff. It had a separate entrance so that the kids didn't have to be subjected to that hospital smell every morning. Through the window I could see healthy children playing with soft balls that were bigger than their heads. A young man showed them how to hold the ball between both hands, put it on the floor and push it over to the child across from them.

Tim had walked up to the hospital entrance as I lingered outside. I rushed after him. We were told at reception to follow the green stripes on the floor to get to the oncology department.

The rubber soles of my sandals made a squishy sound, and I sounded like a nurse walking down the corridors. 'Piotr Mazur was dealing cocaine in the department store,' I said.

Tim shot me a quick glance. He was right to be annoyed.

'Yes, sorry, I should have said something earlier. But you were right yesterday. Those texts between Natalie and Piotr were to set up drug deals. They weren't in a relationship at all. Natalie lied because she was scared to admit to us that she was using.'

'Katja could have contacted him because her sister used to buy from him.'

'Not in the department store, because Piotr didn't start work there until after Sylvie had been fired for stealing. So what reason could Katja have to kill him?' I paused at a rattling noise behind me and quickly stepped sideways to let a teenager race past in a wheelchair.

'Maybe she didn't,' Tim said. 'Maybe she was a witness.'

We arrived at the oncology department and showed our badges, and the nurse, a skinny waif of a girl who surely wasn't able to lift any patient in and out of bed, looked through the appointments to see when Katja Bruyneel was due in next.

'She has an appointment in an hour,' she said with a smile, blissfully unaware that a murder suspect was about to walk into her department. 'Oh, and here is her doctor.'

As Tim called the police station, I talked to the doctor in his examination room. He was only willing to confirm what the parents had told us this morning: Katja was in the final stages of breast cancer and had refused all treatment. He said that in his opinion she had a couple of months left at most and he completely supported her decision to opt for a good quality of life rather than going through the invasive treatment that her parents would have preferred. Unlike the parents, he called her choice 'wise'. I informed him why we wanted to talk to her. He agreed that he would contact us as soon as he saw her and not try to detain her.

There was forty-five minutes to go until Katja's appointment.

We went back to the main hall and on the hospital map I did a quick check where the entrances were. If Katja came by car, it would be the same door we had come through fifteen minutes earlier. There was a metro station by the side of the hospital. The walking route ended up by the car park entrance as well. Perfect: we had one obvious place she would be approaching from.

Unless she had an inkling we were going to be waiting for her.

But then surely she wouldn't turn up at all.

Still, I gave the receptionists in the main hall Katja's photo; the one I'd got from the door in the bathroom, not the blurry one from the security camera in the bar. I told them to call us straight away if they saw her. I hoped our back-up would get here soon, so that we would have more doors covered.

This endless wait reminded me of waiting for Mark Visser at the bar a few days ago. The evening that had started all of this. If only I could stop thinking about him.

Half an hour to go.

'We should wait outside,' I said to Tim. 'Try to keep her away from here.'

He agreed.

As soon as I'd gone through the revolving door, the nursery to the left caught my eye. The kindergarten teachers had taken the group of kids outside to play in the sunshine in the little playground surrounding the school. My heart sank. I looked at my watch. Twenty-five minutes to go. I could warn them and get the children back inside before Katja arrived. 'You stay here,' I said to Tim and dashed up to one of the teachers. It was the same guy who had shown the kids the proper way to roll balls to each other.

I showed him my badge. 'Sorry, what's your name?'

'Vincent de Wolf.'

'Okay Vincent, you need to get these kids back inside,' I said in as calm a voice as I could muster. As I put my badge back in my handbag, I saw the photo of the little boy that Piotr Mazur had had in his wallet. I couldn't get it out of my head that this child had something to do with Katja. If he lived with her, then maybe she had taken him with her when she had her appointments. Patients could place their children here so that they could play as their parents were going through their often stressful treatment.

Twenty minutes. There was time. I showed Vincent the photo as he ushered the group of toddlers back indoors.

They streamed past him in an orderly line, holding hands. 'Have you ever seen this child?' I said.

He took the photo from me. 'Oh yes,' he said, 'he used to come here quite a bit, but I haven't seen him in a while.'

'We're concerned about this boy.' A little girl smiled at me as she went into the school building. She was so cute. Only five children were left outdoors.

The man frowned. 'I didn't know that. I talked to Petra the other day and she said he was fine. He's her grandson.'

'Petra?'

'Petra Maasland. She's a counsellor. She works here. This is her grandson, Oskar. She used to bring him here, but now her daughter has a job where they provide child care as well.' All the kids were now indoors and the teacher was about to follow them in.

Petra Maasland. Sylvie Bruyneel's counsellor. It was okay to delay him for just one question. 'Are you sure?'

Vincent pointed at the photo. 'I recognise the boat. He loves that boat.'

I took the picture back. The teacher went inside and shut the door behind him.

'Lotte,' Tim hissed.

I looked in the direction he was staring and could see her crossing the car park. Adrenaline was soaring through my veins. I put my hand on the gun on my hip as if to ensure that it hadn't mysteriously disappeared in the last ten minutes. I checked my watch. Fifteen minutes early. I walked quickly towards Tim. If I'd sprinted, I might have caught her attention. 'Is our back-up here?'

'Not yet. They're on their way.'

208

She was wearing the same floral dress as the other night in the bar, as if she was trying to make it as easy as possible for us to identify her. She was even carrying the same jacket. She made eye contact with me. I thought she recognised me. I swallowed. This all felt very wrong.

A man with his son, a teenager, got out of their car to my right. If there had been back-up, we could have temporarily closed down the car park. Now I had to deal with more innocent bystanders.

'Please stay back,' I said. Even though Katja looked calm, she was a murder suspect. I couldn't see a weapon, but still it was better to be safe than sorry. The teenager kept walking. He had earphones in. Had he not heard me? His father shot one look at me, then took his son by the wrist and pulled him back.

I concentrated again on the woman walking towards me in her floral dress. I had my hand on my gun but I didn't take it out of the holster yet. 'Katja Bruyneel?' I said. As if I didn't know the answer to that question.

She stopped walking. 'Yes.'

'We need you to come to the police station and answer some questions.'

'I can't see my doctor first?' she said as she held out her hands as if she expected handcuffs. Her composed voice surprised me.

Tim rushed to her side and grabbed her by the upper arm.

'The doctor has to wait,' he said.

'I understand,' she said. 'I guess I need a lawyer more than a doctor.' Her voice was steady. I was willing to bet that her heart rate was slower than mine. This was a very unusual arrest. There were no attempts to justify or explain. I had the distinct feeling that she had known we were waiting here for her. And had come anyway.

She wasn't Piotr Mazur's murderer.

She lifted her head and looked me in the eye.

'I did it,' she said. 'I killed him.'

Chapter Twenty

Katja Bruyneel had her hands loosely folded in front of her. Her nails were short and without any polish. She hadn't lost her poise, not after her confession to murder, not as Tim read her her rights, not as she was waiting in her cell for a lawyer and not as she was sitting here opposite me in the interrogation room.

'I killed him to avenge my sister.' Even when repeating the admission, she was relentlessly calm. She reminded me of one of the solid wooden posts you'd see on the beach; waves would hit it, but regardless of the incoming and out-going tide the stakes would stand rooted in the sand, day after day. She looked older than her twenty-six years.

'My client wants to make a complete confession,' the lawyer said. He was a middle-aged black man. His hair was shaved close to his skull and did not hide a large scar that ran above his left ear. His dark-blue tie was the only item of clothing with any colour in it, an understated but definite contrast with the black shirt and dark-grey suit. 'We're not interested in a reduction of the sentence.'

Of course not. It was likely that Katja would die before the case even came to trial.

'My sister had been clean for so long,' she continued, as if the lawyer hadn't spoken, 'and then this guy tempted her back. It had been so hard for her to stop. She said the drugs made her feel invincible, as if she could take on the world, and that was what she needed to get out of bed in the morning.'

'How do you know that?' I said. 'You were no longer in touch with your sister.'

Bauer sat next to me. The large lump of his body was a clear reminder of the outcome he wanted. He felt more of an adversary than the lawyer.

'I feel very bad about that. I met her counsellor, Petra Maasland. She also works at the hospital and I talked to her after I got my diagnosis. I recognised her from the funeral and she told me about Sylvie. How well she had been doing. Stupid woman, she completely failed my sister. Anyway, I knew I only had a few months left and I might as well rid the world of the person who killed Sylvie and make sure he couldn't do it to anybody else.'

'You're telling me that Petra Maasland told you to murder Piotr Mazur?'

'No, of course not. But she made me realise how much damage he had caused.'

'Did you know the man?'

'No.'

'You had never met him before?'

'No.' Katja held eye contact during the interview. She wasn't fidgeting or scribbling on a piece of paper or biting her nails. She wasn't looking away from me like she would if she was inventing answers to my questions.

'You called him out of the blue.'

'Did you know that I had to identify my sister's body?'

I nodded. I'd seen that in the file.

'Afterwards they gave me her possessions. They gave me her phone. I found his details. I dialled the number and set up a meeting.'

'In the bar? Why would you meet up with him in a bar?'

'It seemed to make sense.' Often people who were interrogated when guilty showed some emotion. Anger, a need to explain or justify, remorse. They would fidget. Katja was completely still, as if her mind was in a different place from her body.

'Why not just set up a deal?'

'He'd be more on his guard.'

'Why did he turn up?'

'I told him I wanted to discuss something with him. About Sylvie's death.'

'And then you stabbed him.'

'Yes.' Katja's voice was so serene it was starting to infuriate me. It was as if stabbing someone was no different from doing the weekly shopping. Even if she hadn't killed him, a man was still dead.

'How many times did you stab him?' I needed to puncture that tranquillity that was surely a facade. I hadn't been this calm in front of the Bureau of Internal Investigation when I had had to explain why I had shot a criminal.

'I stabbed him three times.'

'And what did you do with the knife?'

'I threw it away.'

'Where?'

'In a canal. I can't quite remember.'

'You can't remember. Of course.' I stacked my papers together and leaned forward. 'I don't believe a word you're saying.'

'It is the truth.'

'You're telling me that you called him out of the blue, using a number you found on your sister's phone; you'd never met him before, you wanted to kill him and you met at a bar?'

'Yes.'

'You left together and then you stabbed him to death.'

'Yes.' The girl could be a psychiatrist listening dispassionately to a patient unburdening himself, or a priest remaining unshocked by a parishioner's confession.

'What happened with the German guy with the beard?' I said.

'He came up to us and asked for heroin. The dealer gave it to him.'

'Heroin,' Bauer said.

'Yes.

'Not cocaine?'

'No.' Katja's gaze moved slowly to Bauer. 'He asked for heroin.'

If Bauer could have closed the interview right there and then, he would have done so. Not me, though. 'Are you sure?' I said.

'Yes.'

'Tell me exactly what he said.'

'He said: "I want to score some heroin."'

214

'He snorted it. People don't snort heroin. It doesn't give you a nice high.'

'Maybe he got confused. Maybe he was so drunk he'd forgotten what he'd bought.'

'And Piotr Mazur sold your sister heroin as well?'

'Yes.'

'She didn't want cocaine either.'

'No.'

'Okay, let's talk about something else. What about the child in this photo?'

'It's not mine.'

'We know that. It's Petra Maasland's grandson. Where did you get the photo from?'

'I downloaded it from her Facebook page.'

'You know Petra well?'

'She was Sylvie's completely useless counsellor. Kept telling me how much she'd helped her. She even dared to come to her funeral, even though she was equally to blame for Sylvie's death.'

'The photo has your fingerprints on it.'

'I showed it to him.'

'Why?'

Katja shrugged. 'I just thought he would trust me more if he thought I had a child.'

'Really.'

'It worked.'

'Why did he keep the photo?'

'I don't know.'

'Why did you let him?'

She shrugged again. 'Wasn't my kid. What did I care.'

'Tell me how you killed him. You left the bar together and walked along the canal then turned into the Korte de Wittekade?'

'Yes.'

'Then what happened?'

'The street was empty. I said his name, he turned to look at me and that's when I stabbed him three times. Once in the chest, twice in the stomach.'

'And he didn't try to defend himself.'

'No.' Katja's face wasn't just immobile, it was like a wall. The words bounced from a layer of clingfilm that the woman had wrapped around herself. No emotions were allowed in or out.

'He didn't try to stop you?'

'Maybe he wanted to die. Like me. It can't come soon enough. I'd like to see my doctor. Or at least get some painkillers.'

'You're covering for somebody.'

'I'm not.'

'I don't believe a word you're saying.'

'That's too bad, because it's the truth, the whole truth and nothing but the truth.' She grinned. It was the first emotion she had shown during the entire interview. 'And Mabel would add: so help me God.'

'I thought you said your client wanted to make a full confession,' I said to the lawyer. 'So please stop her from spouting all this crap.'

★ ★ ★

216

Bauer couldn't have been happier. He acted as if all his birthdays had come at once. As soon as Katja had been escorted from the interview room, he went as far as to hug me. I could have done without his sweaty skin touching mine.

I couldn't help but wonder if he knew Katja was lying but didn't care. If she had known what she needed to do to be believed, she couldn't have played it any better. It was Bauer's perfect scenario. Piotr Mazur hadn't swapped heroin for cocaine. His precious previous case was not in jeopardy. We had a confession. We had forensic evidence that linked Katja to Mazur: her fingerprint on the photo in his wallet. We had eyewitnesses who placed her at the scene of the crime. I was one of them. This case was closed: she'd had the opportunity and she had a motive. Nobody seemed to care that she was so obviously not telling the truth.

I moved back to my old team. Bauer wanted me out of that room, to take my doubts elsewhere. He wanted me to stop asking questions. He wanted to keep his team numbers down. I tried not to care but I couldn't help it. There were too many things that hadn't been solved.

'Good job, Lotte,' he kept saying whenever he saw me in the corridor.

It hadn't been a good job. Yes, Katja had been locked up, with constant medical care, but the problem with someone innocent going to prison, or dying in prison, was that there was still a murderer out there. There wouldn't even be a trial. It didn't matter that it was just a drug dealer who'd been killed.

I couldn't stop thinking that Katja had been forced to take the fall for this one. That whoever had really killed Piotr had coerced her into giving herself up. Into taking the blame.

But there was nothing I could do, so we released Piotr's body and his funeral was arranged.

I thought about taking a holiday.

Chapter Twenty-One

Normally Pippi would come to the door as soon as she heard the key in the lock and greet me noisily. This evening there was none of that. There was only silence. The flat was remarkably tidy. The dirty breakfast dishes that I had left in the kitchen had been washed and put away. The cat's litter tray was clean. Her food bowl was full. Only the jelly had gone. She always licked that off first and left the rest to be eaten later; it was a clear sign that she had been fed recently.

'You lucky cat,' I said in the silence.

I had always thought Pippi was happy to see me when I came home. But now I realised that she only meowed at me because she wanted her dinner. Someone else had been feeding her and so I was suddenly less popular. Nice. Having Ronald here told me a truth that I could have done without.

'Pippi-puss, where are you?' I called. I heard the bump of the cat jumping from a height. The sound came from the spare room. I thought of her curling up to me at night when I was sleeping. Was Ronald here? Asleep? It stopped me in my tracks. I listened out for any other sounds, but all I could hear were the cat's paws on the wooden floor as she tripped from the spare room down the hall towards the kitchen. She paused and finally gave me a meow. She was happy to see Mrs Owner, but my return wasn't quite as important as usual. I bent down to scratch her behind her ear.

'Is he here, puss?' I whispered. If Ronald was sleeping, I didn't want to wake him up. 'Lucky puss, you got fed early.' I felt her fur, as if there would be some warmth lingering there if she had slept curled up against him. I stood silently in my kitchen, suddenly unwilling to leave because I might bump into someone.

If he was in the flat, surely he would have heard me. He must be at work. He'd said that he would be out most of the time. That he was on double shifts until they'd hired someone to replace Piotr. Why would he still work there even though they still hadn't paid him? I didn't understand.

Not knowing if I was alone in the flat was unsettling. Why had I let him stay here? It had been a really stupid idea.

I sat down on the sofa and looked out as day turned into dusk, but couldn't get comfortable. The cat jumped up beside me, but I kept her away from my lap. Until I knew that I was by myself here, I would keep listening out for every creeping sound. Even the normal clicking of the water pipes made me think that someone was moving in the spare room.

I got up. This was silly. This was my flat. I could go into whichever room I wanted. The door to the spare room was ajar. I paused outside. There was no light on inside. Surely Ronald would have closed the door if he was actually in there. Unless he had kept it open so that Pippi could get out if she wanted to. I put my hand on the door, palm flat against the wood, as if that would tell me whether there was someone inside. I pushed carefully, inched the door open. My heart beat fast, because if Ronald was there, this would look really weird. He would wonder why I was coming into his bedroom. Why I was coming into my own spare room, I corrected myself.

I could see the bed through the small gap. It was empty. He wasn't here. I noticed the hollow where Pippi had been sleeping. Tension I hadn't been aware I'd been feeling left my shoulders. I took a deep breath in and out. Good thing I'd checked. Now I could enjoy my safe place as I would normally do.

First, dinner. Halfway through cooking it, my phone beeped to announce a text message. It was from a number I didn't recognise. It read: *We need to talk.* I looked at it in puzzlement. Was it from Mark? Did he have a new phone? What would he want to talk to me about? It was probably a wrong number.

We need to talk. Those words never indicated anything good. When my ex-husband had told me that we needed to talk, it had been to tell me that he had got another woman pregnant and was leaving me. I was thinking about sending back a text saying *Wrong number* or *I don't know what you're talking about.* Instead I did nothing. Let whoever this text was for enjoy their last evening without the bad news they were definitely going to get.

I finished cooking – spaghetti in tomato sauce – and ate quickly and in silence, standing up in the kitchen, plate balanced on the work surface. I rinsed the plate and stuck it in the dishwasher.

I should have felt happy to have closed a case, but instead

I felt unsettled. The sense of satisfaction that I normally got was missing.

Even if I could accept that Katja Bruyneel had stabbed Piotr Mazur, there was still something odd about that photo she had given him. Sure, she could have printed out a picture from Petra Maasland's Facebook page, but why had she given it to Piotr? I was concerned about it. Katja had said that the counsellor had failed her sister. If she held her responsible for Sylvie's death, had she tried to use the child to take revenge on Petra as well?

Pippi jumped on my lap. It was a little cooler now so I didn't push her back on the floor. I scratched her behind the ear. 'Hello, puss. I'm good enough again now, am I? You tart.' I smiled.

Katja Bruyneel came at me with her knife pulled. I stared at the blade but couldn't do anything to stop her. She half missed, only nicked my waist, but somehow I still fell to the ground. I heard the thump of my head hitting the street. The doctor in his yellow T-shirt approached me. His footsteps were clear on the pavement. He felt my wrist. 'She's dead,' he said, and walked away again, because now that I was no longer alive, there was nothing he could do for me. The sound of his shoes on the ground rang in my ears. I wanted to call him back and say that surely I was alive if I could still hear footsteps, but the words didn't come. Maybe he'd been right and I was dead after all.

I woke up. It was light outside. It took me a few seconds to realise that I was in my bed and not lying on the street.

What a stupid dream that had been. My mouth was dry. I swung my legs out of bed and welcomed the feeling of the cool wood under my bare feet. I stopped suddenly when I heard those same footsteps again. This time they were actually in my flat. Ronald. Of course. He must have come home after work. The thump of my head on the ground had been the sound of Pippi jumping off my bed.

I got dressed but stayed in my bedroom. I didn't want to bump into him. I wouldn't want to talk to anybody before I'd had my first cup of coffee. I waited until I heard his footsteps go into the spare room. Then I got up with my water glass and filled it in the kitchen. I heard Ronald say, 'Hello, cat.'

I put some food into Pippi's bowl. Just because she preferred someone else's company, that didn't mean I shouldn't feed her. Normally I would have breakfast before going to work, but now I was keen to get out. I would grab something on the way. I quickly left the flat, went down the stairs and opened the communal front door.

I was only halfway out of the house when someone caught me by the arm.

It was Mark. I hadn't seen him standing by the side of the door. 'Who is he?' he said.

I didn't have to ask who he was talking about. He must have seen Ronald by the window, otherwise he would surely have assumed that he was a new downstairs neighbour.

For a second I considered lying, but what would that achieve? 'I'm just helping him out. He needed a place to stay.' I shrugged. 'After all, he saved my life once.'

'That's Ronald de Boer?'

There was something gratifying in this evidence that Mark had been listening closely to what I'd told him about my previous cases.

'I have somewhere he can stay,' he said. 'I still haven't sold the house.'

'I can't ask that of you.'

'I'd prefer him living in an empty house than with you.' He scratched his head. 'Lotte, we need to talk. Can I come in?'

Had he sent me last night's text after all? 'I'm just going to work.'

'Can we stop for a coffee on the way?'

However much I wanted to be in his company, if I spent time with him again it would be even tougher to let go. 'Mark, now's not a good time.' I unlocked my bike without looking at him. It was hard but I did it, and I was proud of myself.

I'd almost got to the police station when I had a text from the same number as yesterday. This time he'd signed his name. It was from Ronald. Everybody wanting to talk to me today. I turned my bike round and cycled back home. I'd been early anyway.

Chapter Twenty-Two

I had expected that Piotr would be buried back in Poland, but he had made a will and had explicitly stated that he wanted to be laid to rest at a cemetery just outside Amsterdam. A small crowd of colleagues, family and friends stood outside in the burning sunshine waiting for the service to start. I stayed far back. I hadn't been sure if I should be here, but Ronald had asked me if I could give him a lift. That was why he'd texted me. Trust him to say that we needed to talk, whereas what he meant was that he needed a favour.

Natalie arrived with Koen. They made a very good-looking couple, both so well turned out and attractive. Even outside work Natalie looked like a walking advertisement for expensive outfits. She was chatting brightly, but Koen didn't say a word. He stared at the ground, looking as if he desperately wanted to be somewhere else. Natalie linked her arm through his, but he took a step sideways and pulled free. She looked as if she was about to cry. Maybe Piotr's death really had hit her hard. Apart from dealing drugs, he had been their neighbour, and Natalie had told us that he had been friends with both of them. Maybe that had been true.

The funeral director gestured that the service was about to start and everybody went inside the church. Ronald followed Natalie and Koen. She had ignored him throughout; there clearly was no need to make casual conversation with a security guard. He glanced around as if he was looking for someone. I took a seat at the back, two rows behind everybody else and as far in the corner as I could.

The hymns were familiar melodies with unknown words in a foreign language. Only the family sang along. They made a frail sound that echoed through the half-empty church and died before it could inspire or lift anybody's soul. A dark-haired priest talked, but the words were just a sound. Part Latin, part Polish. The church was more wide than tall. I counted eleven rows of seating, furnished in an unrelenting modern style with bare pine-wood benches. Funerals were always sad affairs, I thought, especially when parents had to bury their child.

I was probably fortunate that I could not remember anything of the service for my daughter. That day was a blank, as if the grief had erased it from my mind. The only memory I had was of scattering my beautiful girl's ashes out over the sea, standing next to my ex-husband, not being able to look at him or touch him. Standing side by side but each of us terribly alone. If I wanted to be fair to him – which I didn't often want to do but which I was getting better at – losing our child was what had really torn our marriage apart.

The priest's voice droned on. Time for prayer. Everybody got on their knees and bowed their heads. I stared at the ceiling. I was relieved when at a final Amen the service finished and we could go outside again.

The mourners followed the coffin towards Piotr's final resting place. The sun beat down on their heads. Ronald kept a polite distance from the family. The grave was a two-metre-long wound in the ground that was visible from far away. We approached along a path lined by gravestones on either side. On the left, a perfectly maintained plot with flowering bedding plants and a clump of forget-me-nots. Another had a vase with only stems; the petals had long since fallen on the ground and been blown away onto other graves. High poplars, tall and thin, lined the central aisle. Only a plane's vapour trail broke up the everlasting sky.

The procession came to the empty grave. The coffin was lowered. Earth was thrown by the family. Natalie stepped forward. Piotr's father stood behind her, face stern, mouth working hard to keep the tears inside. His wife was a matronly figure in a trouser suit. The couple were probably no more than a decade older than me, but they seemed ancient, like old gnarled trees. Loss aged people.

Koen stepped next to Natalie. She held out her hand to him but he didn't take it.

The priest said a few more words. Ashes to ashes.

A handsome Moroccan man in a suit and tie approached Ronald. I recognised him. It was the man who'd talked to Ronald about his housing situation. They exchanged a silent nod. I joined them. Ronald looked at me but didn't introduce me. He also didn't tell me to leave.

'How are things, Khalil?' he said.

The tall man shrugged, took a handkerchief out and wiped his eyes. 'Sorry, hay fever.'

I remembered that I had used the same excuse myself. A girl from the department store kept looking in Khalil's direction. The pale green eyes in his dark face appeared to mesmerise her.

'The sooner the parents leave,' he said, 'the better.' He gave me a little smile. 'Sorry to say it, but that's the way it is.'

I wondered who he thought I was. I was pretty sure he had no idea that I was one of the police detectives who'd investigated Piotr's murder. Maybe I should have introduced myself, but now that the case was closed, it was probably better to let Piotr's friends talk freely and not feel as if they had to watch their words.

'They keep complaining about burying him in Amsterdam instead of in Poland,' Khalil continued. 'But those were his wishes. He specifically said he wanted to be buried here. He'd taken out this funeral insurance, everything was sorted out. He said it was funny that if he paid seven euros a month, it would get him a funeral with coffee and cake for fifty people.' He shook his head. 'Crazy guy. He probably just fancied the person selling the insurance. Anyway, it means he's ended up here, in a cemetery in Amsterdam.'

'So why did the parents want otherwise?' Ronald said.

'Because they're a bunch of hypocrites. You know they hadn't spoken to Piotr in years. They were angry with him because of . . .' The Moroccan briefly looked at me and shrugged. 'Well, you know why, I don't have to spell it out. But that was his choice, wasn't it? We live our lives. We are what we are. And now' – he turned to Ronald – 'now they wanted to bury him in their home town so that they could easily put flowers on his grave. Who cares about that?'

'Maybe they feel bad. They want to make it up. We all think we're going to live forever, that our children will, that our parents will. We're always wrong. We're always too late to make amends.'

The Moroccan coughed. 'How thoughtful. You're almost a poet, Ronald, who'd have imagined.'

'I just thought—'

'I know what you thought and you're wrong.'

'This is bad, Khalil. You can't live your life in fear,' Ronald said. 'Piotr didn't.'

'And Piotr's dead.'

'That wasn't your fault.'

Khalil didn't reply; just walked away with big strides, as if he could no longer bear to stand by this open grave.

The parents walked slowly away, and everybody else began to file behind them back to the church, where the family would stand in line and receive condolences. I looked at Natalie walking next to Piotr's parents. Why was she doing that?

'Who was that?' I asked Ronald.

He didn't respond.

Natalie was crying. She looked genuinely upset. Then she slowed down as if she'd decided to distance herself from the family. Ronald caught up with her. I followed right behind him.

'Had you met his parents before?' he asked her.

She smiled. 'They know we worked together.'

'You're not repeating that stupid lie that you were seeing him, are you?'

'It's what they like to believe.'

'It's not true.'

'It's easier for them.' She looked round to make sure they couldn't hear her. 'They prefer not to know.'

'Does it matter now that he's dead?' Ronald asked.

She tucked her hair behind her ear in a cute gesture. 'It's perfect now, isn't it? No inconvenient truths can get in the way of their idea of the perfect son. No wonder he left Poland and ended up in Amsterdam.' She seemed brittle, too bright. I wondered if she was on drugs. Her make-up was less than perfect. She looked vulnerable. Fragile. Scared, even.

Koen came over and joined her. She hooked her arm through his. This time he didn't pull away.

'I'm going to head home. This isn't really my thing.' Ronald looked in my direction, to check whether I was ready to leave as well. I nodded.

He got a cigarette out of a packet and put his sunglasses on. 'If you need anything, call me.'

As I took a step towards them, Natalie's voice stopped me.

'That stupid little bitch.' Her tone was perfectly pleasant on the unexpected swear word. She looked at me. She wanted to make sure I was listening to what she was saying. 'Meeting him in a bar. As if that would sort anything out. As if she could stop him asking those questions. Trying to protect the child.'

'Natalie,' Koen said. 'Be quiet.'

'You know why he got killed?' Ronald said.

'That stupid little bitch,' Natalie repeated as if she hadn't heard him. 'She killed an innocent man.' She smiled brightly, her eyes small in the smudged mascara. 'But maybe it's better this way.'

She freed her arm from Koen's and dashed away towards Piotr's parents.

I wanted to follow her, but Ronald stopped me. 'Later,' he said. 'Talk to her later.'

He was right. I couldn't ask the questions I wanted to with Koen here. I would go to the department store, or call her into the station for questioning later. Do it officially. Not just meddle in a case that had been closed.

Chapter Twenty-Three

I could see what Maarten Wynia had meant when he'd said he'd moved all Tim's stuff from this spare desk. In the few days since I'd been gone, it seemed that he had transferred it all back. Clothes hung over the chair I'd sat on. Gym kit was piled up on the corner of the desk, giving the place a hint of sweat. My plan had been to talk to Bauer by himself, but as Tim and Maarten were here as well, I might as well tell everybody in one go. A couple of days ago, my mother had told me that I needed to ask for help every now and then. I was going to follow her advice. I didn't have to do this by myself.

'We need to look at Piotr Mazur's death again,' I said. 'It was about a child, not drugs.'

'What are you talking about, Lotte?' Bauer said.

'Earlier, at Piotr's funeral, Natalie Schuurman said that Katja Bruyneel had killed an innocent man. She was trying to protect a child.'

'I didn't know you went to the funeral.'

'Yeah, well, I had to give someone a lift there.'

'We're not doing it,' Bauer said.

I frowned. 'Not doing what?'

'We have a confession. We have the motive. The forensic evidence agrees with Katja's version of events. We're not reopening this case just because a woman said something at a funeral. Plus nobody is saying that Katja didn't kill him, right?'

'But that photo has been bothering me from the beginning. If Katja killed the wrong man, then who was the right man? If she killed him to protect the child, this child is still in danger.'

'No.'

'No?' That was all? That was all he was going to say? 'What do you mean, "no"? No, the child isn't in danger? No, Katja didn't kill the wrong man?'

'I meant: no, we're not looking into this again. That other dealer's case is going to court in a couple of weeks. I want to protect the conviction. I'm grateful for the work you've done on solving Piotr Mazur's murder and ensuring my other case didn't fall apart, but now you need to leave this alone. If we had locked up an innocent person, that would have been different.'

I still thought we had locked up the wrong person.

'We're not going to follow up on what this woman said.' Bauer's tone was final.

I shook my head. This wasn't what being a police officer was about. If there was a child potentially still in danger, how could I ignore that? Even if I didn't yet know the identity of that child, how could I stand here and be happy that we'd solved another case? If I did that, then what was the point of it all?

I left the office because I knew there was no arguing with Bauer. Instead I sent Tim a text and asked him to join me for a coffee in the canteen.

He came down only minutes later. 'No, Lotte,' he said without even sitting down. 'You know I can't help you. I'm not going to go against Bauer. I've finally done something he approves of and I'm not going to risk that for a wild goose chase. If you had some concrete evidence . . .' He scratched his head. 'No, I have to be honest with you. Even if you had concrete evidence, I probably wouldn't help you.'

'You don't care that a child is in danger?'

'You don't know that. A woman said something at a funeral and now you have to go running off like crazy and potentially damage the trial of someone who's killed six people? What do you think is more important?'

I looked at him in silence for a second. 'Protecting some-one is more important than putting someone in prison.'

'Think about what you're saying. You don't believe that.' It almost looked as if he felt sorry for me. 'We didn't find any evidence of a child. Piotr didn't have a child. Katja didn't have a child. She used a photo from Facebook. We only have Natalie's word for it, and she made up the story that she was sleeping with Piotr Mazur, remember? She isn't exactly credible. So now you're suggesting that we should put a trial at risk because of something a known liar is saying?'

'And you're not going to help me, because Bauer is finally happy with something you've done.'

'And because I think it's the right thing to do!'

'I get it.'

234

'I'm not sure you do. But that doesn't matter. I can't help you.' He walked away. I wanted to shout after him that he'd only managed to do something that Bauer approved of because I had helped him. That maybe he owed me something.

It didn't matter. There was someone else who owed me something. Who kept telling me that she owed me a big favour for saving her life.

I calmly finished my coffee before I went back to my office.

Thomas had gone out but Ingrid was waiting for me. She stared at me as I entered the room. 'Tim just told me,' she said.

'Told you what?'

'He said that you would probably come to me.'

'We need to look for this child.'

'No. No, we shouldn't. It was Natalie Schuurman who told you, wasn't it?'

'Yes. So what?'

'So you accept a story told by a woman who lied to us before.'

'But it makes sense! You know Piotr had that photo on him. You know this bothered me from the start.'

'A photo that Katja Bruyneel just pulled from Facebook.' She put a hand on my arm. 'Lotte, be honest with yourself. If this wasn't something that fitted with your theory – your preoccupation – you wouldn't have believed it either. You *want* to believe this. You want to think there's a child out there that you can save from whatever is threatening him.' She closed her eyes for a second.

To be fair to her, I would later think, she hesitated before ploughing on. Before stabbing in the knife so deep.

'You're obsessed with saving children,' she said, 'because of your daughter.'

Even though I'd had an inkling of what she was going to say, I felt sick. 'I saved your life and this is how you repay me?' I could barely get the words out. 'By siding with your new boyfriend? Because to look into this more closely could ruin the one time that Bauer thinks he's done something right?' I grabbed my handbag. 'And then you dare to talk about my motives. How about you examine your own?'

I almost ran out of the office.

'Lotte,' Ingrid shouted after me, 'Lotte, I'm sorry. I shouldn't have said that. I'm so sorry.'

I walked along the corridor to CI Moerdijk's office.

'I know why you're here,' the boss said. 'Bauer just called me.'

Everybody had been quicker off the mark on this than me. 'Please,' I said.

'I'm sorry, Lotte, we can't.' The boss looked surprised that I had asked it as a favour rather than demanding that we keep investigating. 'We have a confession and it matches up with the forensic evidence.'

'It's a false confession.'

'That's just your opinion. And this woman who killed Piotr Mazur says she did it purely to avenge her sister's death,' he continued as if I hadn't spoken. 'I don't want you to do anything that jeopardises either of Bauer's cases.'

'And that's the only thing that's important?'

'It's key at the moment.'

I shook my head. 'This is wrong.'

'Take the rest of the day off, Lotte. I'll see you tomorrow.'

I listened to him. I left the police station. Why would I want to spend the day with people who had all betrayed me even though I'd helped them?

Instead I went home.

It was in this state of mind that I couldn't refuse Ronald a huge favour when he asked for one.

Chapter Twenty-Four

An hour and a long phone call later, Ronald and I were driving in my car to Alkmaar. It had been more than a week since I'd been there to see my father.

Ronald gave me the directions to get to his ex-wife's house. He was hyper, probably because he couldn't have had more than four hours' sleep, and he told me story after story about his kids until he drove me crazy. He had this amazing ability to make me regret whatever I was helping him with.

'Natalie didn't tell you anything more about the child?' I asked, to interrupt a story about his daughter's amazing ability in gymnastics.

'She didn't come back to work after the funeral.'

'She wasn't at her flat either.' Of course I had tried to talk to her, but nobody had opened the door. 'Do you think Katja killed Piotr because of this child? To protect the child?'

'Lotte, you have Piotr all wrong. He wouldn't have harmed anybody. I think she used that photo as bait.'

'To get him to come to the bar? So she could kill him?'

'I never understood why he met up with her.' Ronald had maintained that Piotr was innocent of everything. That he wouldn't have had anything to do with Katja's sister's death.

Natalie's claim that Katja had killed the wrong man made perfect sense to him.

To me it brought up entirely different concerns. Not about clearing Piotr's name but about keeping the child safe. 'But Natalie said something about Piotr asking questions. What do you think she meant?'

'Lotte, I told you, I have no idea. He didn't mention anything to me.'

The road was clear until we got to the main roundabout at the end of the A9. Then cars were backed up because one set of traffic lights had gone on the blink.

'Which turning is it?'

'Just take the first one. I'll direct you.'

'Is she . . .' I wasn't sure how to ask it tactfully. 'Was this your house?'

'Yes, she still lives there. She needs to sell it at some point, but this is not the right time to do it. The house is worth less than we bought it for. I'll just let her live there with the kids. Doesn't make sense for her to move somewhere smaller.'

'Sure.' The house was in one of the newer areas of Alkmaar, to the north of the city. This used to be all farm-land, my father had told me once. Now it was covered with semi-identical new builds. No wonder they had lost their value.

We parked in front. Ronald's ex-wife, Ilse, had already opened the door. She looked like a farmer's daughter, with skin the colour of cream and hair the colour of butter.

She didn't look happy to see us. 'It's what the kids wanted, but I'm still not sure.'

I could have told her that I wasn't keen on being here either but that I thought I'd needed to help someone even though nobody had helped me. It meant a lot to Ronald to see his children.

'The only reason I agreed to this,' she said, 'is that I respect you, Lotte. I don't like you but I know you're a good detective. My kids will be safe with you.'

'They are,' I said. 'And maybe you should give Ronald another chance. He didn't do anything wrong.'

He glared at me. I shouldn't attempt to reconcile a recently divorced couple. I had no idea what had happened between the two of them. I could only imagine it had something to do with the fallout from the shooting.

'If you promise to accompany them for the whole afternoon,' Ilse continued as if I hadn't said anything, 'I'll let them go with you. It's the school holidays anyway and this will give me a chance to do some things I need to do. You have to be there for the first five visits. Then we can reassess.'

'But—' I said.

'Agreed,' Ronald said.

The beach was a wide expanse of sand that burned hot under my bare feet. I drew them back onto the beach towel. I wished I had brought a bathing suit; the sea would be mercifully cool. I scratched my arm. The heat of the sun only made the mosquito bites itch more fiercely. The water was far away and left plenty of space for the hundreds of sun-worshippers dotted all over the beach. The outgoing tide had stranded a row of jellyfish. There were always more of them with an easterly wind. I turned on my stomach and with my chin on my hands watched Ronald and his children ineptly throw a Frisbee around. Wind drifted over the beach, just strong enough to dust loose sand over bodies covered in sun cream. To my left, a group of teenagers were handing a bottle of lotion round, taking full advantage of this opportunity to rub hands over bare backs.

I couldn't understand why Ilse had insisted on me accompanying them. Did she worry that Ronald would do something to his children? First of all he wasn't the type, and secondly, his son was already taller than he was, even though he was only thirteen. His daughter was fifteen.

Ronald put an arm around his son's shoulders. Whatever his father wanted to tell him, Fred didn't seem too interested in listening. His face was set in a constant scowl; no matter what Ronald said to get him to relax, he didn't smile. Even in the car the two kids had been quiet. The girl had sulked and said she didn't want to come with us. God knows what she thought was going to happen. 'This is Lotte,' her mother had said. 'She's here to protect you.' Both teenagers had squirmed at those words. Nice start to an afternoon out, that was. She'd made sure I sat with the girl in the back, making Fred sit next to his father. He had kept his earphones on for the entire journey. Now he fished them out of the pocket of his shorts again and stopped his father's words as effectively as he could.

The seagulls floated effortlessly on the air currents, staying afloat like ducks on a pond. The sea itself was flat; there were no waves. I looked at my watch. There was still two hours to go before Ronald had to bring them back. I put some more Factor 30 on my face and studied the skin on my arms. I wished I had brought something with long sleeves.

We were on the part of the beach where all the windsurfers would have gathered had there been wind. When I'd stayed on the coast four months ago to recover from my shoulder operations, I'd walked on the beach every day, rain, sun or wind. It had been my daily exercise.

I put my headphones in and listened to Radio Tour de France. That really was the sound of summer. In this temperature, it was hard work lying here on the beach, let alone cycling up a mountain. The forecast said the hot weather would stay for another couple of days. It was a proper heatwave.

When the three of them got back to me, Ronald's face looked greyer than ever. He almost fell onto his towel. I handed both kids a can of fizzy orange.

'Are you all right?' I said.

'I'll be fine. You know I've come here straight from my night shift.'

'How long have you been awake?'

He looked at his watch. 'Twenty-two hours. You can't think straight when you don't sleep. I don't think I've been thinking straight for a while.'

It almost sounded like an apology. 'And you insisted we came here today? Are you crazy?'

'No. I'm fine.'

I took hold of his chin and looked into his eyes. 'You don't look fine to me at all.'

'You have no idea what it means to me to see my

children. I hadn't seen them in four months. I'm not going to get them home early today.'

I took my mobile out. 'Leave it with me.' I called my father and asked if he was doing anything that afternoon. He wasn't, so we drove to his house. Ronald crashed in the spare room for an hour's sleep, with strict instructions about when we were to wake him up, and my father, my stepmother, Ronald's daughter and I played Cluedo. Fred sat on the sofa with his headphones in, playing games on his iPhone or maybe texting his friends about what a crap afternoon he was having. Something that required him to move his thumbs over his phone at lightning speed.

I went upstairs to wake Ronald after his sleep. I said his name four times but that didn't make him stir at all. In the end, I shook him by the shoulder. He opened his eyes just a slit and said, 'Go away, Lotte' in a tone of voice that told me he was barely awake. I gave his arm another good shake. He growled and stretched himself.

'Your kids are here, remember?' I said.

'Ah yes. I thought I was just having another nightmare and that was why you were in my bedroom,' he said with his eyes still closed.

'We need to get them back in an hour.'

He sat up and swung his legs out of bed. He hadn't undressed at all. His face was crumpled and his eyes no bigger than peas, trying to keep as much of the light out as he could. He managed to stay awake for two more games of Cluedo, losing both of them, and sat in the back seat of the car as I drove them all back to Ilse. He said goodbye to his children, getting the afternoon's first smile from Teri – it had been worth letting her win that final game – and climbed back into the car. As soon as he had clicked the seat belt shut and leaned his head against the window, the snoring started, a match for the engine. I didn't bother turning the radio on, not wanting to wake him up and unable to hear it anyway. By the time we stopped outside my flat, he'd had another hour of solid sleep.

'Thanks for that, Lotte,' he said as he undid the seat belt. 'You're a good friend.'

As we went in, I thought I saw Mark on the opposite side of the canal. I must have imagined it.

Chapter Twenty-Five

The next morning my legs were heavy as I cycled into work. The afternoon on the beach had turned my skin to a colour between red and deep pink. A couple of days would tone down the burn into a healthy tan, but today the cloth of my shirt chafed painfully against my arms and back, and even a thick layer of after-sun moisture cream hadn't managed to take the sting away. I should be grateful we'd only been out for a few hours. Had I been baking in the sun the entire day, I would probably have had a second-degree burn. Mosquito bites, sunburn, ongoing heat: I was starting to get really fed up with summer. Maybe it would rain again soon.

The rainbow flag was flying cheerily on top of the police station, the blue stripe matching the colour of the sky. My feet didn't want to carry me up the stairs to the office and the people who had chosen not to help me. In the past I'd had run-ins with my colleagues, but then I had understood only too well. After all, there were things I'd done that hadn't been right, and Thomas especially had known about it. But now all I wanted to do was look into a case a bit longer.

That confession still didn't make any sense to me and Piotr's murder really wasn't solved as far as I was concerned.

'Good morning, Lotte,' Ingrid said as soon as I'd come through the door. 'How was your day off?'

'Fine.'

'What did you get up to?' Thomas said with a grin.

What were they so happy about? 'I went to the beach.'

'It shows. That red glow isn't healthy. You should have used better sunscreen. Your nose wouldn't look out of place on Pipo the Clown.'

I put my hand against my face. 'Very funny.'

'Instead of going to the beach, we worked hard,' he continued. 'We looked at the tapes of Katja Bruyneel's interview.'

That brought my head up. I looked at Thomas. 'You did what?'

'We looked at the recordings and we think we should definitely talk to Petra Maasland again.'

I felt as if a weight that I had been carrying all the way to the office had now dropped onto the floor. I wanted to give them both a hug. 'Did you tell Bauer?' They were my team after all.

Ingrid shook her head. 'I haven't even told Tim. But I think you're right. There are too many open questions.'

'About the child—'

Thomas raised his hand. 'There's no evidence of a child, Lotte.'

'But—'

'Either way, the confession of Katja Bruyneel is very

flawed,' he continued, as if I hadn't said anything. 'We know she could pass away in a few weeks, or even less.'

'That quickly?'

'We spoke to her doctor. She could ask to have her life terminated at any point. We would be in a tough situation because we couldn't refuse. Her cancer is terminal, and as soon as she feels the pain is unbearable, she could ask for euthanasia. We would be crazy not to follow up now while we still can.'

'We're not saying that you're definitely right in your concerns,' Ingrid said. 'But Thomas and I agreed that if we're going to do something, it needs to be now.'

I nodded. That was good enough. 'Did you tell Moerdijk?'

'We haven't told anybody,' Thomas said. 'And we should probably keep it like that.'

'So we should interview Katja again.'

Thomas and Ingrid exchanged a look. 'We should do that last. If we call her in, and her lawyer, then everybody will know immediately. Bauer will stop us. The boss too. We should find concrete evidence and then talk to Katja.'

I didn't like it but I knew he was right. I gave Ingrid a quick hug. When she put her hands on my back, it hurt my painful skin but I didn't pull away. 'Thank you so much,' I said. I knew she had chosen me over her boyfriend. I moved across the desk to hug Thomas as well.

But he moved out of the way. 'Just go to the canteen and get me a coffee.'

'Sure.' I grinned.

'And try not to look so happy. Everybody will know within seconds.'

But before I skipped down the stairs to get his coffee, I called to check that Petra Maasland was at the hospital today.

'When did you first meet Katja?' Ingrid asked. She was sunk deep in the person-eating sofa. Even though her tall, angular figure clashed with the softness of the room, it seemed appropriate to just have women in this place that looked like a boudoir. Petra's appointment was sitting outside, waiting until this interview was finished to get back to their counselling session.

Thomas had stayed behind at the station to check the initial reports on Piotr's death again. I'd told him that Bauer and his team hadn't done much with either the forensic evidence or the crime-scene reports. After all, Tim hadn't even known that Natalie had claimed to be Piotr's girlfriend. Anything that had come up after the case had gone upstairs could well have been ignored.

'I met Katja at Sylvie's funeral,' Petra said. 'We didn't really talk but she said that I'd caused her sister's death.' She nodded thoughtfully at her own words, but the way she was clenching her hands together showed that she was nervous.

I could understand that. Katja had thought Piotr Mazur had been responsible for Sylvie's death too, and Piotr was now dead. 'Why didn't you tell us this when I first interviewed you?'

'You didn't ask me about Katja.' I had chosen the chair that Tim had used last time we met with Petra. It was much more comfortable. At that point we hadn't known that

Sylvie's sister had been in the bar with Piotr. We hadn't known that she was going to confess to having killed him.

'You told me she was unreliable.'

'Yes, she was behaving quite irrationally. Probably because she was angry. She felt guilty about Sylvie's death,' Petra continued.

'Guilty?' That was surprising, given that she wasn't feeling guilty over what had happened to Piotr.

'Sylvie came to Katja's flat a few hours before she overdosed. But Katja refused to let her in because she was asking for money. She told me that Sylvie had a massive bruise on her face and she was worried that she was using again. It was the first time they had met since Katja had kicked her out.'

'She hadn't seen her sister in three years?' Ingrid asked.

'That's why she was feeling so guilty. She thought Sylvie must have been at the end of her tether and overdosed on purpose because she didn't help her. To be fair, she'd kicked her out originally because she realised that Sylvie had taken all the money from her bank account.'

'So Katja thought that Sylvie had committed suicide?'

'Yes. We had an argument at the funeral. She said that it was ironic that only the three people responsible for Sylvie's death had turned up. She said I had clearly failed her sister but that she was the one who'd been ultimately responsible.' She shrugged. 'After she told me that, I stopped talking to the police. I thought that maybe she was right.'

'Three people?'

'Piotr Mazur came to the funeral. Can you believe it?'

'Is that when Katja decided that it was Piotr Mazur's fault and that she would have to kill him?' I leaned forward on my seat. 'What did you tell her?'

'Only that he'd been her dealer.'

'Are you sure he was?'

'Yes. During our sessions Sylvie had told me that her boyfriend used to supply her with drugs. She had to break off the relationship to help break her dependency.'

'And Piotr was that boyfriend?'

'He asked a lot of questions about where Sylvie had been for the last two years. He came to the funeral.'

'Sylvie was in a relationship with Piotr Mazur in the years that she shared a flat with Natalie?'

'Yes, I guess so. She shared with Natalie until they had a huge falling-out. Then Natalie accused her of stealing from the department store.'

I remembered that Ronald had said that Natalie had helped Piotr get a job at the store. She must have first met him when he was going out with Sylvie and they'd shared a flat. Why she'd thought he'd make a good security guard was beyond me.

'Sylvie was very angry about getting caught stealing.'

'Wasn't she guilty?'

'Oh, she was. She stole the dresses. She just thought that her friend could have helped her instead of reporting her to the police. She was in a messed-up frame of mind. She was a drug addict, you understand.'

'So why didn't you tell us about this last time?'

'I thought I had. Anyway, Sylvie told Katja that she had no choice but to go to her old boyfriend for money.'

250

She went for money to her old boyfriend, who'd been a dealer. Then she overdosed. It all started to come together. 'And he came to the funeral. Nobody else?'

'No, just the three of us. But as I said, I didn't really talk to Katja or Mazur much. It was a few months later, when I saw her at the hospital, that she started to ask me all these questions. She was crying outside – she'd just had her cancer diagnosis – and I recognised her. I thought that talking about her sister might help her.' She pulled her hands through her thick curls. 'I now know that was a huge mistake, because she ended up killing that guy. Even if he was just a dealer.'

It reminded me of Natalie saying that Piotr was 'just a security guard'. 'And finally, can I just confirm,' I said, 'that this is your grandson?' I showed her the photo.

Petra held her hand out for it. 'Yes, that's Oskar,' she said.

'Your daughter's son?'

'Yes, that's right.' She looked at the picture with a beaming smile. 'Where did you get this from?'

'Katja gave it to Piotr. She told us she printed it off from your Facebook page. You should be more careful about what you share online.'

We sat outside, at a café along one of the canals. I was in the shade, as I should have been yesterday.

'Did that tell you anything new?' Thomas said when he joined us.

'Maybe not.' I pulled out a chair for him. If Ronald hadn't been staying at my flat, we could have gone there. Instead we had to make the best of things here. I couldn't go to the police station and draw on the whiteboard there. The boss would be furious if he found out, and I didn't want to get Thomas and Ingrid into trouble for going so directly against the CI's directive. 'But it's made the timeline clearer for me,' I said. 'Of Sylvie's past.'

'You think that's important?'

'Yes, because Katja said that Sylvie's death was her motive for murdering Piotr.' I got my notepad from my handbag and moved the coffee cups out of the way so that I could put it in the centre of the table. I started drawing a timeline. 'Three years ago, Katja threw Sylvie out of her flat. She gets a job at the department store and shares a flat for a year with Natalie.'

'Who then kicks her out when she's caught stealing. That's two years ago.'

'Not only kicks her out,' Ingrid said, 'but also shops her to the police.'

'Did Piotr Mazur already work at the store then?' Thomas said.

'No. I checked the dates; he only started at the department store eighteen months ago. That's six months after Sylvie was arrested. Natalie got him that job. She must have met him when he was going out with Sylvie.'

'And of course he was Sylvie's dealer,' Ingrid said. 'If Natalie continued to do coke, she was probably buying from him all that time.'

'That makes sense. And then six months ago, two years after Sylvie got kicked out of Natalie's flat and the department store, she decides to go to her ex-boyfriend Piotr to get money from him.'

'And dies from an overdose,' Ingrid said.

'Right. Then Katja meets with him and shows him a photo of a child. A child who's about two years old.'

'You think that's Sylvie's child,' Thomas said. It wasn't a question.

'No, we know he's Petra Maasland's grandchild,' Ingrid said. 'But Katja could have pretended, couldn't she? She could have said he was Sylvie's child. Piotr Mazur's child.'

'So Sylvie tried to get money out of him by saying he had a child and he gave her heroin?' I said.

'He gave that German heroin instead of cocaine,' Thomas said. 'What if he did the same with Sylvie? She came to him but he wasn't keen on paying for his child and decided to kill her instead?'

'He was happy when he saw the photo.' I remembered that clearly. 'He smiled so widely that it made his face light up. He'd had this intense, maybe even worried look on his face before.'

'Let's go back to the station,' Ingrid said. 'We can check the registers. See if Sylvie ever had a child.'

We rushed back to the office and checked the birth certificates, but our theory was ruined when we could find no mention in the register that Sylvie Bruyneel had ever given birth to a child. My best guess was that maybe Katja had known about the lie that Sylvie told Piotr and just run with it. Everything we'd found out confirmed the story Katja had been telling us all along. She'd killed Sylvie's old boyfriend. Her dealer.

Chapter Twenty-Six

The next day was my favourite Saturday of the year: the day that Amsterdam's centre turned into one big party. I was having lunch quietly so as not to wake Ronald. They'd finally hired more staff at the department store and he'd warned me that it was the end of double shifts. I'd heard him get back to the flat around 4 a.m. That meant he'd had eight hours of sleep by now, probably the first normal night since Piotr had been murdered. I was just examining the skin on my arms, which almost matched the fuchsia pink of my polo shirt, when he burst out of the bedroom dressed in a T-shirt and jeans that looked as if he'd been wearing them yesterday too. I didn't blame him; I did that often enough myself, just putting on what I'd dropped by the side of the bed.

'Aren't you going?' he said.

I didn't have to ask him what he was talking about. Enough people were already walking along the canal dressed in pink. They were going to the bridge to cross onto the Prinsengracht. It was just after twelve, so there was another hour and a half before the boats would even get going. I had the day off, but the news that yesterday someone had been stabbed at Jerusalem's Gay Pride parade meant that I felt we could do with an extra pair of eyes. Not that I expected trouble – this was Amsterdam, not Jerusalem – but I also knew from experience that problems always came up when I didn't expect them.

'I was planning on it. There's plenty of time. Have lunch. I've got a space lined up.' I gestured at my polo shirt, 'Why do you think I'm dressed like this?' This shirt only saw the light of day once a year. Pink wasn't really my colour.

'Good.' He sat down.

'Please tell me you have a nice reason for asking that.'

'I just got a text from Khalil telling me to come to the parade. He's asking where I'm going to be.'

'The guy who was at Piotr's funeral?'

He was quiet for a bit, as if figuring out what to say. 'He was a friend of Piotr's.'

'A friend of your drug-dealing colleague wants you to come to the parade.'

'Yes.'

'His name sounds Moroccan.'

'He is.'

'Is this going to be trouble?'

He shook his head. 'You shouldn't believe all the stereo-types. But to be honest, I don't know. I really don't know.' He went into the kitchen to get a plate, then sat down and helped himself to some bread. 'I talked to a friend of yours yesterday,' he said. 'Really tall guy. He seemed interested to know why I was staying at your place.'

'When was this?' I spread some butter on a slice of bread and pretended that that needed my full attention.

'As I was going to work. Who is he? Your boyfriend? I'm sorry, I never asked.'

'No, nothing like that.' I reached out for the cumin cheese.

'He's clearly interested in you.'

'I don't want to talk about him, Ronald.'

'He seemed like a nice guy.'

'It's none of your business.'

'You split up?'

'In a way, I guess.'

'You didn't split up? This is getting more and more mysterious by the minute.'

'I don't think we were ever really in a relationship.'

'You should talk to him.'

'Why?'

'He clearly likes you enough to want to get me out of your flat. Seems to me like he's trying to make up for something.'

'No, you're wrong. It's me who has to make up to him. I got a bit obsessed. It wasn't particularly healthy. I wasn't behaving sensibly around him.'

'What did you do?'

'I sat in a car outside his house for hours on end just to catch a glimpse of him.' I buried my face in my hands. 'It's so embarrassing.'

Ronald grinned. 'My daughter did that with a boy she fancied.'

'You're telling me I'm no better than a lovesick teenager?'

'Some people take a while to grow up.'

256

'Very funny. I think I was more like a crazy stalker. What we did to him was awful.'

'What did you do?' Without waiting for my answer, he went into the kitchen to get a glass of water. He was getting far too comfortable in my flat.

It did give me time to think about how honest I wanted to be with him.

When he sat back down, I still hadn't made a firm decision but the truth came out of my mouth anyway. 'I slept with him. And then we wrongfully arrested him.'

To give Ronald credit, he didn't spurt his water all over the table at this. In fact, he stayed remarkably calm. There was just a little grin on his face that I could tell he was doing his best to suppress. 'When was this?' he asked.

'Three months ago.'

He slowly nodded his head. 'You never cease to amaze me. Let me get this straight. You really like this guy, you had sex with him, and you feel bad for having arrested him by mistake.'

'I didn't personally arrest him.'

'Whatever. But you haven't actually spoken to him about any of this and instead sat outside his house in your car.'

'Something like that.'

'You have to talk to him.'

'No, I need to stay well away from him.'

'Why?'

'Because I scare him.'

'When did he say that?'

'We were on a picnic. He told me how hard it had been for him to see Piotr Mazur's body, and me covered in blood.'

257

'That's perfectly understandable.'

'And it made him throw up.'

'You had been drinking all night and he was confronted with a rather bloody scene. I don't blame him. And that's when he said that you scared him?'

I nodded.

Ronald narrowed his eyes. 'You rushed to a murder scene. It scared him. Isn't that perfectly normal?'

'He didn't mean that he was scared for me, but scared of me.'

'Okay, so he said you were scary. What did you do?'

'I left.'

'What?'

'Well, it wasn't great to hear.'

'You stormed off.'

'And then he said he'd seen me outside his house,' I said softly to my coffee cup.

'You're an idiot. You need to talk to him. If you're interested in straightening things out with him.'

'And I sent him some drunken texts.'

'I'm sure that improved matters enormously. Here's what you do. You go to his house and you have a conversation. None of this immature teenage behaviour. You need to apologise.'

'I did.'

'What did you say?'

'I said that I was sorry. When I took his statement.'

'When you were on official police business. Nice. That's not a proper apology.'

I kept quiet.

'Seriously, go talk to him,' Ronald said. 'Up you get. On your bike.'

I didn't move.

'What's keeping you?'

'I'll do it later.' I took a sip of my coffee. 'We need to watch the Gay Pride parade first.'

'When I gave my daughter this same advice, she said she was scared to talk to this boy. But surely that can't be the case with you.' His voice was sarcastic and teasing. 'You can't be scared to talk to this man.'

'It's not funny.'

'Oh it really is. I'm enjoying this tremendously.' He grabbed a book from the shelves. It was *Men Are from Mars, Women Are from Venus.* 'I don't think those books are helping you at all.'

I took it from his hands. 'Give that back.' I hated that he'd probably paged through half my self-help books. But he was right: they didn't help at all. 'So what happened with your daughter and this guy?'

'He didn't like her that way, but he was nice about it. For a teenager. She stopped following him everywhere and her school grades improved massively.'

'Okay, so you say I should go and see Mark and tell him I like him and—'

'No,' Ronald interrupted. 'Go and apologise to him. Properly. Have a grown-up conversation about what happened.' He shrugged. 'Then he'll tell you he doesn't fancy you and you can concentrate on work again instead of sitting here moping like a middle-aged teenager.'

'I'm not moping.' I couldn't possibly be, because I smiled. Even though it didn't change what I'd done, it was better to think that I'd behaved like a teenager rather than a stalker.

My friend Alex lived in a houseboat along the Prinsengracht. I'd arranged to see the parade from her roof. The best view in town. I'd texted her to check that she had room for one more – she did – and dragged Ronald with me. Hundreds of thousands of people lined the canals to cheer on a flotilla of partying drag queens and party boys. Pink was a very happy colour. When we got to the boat, the crowd was already five deep. I had to skirt my way past a group of tourists with wheelie bags, and a grandmother with a hearing aid, dressed in fluorescent pink, who was lighting a cigarette with a lighter adorned with a kitten. Alex and her husband were dressed in matching outfits, she in a white shirt with pink trousers and he in a pink shirt with white trousers. I refused the glass of champagne that was offered and asked for a soft drink instead. Expecting trouble wouldn't damage my enjoyment of the parade. It was pretty close to my default state of mind anyway.

On the canal bank opposite, a young man was sitting on a pink towel, his legs dangling over the edge. His friend, a chubby woman wearing pink bunny ears, had taken off her shoes and showed pink toenails. On the boat next to us, a man dressed in pink hot pants and a pink singlet and a black gimp harness was twerking. He was bald and overweight and probably my age. I bet he dressed really conservatively during his nine-to-five and that the pink socks tucked into combat boots didn't come out too often. Unless this was his normal weekend gear.

All over, the rainbow flags were dangling proudly. A boat with policemen came past. The people watching from the canal cheered loudly. They were bored with waiting for the parade to start, so anything was better than nothing. My colleagues gamely waved at their adoring fans, which drew loud applause. Today everybody loved each other.

Which was why the text from Piotr's friend bothered me so much. Ronald was staring at his phone and typing something with extreme concentration.

'Who are you texting?' I said.

'I'm letting Khalil know where we are. In case he wants to meet up.'

'You what? Why did you do that?'

'Because he asked. He's fine. There won't be any problems.'

I wished I could believe him. I heard loud disco music in the distance, the first notes of 'YMCA'. An even louder cheer went up. The parade was arriving. On the first boat, a group of men in very tight sailor outfits were dancing to the Village People, and half the people on the canal joined in. So did I. Who cared? It was a Saturday and the sun was shining. And I had a good reason to see Mark later. 'Come on, Ronald, where's your party spirit?'

'I might have forgotten to bring it.'

Yes, this really was my favourite day of the year. Pink seemed to be our new national colour. It was much more flattering than orange. The next boat brought a huge inflatable version of the Amsterdam bollards, striped in rainbow colours. It had to be lowered to clear the bridge and then rose again in its full glory. A bollard had never looked more phallic.

'That's crazy,' Ronald said.

It was glorious. Ridiculously, gloriously camp. The boat celebrated the gay people working for the Amsterdam council. I recognised one of the councillors. I'd had dealings with him in the past. Then he'd worn much more than he did now, his bare torso spray-painted in gold, with matching gold trousers.

The next boat brought three semi-naked dancers. Their tight white hot pants left very little to the imagination, and that was all they wore apart from rainbow-coloured angel wings. They danced in synchronised abandon to 'Relight My Fire'.

'Oh my God,' I heard Ronald breathe beside me.

'What?' I immediately scanned the boats and the crowd along the canal front to see what had concerned him.

'He clearly doesn't do things by half.'

'Who?'

The dancer in the middle, a man with sculpted muscles and dark skin, looked across at Alex's houseboat. A big grin split his face and he stretched both arms to the sky in a gesture of pure abandon.

'Fucking hell!' Ronald laughed. 'Khalil, you idiot!' he shouted jokingly at the boat.

'Friend of yours?' asked Alex in an impressed tone of voice. 'Great dancer.'

'When I told him he shouldn't live in fear, I didn't mean he should out himself in just hot pants and a pair of angel wings in the middle of Gay Pride.'

'Isn't that what the parade is all about?' Alex said.

But Ronald shook his head. I sang along to the song. The sun was shining over the city and Ronald's friend had only texted him to make sure someone he knew saw him dancing. The incongruity of it made me laugh out loud. Nothing could spoil this day. I gave Ronald a prod to make him dance with me. He didn't respond, and I looked at him. His expression was too serious for the party atmosphere. 'What's up?' I said.

'Couldn't you see the desperation in his face? Even today hasn't made the hurt go away.'

The words surprised me. I stopped moving. 'What hurt?'

'We buried his long-term partner a couple of days ago.'

It took me a moment to work out what he was saying. 'Oh my God. He and Piotr, they were together? Did Natalie know?'

'They were neighbours. Of course she knew.'

That was why she had said that Katja had killed an innocent man. If she'd killed him because she'd thought he had been Sylvie's boyfriend, she had been very wrong.

'We should talk to him,' Ronald said.

Chapter Twenty-Seven

Ronald and I caught up with Khalil immediately after the Pride parade had finished its cruise through the canals. By the time we found him, he was in the middle of getting changed, standing apart from the colleagues who had been on the boat with him. He had replaced his white hot pants with black jeans but was still wearing his feather wings. The gold highlights on his torso and face brought out his muscles and features. He made quite a beautiful angel.

'Can you help me with these?' he asked Ronald.

'Of course,' Ronald said, but he sounded reluctant.

Khalil turned to give him access to the buckles on the harness that connected the rainbow-coloured wings to his body.

'You need to give us a statement,' I said.

'What difference does it make?' he said as Ronald undid the straps. 'Piotr is dead and you've got his killer. Nothing else matters.'

I got the impression that it was only because I was here with Ronald that Khalil was willing to talk to me. 'I'm not sure we do have his killer,' I said.

Khalil threw a glance at Ronald. 'I thought you had?

Wasn't this about drugs? Some deal gone wrong?' He shrugged out of the wings as if he was taking off a jacket. 'That's why I got up the courage to do what I did today.'

This was clearly something that the two of them had discussed at some point in the past. Then I remembered Ronald telling Khalil at Piotr's funeral that he shouldn't live in fear. Was this what he meant? That Khalil shouldn't be afraid to come out?

'My parents, my cousins,' the Moroccan man continued, 'they're very traditional. I was worried that they'd had a hand in Piotr's death. It's horrible to think that about your own family, but because he'd been stabbed to death, I couldn't help but wonder. When I heard it was about drugs, that it had been a white woman who'd killed him, it actually made me feel better. That he didn't die because of me. That it wasn't about me.' He scrubbed his hands and arms as diligently as a surgeon, to remove any trace of gold. 'Piotr had come to Amsterdam, only to end up with me and be more afraid than he'd ever been back at home.'

'We don't think Piotr was killed because he was gay,' I said. After all the years of tolerance, it made me sad to think that people were still scared to come out. In recent years, violence against gay people had increased, and in certain areas men didn't even dare to walk hand in hand any more. Whatever had made Khalil come out today, if his family were that strict, it might have been sensible for him to have stayed in the closet. 'Someone said it was about a child,' I said gently. 'Because Piotr was asking questions.'

Khalil rummaged through a bag by his feet. He didn't clean his chest but just hid the gold paint on his torso with a black T-shirt. 'You found the child?' He said the words as if it was definite. There were no doubts in his mind about the child's existence.

'We think Katja used a photo of a child to lure Piotr to the bar. Isn't that why he met her there?'

Khalil nodded. 'He loved children. He was hoping we could adopt at some point, but I wasn't ready for that.' He sighed. 'I wasn't even ready to be open about our relationship. And he was worried about this child. The girl's child.' In the mirror I could see the gold glitter hugging his face, and it brought out the incredible greenness of his eyes.

'Which girl?' I said.

Khalil ignored the question. 'I thought he was nuts. I told him to let it go.' Tears welled up in his eyes. 'I hadn't realised it would be the child that would kill him and not the coke.' He started to attack the golden sequins on his cheekbones with a nailbrush, as if they now offended him.

'What do you know about this child?'

'Only what Piotr told me. He was at his neighbours' flat; they all liked to do a line together every now and then. It wasn't my scene so I never joined them. But this one night, a girl turned up. Piotr had never seen her before. She was pretty, he said. Blonde hair, blue eyes, very Dutch-looking, you know. And she said she had a child. She was the neighbour's ex-girlfriend.'

'Sylvie Bruyneel,' I said.

'She was Koen Westerfaalt's ex?' Ronald said at exactly the same time.

'That's it.'

'And Natalie was there too?' I asked. Sylvie used to go out with Natalie's fiancé?

'Yes. So this girl turns up and claims that the guy is the father of her child. Natalie screams that she's lying. That she doubts there even is a child.'

'There's nothing about Sylvie's child in the birth register.'

'I know. Piotr checked that too. Anyway, Piotr said that Koen got upset. Angry. The three of them disappeared into the bedroom. Why they didn't just ask Piotr to leave, he couldn't understand. He would do that a lot, talk about Dutch culture to me, as if I understood all of it.' He smiled a small smile. 'That's what got us together, you know, that we were both outsiders in a way.' He started to cry and reached for a tissue. 'Sorry, just give me a moment.' He worked visibly hard to compose himself before he could continue. 'There was a lot of shouting, a crash, and when they came out, the girl is crying and her face is red as if she's been hit.'

I nodded. That made sense. Petra had told us that Sylvie had had a bruise on her face when she'd gone to Katja's flat, desperate for money. She must have gone to Katja after she'd been at Natalie and Koen's flat.

'After she'd left, Natalie told Piotr that the girl had been trying to blackmail Koen but that it was all a lie. Fine. Piotr left to go home, but he talked to Koen in the doorway and told him that if he was a father, he had a responsibility and he should look after his kid.'

'And that was the last time Piotr saw the girl?'

'The last time he saw her, yes, but he heard her again later. He heard the doorbell. She had come back, and he was worried that there would be another argument.' Khalil rubbed his eyes. 'But he told me the voices sounded happy and there was laughter. So he went to bed, thinking it was all solved.'

I remembered that time I'd searched Piotr's flat. I'd been able to hear every word that was said from the other side of the wall. No wonder Piotr had known exactly what had been going on.

'But the next morning the girl was dead and that's when Piotr started to get obsessed,' Khalil said. 'He had this odd idea that the girl had been telling the truth, however often I told him that maybe she had just been a very good liar. That she was a junkie out to score cash for drugs and she'd clearly managed it because she'd OD'd. But Piotr kept insisting she looked clean.'

'Why didn't you tell us this sooner?' Ronald sounded angry. 'You made it sound to me as if it was about drugs.'

'That's what I thought. In a way, that's what I hoped.'

'That was why Piotr went to Sylvie's funeral,' I said.

'Yes. I told him he was crazy, attending the funeral of a girl he'd only seen once, but he thought the child would be there. He wanted to see him with his own eyes and check that he was being looked after.'

'I guess he asked Koen directly?'

'Yes, he asked both Koen and Natalie. But they both maintained that Sylvie had been telling stories and they denied knowing anything about it.'

No wonder Piotr had come to the bar when Katja had shown him that photo. She must have known that he had been looking for Sylvie's son – Koen's son – and had used that to get him to meet her. I would call Ingrid and ask her to get Katja ready to be interviewed again. We would have to inform her lawyer, of course, but we needn't tell Bauer. Now that I knew what Piotr had heard, I was only more certain that the little boy existed somewhere.

Khalil leaned towards the mirror, examining his face, and peeled the last shiny flecks from his skin. All signs of today's celebration and abandon had been scrubbed away. The beautiful angel had disappeared. 'I made a huge mistake today, didn't I?' In his black T-shirt and jeans, he looked as sombre as he sounded.

Ronald put an awkward hand on his shoulder. 'You couldn't have honoured Piotr better.'

Chapter Twenty-Eight

We got back on the tram. Half the people around us were wearing something pink. My own fuchsia T-shirt seemed very much out of sync with my thoughts. It was too festive. I pulled on the bottom of the shirt and straightened it. 'I'm sorry,' I said.

Ronald had been looking out of the window, but now he turned back to me. 'What for?'

'You told me the truth from the beginning about Piotr. That he hadn't been sleeping with Natalie. That he hadn't been dealing drugs. I should have believed you.'

'I should have taken you to Khalil sooner, but he wanted to keep his relationship with Piotr secret.' He put his hands on the headrest of the seat in front of him. 'I went to their place and had dinner. That was a big deal. They hadn't told many people but they trusted me to keep their secret. Maybe I shouldn't have kept quiet. I don't know.'

'It's fine.'

The tram took us closer and closer to Koen and Natalie's flat. I was reminded of when I was there a week ago and had heard them argue. Had that been about Koen's child? The tram took us slowly through the post-parade crowd.

270

I wished we could move more quickly, but I knew that this was still faster than if I had driven. But I was worried about what we were going to find.

We got off at the nearest stop and went up to the fourth floor. It was a massive anticlimax when all we found was a closed door. There was no response when I rang the bell.

'What now?' Ronald said.

I didn't think we had enough to apply for a search warrant. 'Call Natalie. You have her number, right?'

He nodded.

'Find out where she is.'

Ronald got his mobile out. After a few seconds' conversation he turned back to me. 'She's at work,' he said.

We went back into the centre of the city, to the department store. It was nearly closing time when we got there and the store was almost empty of shoppers. I stepped on the escalator to get to the second floor. I stared at my bare toes in my sandals, then further down to the striped metal steps. Each of the steps might think it was going somewhere, but at the top it was being dragged right back to the bottom to start its aimless journey up again.

When I got to the top of the escalator, I could see Natalie Schuurman wrestling with a mannequin. One naked arm lay discarded on the floor. I tried not to look at it. It reminded me too much of the time when I'd seen a real one severed just like that. That had been a horrible traffic accident. At the time, we'd just dealt with the aftermath and tried to keep the woman alive until the ambulance turned up. We'd managed. She'd lived.

'We have a couple of questions,' I said.

The rest of the mannequin seemed to be clinging on to the expensive dress. Natalie wrenched the other arm free from the body. 'What do you want to know?' she said.

'Tell us about the night that Sylvie Bruyneel came to your flat. We know that Piotr Mazur was there.'

Natalie sighed. 'That was what started it all.' I thought she meant Piotr's murder, but she continued, 'All the trouble between Koen and me.' She held on to the edge of the sleeve of the dress and stripped it from the loose arm.

'Because of the child?'

She bent her head and her hair fell forward and covered her face. 'There is no child. Koen hated the idea. He refused to believe it was true. We were both so happy when it turned out she'd been lying.'

'Where is Koen?' I said.

'I don't know. I haven't seen him for a few days.'

'Let me give you a hand.' Ronald stepped towards the mannequin, but Natalie pushed him away. She dropped the bare pale arm, still slightly bent, on the floor. 'I don't need a security guard's clumsy fingers all over a five-thousand-euro dress, thank you very much.'

'Are you okay?' Ronald asked, seemingly unperturbed by the rebuff.

She turned back to the mannequin and yanked the doll's head from its shoulders. 'Oh Ronald,' she said, 'I think he's going to leave me.' She dropped the head on the floor. Its dark nylon hair spilled across the carpet like a puddle and the blue eyes stared lifelessly at the ceiling. 'What am I going to do?'

He hugged her and she sobbed on his shoulder. It was

sincere, unlike her tears for Piotr Mazur the first time I'd met her. 'He won't leave you,' he said. 'How could he? It will be okay.' His voice was soft.

I frowned. 'Piotr Mazur believed Sylvie. He thought there was a child.'

She stepped out of the hug, managed to stop crying and dried her eyes on a tissue.

'Yes, I know. He kept asking questions about that night. Why Sylvie had OD'd.' She tucked her hair behind her ears and looked at Ronald. 'But it was so obvious what had happened. Sylvie needed money for drugs, and when she got it, she ended up using too much.' She tipped her head sideways and gave me a look from under her eyelashes that probably would have made Ronald's heart beat faster but didn't do much for me. 'Piotr just wouldn't believe it.' The look wouldn't have done much for him either.

'Why did you say that Katja killed an innocent man?'

Her eyes moved sharply to Ronald. 'Because Katja wanted to kill whoever had sold Sylvie those drugs and it wasn't Piotr.'

'Do you know who it was?'

'Not Piotr, because he had never seen Sylvie before she came to our flat that night. I know that for sure.'

'Was Koen her boyfriend?'

Ronald threw me an angry glance.

'No,' Natalie said. 'He was always mine. He just cheated on me with her.'

Behind me, the escalators whispered of secrets as they continued their pointless journey.

★ ★ ★

Ingrid was ready with Katja and her lawyer by the time I got to the police station. The rainbow flag still flew proudly from the flagpost on the roof. I swiped my card and went to the interview room.

Katja was calm, like last time, but she seemed drawn into herself. Her hair was limp around her square face and her eyes were deeply sunken, as if the effort to stay alive was sucking them into her brain. She was looking down. We might be running out of time to get to the truth. Her lawyer hadn't changed at all. I thought he was wearing the same suit, and maybe even the same tie.

I pressed the record button on the equipment, but after stating our names and the time, I let the silence grow. Normally people talked if it lasted too long. It was a human impulse to fill silence with words, to tell stories or to share impressions. Katja didn't say anything.

In the end, I was the first to speak. 'The wrong man is dead.' I said it softly but still pushed the words across the table towards Katja. I'd been waiting to say this ever since I'd heard Natalie talking at Piotr's funeral, but only now did I have enough information to go directly against Bauer's wishes.

Katja lifted her gaze from my chin and looked me in the eye.

'Natalie Schuurman said that an innocent man was killed,' Ingrid said. We had agreed beforehand to focus on finding out the motive for Piotr's murder. Later we could move on to finding out who actually killed him. As I'd said to Tim, sometimes protecting the vulnerable was more important than convicting the guilty.

274

'Whatever you meant to do, whatever you were trying to achieve, you failed,' I said, 'because the wrong person was stabbed.'

Katja frowned, the first outward sign that she was actually listening to what was being said.

'So you'd better tell us what the point of killing Piotr was. Were you trying to protect someone? Whatever was going on, if you do not tell us, that person will still be in danger.'

'No.' It was a hoarse whisper. 'He wasn't the wrong man.' The words were slow and drawn out, as if Katja had lost the ability to speak fluently. 'She's lying.'

'This was about Sylvie and her child.'

'There is no child. I told you: I wanted revenge on Sylvie's dealer.'

'Petra Maasland told you that her dealer was also her boyfriend?'

'Yes, that's how I figured it out. Because Piotr had been her boyfriend.'

'Why did you think that?'

'He came to her funeral. He kept following me. He kept asking me all these questions about her. Where had she been? What had she been doing in the last two years? So I started to suspect that he'd been her boyfriend. Then I saw him give that German the drugs and I was sure. He killed Sylvie; he gave her the drugs that made her OD.'

'Katja, he wasn't Sylvie's boyfriend,' I said.

Katja shook her head. 'You're wrong.'

'Piotr was in a long-term relationship with a man,' I said.

'That doesn't mean anything.'

'He didn't know Sylvie until she came to Koen and Natalie's flat.'

'He gave that German the drugs,' Katja said. 'That's when I decided . . .' She stopped.

'Decided what?'

She lifted her head and looked me in the eye. 'I decided to kill him.'

I shook my head. That wasn't what she had been going to say. 'What happened that evening? Tell me about the German.'

'He kept pestering us. He kept asking for drugs. He was hassling everybody. And then Piotr took this little bag out of his pocket, gave it to the guy and told him to get lost.'

'Gave it to him?' Ingrid said. 'Did he take money for it?'

I inhaled sharply at the question. It only occurred to me now: Ronald had told me from the beginning that Piotr hadn't been a dealer. Khalil had talked about him doing lines with his neighbours. That footage of Piotr and Natalie in the changing rooms hadn't been about Piotr selling drugs to Natalie. What had she texted him? *I'll give u what u want.* Not money for drugs, but drugs themselves. He hadn't been selling; he'd been using.

Katja's face was pale. 'No, the guy didn't give him any money,' she said reluctantly.

'He had no other drugs on him when we found him. Did you steal anything?'

'No, I didn't touch him afterwards. I just left.'

'So he was carrying a single hit and gave it to the German,' Ingrid said. 'What if it was for his own consumption?'

Katja buried her face in her hands just as the door to the interview room opened.

'What the hell are you doing?' Bauer said. He grabbed my arm and dragged me out of the room. He pushed me into the corridor and slammed the door behind me. 'Are you crazy?'

'There's been a development—'

'I listened to you from the observation area. You've got nothing! You're ruining my case for nothing! Don't you understand what you're doing? If I see you anywhere near Katja Bruyneel again, I'll report you. I'll have you fired. Get out of here.' His face looked as if it was ready to explode. 'Get out of here right now!'

'Don't blame Ingrid,' I said. 'This is my doing.'

'As if I don't know that!'

Maybe I would have argued for longer if it had just been my career, but for Ingrid's sake I capitulated. I knew that the outcome would be bad for her if I stayed.

Plus I knew Bauer was right – I had nothing. Everything pointed towards Katja having killed Piotr because she'd mistakenly thought he had been Sylvie's dealer. Piotr's concern for Sylvie's non-existent child had given everybody the wrong impression.

So why did I still feel it was all a lie?

I went to my office, grabbed the files on Piotr's case, stuffed them in my bag and went home.

Chapter Twenty-Nine

I was woken up by Ronald bursting into my bedroom. The cat jumped from my bed with an annoyed meow. I was just about to ask what the hell he thought he was doing when I noticed he had his mobile in his hand. It was on speakerphone.

'Doesn't feel right.' A woman's voice.

'Who is it?' I said.

Ronald didn't respond and the voice on the phone continued. 'He gave it. It's not right.' The words were slurred.

I recognised the voice and was fully awake instantly.

'Stay upright,' Ronald said into the phone. 'Don't lie down.'

A soft laugh. 'I listened to you. I called you.'

'Where are you?'

'Home.'

I got out of bed. Ronald was chivalrous enough to turn his back. I threw some clothes on. The same ones I'd been wearing all day because they were on the floor by the side of the bed.

'Is Koen with you?' Ronald said.

'No. He left again.'

'Give me the address.'

'I know where it is,' I said.

'I'm on my way,' Ronald said. 'I'll get an ambulance.'

'Fine. It's fine,' the slurred voice on the phone responded.

'Sit upright. Your back against something.'

I heard her shuffle. Good, she was with it enough to listen to Ronald. If she had her back against something and passed out, she would hopefully stay upright. Then she would at least not choke to death on her own vomit.

'Natalie,' he said, 'I'll be there in ten minutes. Whatever you do, don't lie down.'

I grabbed my mobile and dialled 112. 'Ambulance. It's an emergency. A drug overdose.'

'Do you know what drug?' the operator said.

'Heroin possibly. Or cocaine. We're on our way there now. She's still conscious. But hurry.'

The operator said something but I had already grabbed my car keys and was running down the stairs.

Ronald followed me.

'How's she doing?' I said.

'She's cut the call.'

I drove back to where we had been only a few hours before. Even though it was the night after the Gay Pride parade, once we were away from the canal, traffic was remarkably light. I pushed the gas pedal down and my green car responded pleasingly quickly. The streets were empty enough that I didn't stop for red lights. I didn't need a siren on top of the car to drive as if there was one. It didn't matter: there were no cars that needed to pull over. A flash followed me as I hit the third red light. I would have a few minutes with Natalie before the ambulance arrived. Ask her some questions. Who had given her the drugs? Natalie had told Ronald that Katja had stabbed the wrong man. Did she know who the right man was? Was this about drugs after all?

Another car came towards the junction from the right. That car had right of way. He headed towards me, fully expecting me to stop. Instead I sped up and shot across in front of him; there was no time to lose. I heard the screeching sound of the other car's tyres.

How much time would I have before the ambulance arrived? Would she talk to me? Probably not, but she would talk to Ronald. I started to believe that Natalie had known exactly what had been going on. It had now put her in danger.

I turned the corner and was surprised to see blue swirling lights already there. How had the paramedics beaten us to the address? Two men in white were wheeling a stretcher into the back of the ambulance. Was this someone else? It wasn't possible that they could have got here more quickly than we had. I stopped the car and jumped out. It wasn't parked properly but that didn't matter. Ronald ran up to the ambulance. The paramedic, a man with a shaven head and a handlebar moustache, stopped him with one hand.

'I got a call,' Ronald said. 'A woman overdosed.'

'We've got her.'

'Natalie Schuurman?'

'That's her. She'll be fine.' He put the hand on Ronald's arm. 'We got there in time. Don't worry.' He climbed into the ambulance.

Ronald grabbed the handle to keep the door open. 'We'll follow you.'

The ambulance sped off. I would have thought that the hospital was further away from here than my flat. That had been a nifty bit of driving by the ambulance crew.

Was there a rule in the architect's handbook that said that hospitals always had to be white? This place couldn't be anything other than a cathedral dedicated to healing. The nurse at the reception area stared at me bleary-eyed. 'You can't see her yet,' she said. 'She's being treated.'

'I'm a police officer. We need to talk to her urgently.'

'You can see her as soon as the doctors are finished with her. Just wait here.'

We sat down in the waiting area on orange chairs that were linked together. They were uncomfortable, and after ten minutes, the edge started to dig into my upper legs. A steady stream of injured people kept the nurse in the reception busy. I might be imagining it, but it seemed that she had to speak more English than Dutch. A few people wore pink, but then I was wearing my fuchsia-pink top as well. I had just picked it up off the floor when Ronald had woken me, without giving it any thought.

We sat without talking. A woman came out with a leg in plaster. A man walked slowly with a bandage around his head. It was a normal Saturday night.

Finally, the nurse called my name. 'You can see her now. She's in A17. It's a left here, then right, then follow the red line on the floor. That will get you there.'

'Thank you.' Ronald smiled at her, but the woman's eyes had already gone back to her screen.

Natalie looked younger without the thick make-up. She had a drip attached to her arm.

'Natalie.' Ronald touched her other arm. 'What happened?'

She opened her eyes. 'Hi, Ronald. Did I spoil your Saturday night?'

'It doesn't matter. I'm glad you're safe.'

'I was stupid, wasn't I? You warned me.'

'You will talk to the police, won't you?'

She bent her head forward until her hair covered her face. 'Not now. I want to sleep.' She raised her head again and looked me in the eye. 'This isn't a matter for the police. I was stupid but I won't be any more. I don't think I really wanted to kill myself.'

'You nearly died. If we hadn't called the ambulance . . .' He stopped at her small smile.

'Oh Ronald,' she said. 'You must have known I'd called the emergency services before I called you.'

Chapter Thirty

In the morning sunshine, I took out the files I'd taken home yesterday. Ronald was still asleep; we'd got home from the hospital in the very early hours of the morning. I was wide awake. I took all the photos of the scene of Piotr's stabbing out of the files and spread them out in front of me. Had I been too close to it all along? Had I inserted my memory of that night into every picture that I looked at? I normally started with the photos. I liked looking at the photos. Why hadn't I done that this time?

Maybe I'd thought I had no need of crime-scene photos because I'd actually been at the scene. I'd seen the aftermath in person. From up close I'd witnessed the exact moment that Piotr Mazur died.

Or maybe it had been because Piotr's death had been so mixed up with my personal thoughts about that night.

Or, if I wanted to be kind to myself, maybe it was because I had moved to Bauer's team and all he cared about was protecting his previous case.

Either way, it didn't matter. I examined them now. I no longer saw a dead drug dealer, but a dead innocent man who had been killed by mistake. I picked up the first photo.

Look at this objectively, I told myself. Forget about pushing the T-shirt against his stomach and look at this photo as if you had never seen him before. What would his body position normally tell me? That someone had turned him on his back. That someone had done CPR. He wasn't lying how he had fallen. Nothing else.

This was hard. Even though I was really trying, I kept putting myself into the photos. Me and Gerard Campert both. I could picture the doctor, his chest bared because I was using his T-shirt to try to staunch Piotr's blood. I could see his large facial features in profile, his face turned away from me.

This was no good.

From the photos in front of me I took all the ones that showed Piotr's body and pushed them into a pile. I turned them over. It was still so hot. I could feel the sweat running down from my armpits, and a film was forming on my upper lip. I got up and splashed cold water on my face. I sat back and closed my eyes to clear my mind.

When I looked at the photos still in front of me, one of them jumped out at me. It showed the drawn outline of where the body had been. But it also showed the cars parked along the street.

I'd been an idiot.

I picked up the picture. I looked again at the position of Piotr's body. I looked at the gap in the row of cars just ahead of where his body had been.

A gap the size of a car.

Katja had driven to the murder scene. When she and Piotr had turned into the side street, he had walked her to her car.

She hadn't been on foot. No wonder we hadn't been able to find any footage of her leaving.

I could feel the excitement racing through my veins. I saw the series of photos of the parking payment machine with my bloody handprint on it. I remembered leaning on it after feeling dizzy that night. Either Katja had got a fine, or she'd paid for parking at that machine. Either way I would be able to get the car registration plate. Maybe it was useless but maybe it would give me something. It was worth a go.

It didn't take me many phone calls before I got some answers. Not a single parking fine had been issued in that area that evening. The list of the tickets issued by the machine wasn't long. Most cars belonged to local residents. Only seven cars had paid for parking. I got the number plates.

I looked up the cars. I looked up the owners.

I swore when I saw whose car had been parked in that area. Next to where Piotr died. I looked back at the time the ticket had been issued. Nine thirty-three. Katja had already been in the bar with Piotr when Petra Maasland had parked her car and paid.

I'd been a fool. I pulled up Petra's personal records. She didn't have a daughter. She didn't have a son either. She had no children at all.

Why had I ever believed the story that Oskar was Petra's grandson? He wasn't her grandson; he was Sylvie Bruyneel's son. It all seemed so obvious now. Sylvie must have told her counsellor that she was pregnant and Petra had helped her keep the baby a secret. So had Petra killed Piotr? Had she been the one to wield the knife?

285

I knew someone had to come with me to bring Petra in. We had to question her. Was this enough to get the boss and Bauer to agree with me?

I didn't have time to argue with them. Instead I called Thomas. He wasn't even annoyed with me. He was at my flat within ten minutes. I'd called ahead to the hospital and they had confirmed that Petra was working today. Apparently Sundays were very busy days for counsellors specialising in drug-related issues.

Thomas drove me to the hospital. I filled him in on exactly what I'd found out. That Petra's car had been parked in the side street. That she'd lied to us. That Katja had lied to us. It didn't take long, and I had finished well before we pulled in to the car park of the hospital.

We came past the nursery on the way to the entrance. I recognised Vincent de Wolf, the guy I'd talked to when we'd arrested Katja. He called me over. 'That child you were worried about; I wanted to let you know he's been coming here again.'

'Is he here now?'

'No, not yet.'

'Come on, Lotte, we need to interview Petra Maasland. We can come back here afterwards,' Thomas said.

I gave Vincent my card again. 'Let me know as soon as he gets here.'

I followed Thomas into the hospital, throwing one last glance at the nursery before I entered. We went up to Petra's floor, pushed into her office and told her patient that she had to wait outside until we were done.

'I hope this is urgent,' Petra said.

We were back in the boudoir, and this time it seemed overwhelmingly cloying. 'Did you kill him?' I said. My voice was harsh. Petra had helped Sylvie to hide her child. How far had she been willing to go to keep that child's existence a secret? Far enough to actually kill a man?

'Kill who?'

'Don't pretend you don't know who I'm talking about. Did you kill Piotr Mazur?'

'Of course not.'

'But you were there.'

'No.'

'Your car was there.' I showed her the records from the parking machine.

'Katja must have stolen it.'

'No,' I said. 'Stop this. You keep saying that you don't know Katja that well, and now you want us to believe that she stole your car and took a photo of your grandson to lure Piotr to the bar?'

'Isn't that what she told you?'

'How do you know that?'

Petra didn't respond, just shook her head, which made her dandelion hair bounce.

'Did you report your car stolen?'

'No.'

I was reminded of the first time I'd met Petra; learning how she had been upset that Sylvie had overdosed and had flagged it up with the police, but had then withdrawn her concern. Now I knew that it hadn't been because Katja had told her it was suicide but because she had Sylvie's son living with her. A boy who hadn't been registered as Sylvie's child.

'Oskar is Sylvie's child, isn't he?'

'No, he's our grandson.'

'Your daughter's child?'

'Yes.'

'You don't have a daughter.'

She didn't miss a beat, I had to give her that. 'My husband's daughter from an earlier relationship.'

I shook my head. 'I'm calling Social Services. I'm going to have them look after him until I can see some paperwork. I need to see birth certificates.'

Petra deflated. 'I want a lawyer.'

I wanted to swear and sank back in the sofa.

'Sure,' Thomas said. 'That is your right.'

It was going to be hard to prove who had actually killed Piotr unless Katja would retract her statement. Unless Petra confessed. Thomas and I looked at each other. That was the end of our questioning. I rested my head against the squishy sofa.

'You know the real murderer is only just around the corner, don't you?' Petra said.

At her voice I quickly brought my head up. 'Who do you mean?'

'All out of jealousy. She told me.'

'Who are you talking about?'

But Petra glued her lips together and shook her head. Why tell me anything that she could use as a bargaining chip later? I thought bitterly.

Thomas took Petra to the station to wait for her lawyer so that she could be interrogated later, and I told her patient that she should go home; that Petra wouldn't be able to listen to her any time soon.

I stared out of the window as I called Social Services. I would wait at the hospital for them to turn up. Downstairs I saw Ronald de Boer cross the car park and enter the hospital. I could guess why he was here. Had he come in my car?

Chapter Thirty-One

I found Ronald easily enough. I stayed outside the door and out of sight. I knew Natalie would be much more willing to speak if she didn't know I was here. I trusted Ronald to ask the right questions. He still knew how to do this job and Natalie seemed to like him.

'Nobody has come to see me.' Her voice was petulant.

'Not even Koen?' Ronald said.

'No. I called him but he refused to come.'

'Are you being discharged already?'

'Yes, just a couple of forms left to fill in and then I can go. I'll be an outpatient and just "under observation".' She made speech marks in the air with her fingers.

'Because you told them you tried to kill yourself.'

'I'm so tired, Ronald.'

Compared to Ronald and the few hours of sleep he was getting, she was probably well rested. I knew she wasn't talking about sleep, though, but of that deeper tiredness that sadness brought. She must have been if she'd tried to take her own life. I peeked into the room. Natalie was fully dressed. She stood with her back towards me.

'You used to be a cop, didn't you?' she said.

'I was.'

'What happened?'

'I don't want to talk about it.' As he grabbed her bag, he threw me a quick glance. He'd noticed that I was here. I didn't think Natalie had.

'You tell me your secret and I'll tell you mine,' she said.

'Just tell me yours. You'll feel better for it.'

'I could have saved my friend.'

'Who are you talking about? Sylvie?' Ronald sat down on the edge of the bed with his back towards me. He patted the space next to him. Natalie slumped down. It was clever of him, because now I could step closer to them and there was less of a chance that Natalie would see me. I took my phone out and pressed record. It wouldn't be admissible in court, of course.

Natalie dropped her head into her hands. 'I hadn't seen her in almost a year. She looked well. Much better than she had in a while. We were all together, me, Koen and Piotr. He'd popped round to see us. He stayed for a drink. Anyway, we'd done a couple of lines and Sylvie came round. Said she needed to talk to Koen. They went into the bedroom together. Piotr and I stayed behind.'

'Did another line?'

'Something like that.'

That was different to what Khalil had told us. He'd said that Natalie had gone into the bedroom too. Maybe Piotr hadn't wanted him to know that he and Natalie had stayed behind to do a line of coke.

'We heard the screaming and shouting behind the door,' Natalie continued. 'Piotr wanted to interfere but I held him

291

back. Koen is always so wired after. I'm good at staying out of the way when he's like that.'

I remembered Natalie's black eye. I wanted to step into the hospital room but I knew she would stop talking. It was better to listen in and to get her to give me an official statement afterwards. It was always hard with these domestics. Women who'd been beaten were often afraid to testify, or they changed their minds when things were 'better'.

'When Sylvie came out,' Natalie continued, 'I couldn't look her in the eye. He'd hit her, I could tell that. She was quiet for a bit. Then she said: he's your child. At that I could have hit her myself, so I didn't feel too bad that he'd punched her.'

'What did Piotr do?'

'He stood up as if he was going to interfere. But I think maybe he was scared to. Sylvie left.' Natalie stopped talking.

'You didn't kill her. You didn't get between her and your boyfriend but you didn't kill her.'

Natalie grimaced. 'Not then. But she came back. Two hours later. She stood outside the door of the flat and screamed that she was going to go to the police, tell them about the drug dealing. Unless he paid. He opened the door really quickly and got her to go inside.'

'Was Piotr still there?'

'No, he had left. Anyway, Koen said that she was right, that if the kid was his child, he would pay child support. Sylvie smiled. She looked so pretty, even though the bruises were already showing on her face. He had split her lip. I don't know why she believed him. He suggested we

292

celebrate. He gave her a line. To make up for hitting her, he said. It would make her feel better.'

'And she overdosed.'

Natalie closed her eyes. Tears were running from the corners. 'Swapping the drugs. It was such an easy thing to do. And I' – she looked at him – 'I hated her so much, because she'd slept with him. Because she'd always have this tie with him. His child. I forgot that she used to be my friend.'

'It wasn't your fault.'

'I never called an ambulance. I watched her and she died.' She laughed, a joyless sound. 'I called an ambulance for myself while I still could. But Sylvie, I just helped carry to the alley around the corner.' She tied her hair into a pony-tail, getting ready to leave the room. 'I've got this counsellor, because of the suicide. I told her the story. She called me a callous bitch.' She looked at Ronald. 'I thought she was going to hit me. I actually was scared. Do you think I should report her? I've got her name and address. That fat cow. And she had such terrible hair.'

'What happened to the child?'

'That's what I asked Koen yesterday afternoon. He said: what's with all the questions? Then he said he was going to sort it out.'

'He was going to sort it out.' There was clear anger in Ronald's voice. 'You didn't try to kill yourself at all, did you?'

He didn't think this had been an accident or a suicide attempt; he thought someone had swapped Natalie's drugs as well.

293

Chapter Thirty-Two

My phone rang with an unknown number. I gave up listening to Ronald trying to convince Natalie to make a statement and walked down the corridor to take the call. It was Vincent de Wolf. Oskar had arrived at the nursery. I rushed over there.

'You were worried about this boy, weren't you?' Vincent said. 'Well, you needn't be. His grandfather just dropped him off. I didn't mention anything to him. I wasn't sure what to do.'

'His grandfather? I thought you said Petra Maasland always brought him here.'

'Oh yes, she does sometimes as well. But her husband works here too. Gerard Campert.' He nodded towards the hospital entrance, where a man was just going inside. I must have missed him by seconds.

He needn't have said the name. I recognised the man immediately. The last time I'd seen him, we'd both been sitting on the kerb drinking tea, covered in Piotr Mazur's blood. It was the man in the yellow T-shirt, the doctor who'd tried to keep Piotr alive until the ambulance turned up. Or had he not tried as hard as he should have?

I wasn't sure what to do next. Should I get the child out of here, or should I talk to the doctor? The husband of the woman who had just been taken to the police station to be questioned over Piotr's death. I turned to Vincent. 'Social Services are going to come and pick the child up soon. I had to contact them. Keep Oskar safe here until then. Don't let him out of your sight.'

Vincent frowned. 'Social Services? Why?'

'No time to explain,' I said, and ran after the doctor. I caught up with him just as he was waiting for the elevator and grabbed him by the arm. 'What did you know?' I said.

He didn't even ask what I was talking about. 'I was wondering when you were going to come here,' he said. There was none of the defiance his wife had shown. He just looked tired. 'Do you want to come to my office?'

'Sure.' I felt some connection with him because we had tried to save a man together. I still believed that. Just look-ing at him brought that night back to me. The heat, the smell of Piotr's blood, the yellow T-shirt in my hands. I cut him some slack because of that.

He also seemed very willing to talk to me. I looked at his face. If anything, he seemed relieved that I was finally here.

We went up in the elevator to the third floor and along a corridor. He opened the door to a small room and offered me a seat.

'I knew you'd come. It all went so wrong.' He didn't even wait for me to start asking questions. He just started talking. 'We wanted to show him Oskar. We thought that if he saw the child, saw that he was well taken care of, he would stop all the questions. Katja would meet him in the bar to talk to him and see what kind of man he was. I was there as well to keep an eye out, in case things went very wrong. Katja somehow thought that maybe he wasn't so bad; after all, her sister had liked him.'

'And what changed?'

'He gave those drugs to the guy with the beard. Suddenly Katja said that we couldn't introduce Oskar to his father as the guy was a drug dealer. She said: I can't do it.'

'He wasn't Oskar's father.'

'He was. He was watching our house all the time. We would see him outside in his car. It was actually getting worrying. I would leave to go to work and he would be there. We couldn't go to the police.'

'He'd heard Natalie and Koen arguing over the child. When Sylvie OD'd, he was concerned. That's all. He liked children. He was worried about the child's welfare. And you killed him because of his questions.'

'Petra should never have told Katja, but she thought it would make her final months better, to know that her sister had a child. We agreed that Katja could move in with us and look after Oskar. That way we didn't have to bring him to the nursery here. But Piotr followed Katja. He saw her in a toyshop and followed her to our house.'

I was reminded of how happy Piotr had looked when Katja showed him the photo. Now I knew that he'd been happy because the boy was safe. How ironic that really everybody had wanted the same thing. 'Why did she kill him?'

Gerard paused before answering the question. 'I'm not sure what happened. All I know was that Petra was waiting in the car with Oskar. There must have been an argument.

I don't know. Petra won't tell me.' He sighed and folded his arms. 'When I heard that guy shout for help, I was so worried that it was Petra or Katja who'd been injured. When I saw Piotr on the floor, I was relieved.' He rested his head in his hands. 'It was awful that a man died and I was happy about it.'

'You ran so fast you almost overtook me.'

'We could never have kept him alive.'

I looked him in the eye. 'I believe you.'

'If we hadn't invited Katja to live with us, none of this would have happened.'

'It would have come out at some point. The child isn't registered as Sylvie's.'

'She was worried that Oskar would be taken into care. The closer it came to the due date, the more fractious she got. She became hysterical, so in the end, for her safety and the baby's, we agreed. She had the child at our house. I helped her but we had no midwife. We had agreed that we would call an ambulance if it looked as if anything was going wrong, but luckily there were no complications. I'd been present at the birth, so I could register him. I used Sylvie's original name from before she was adopted. Sonja Aak.'

'So why did Sylvie go to Katja that night? And then to the father?'

'She'd argued with Petra. It was just a stupid little argument over vaccinations, but Sylvie got it into her head that she wanted to leave and live by herself. But of course she needed money for that. She'd probably thought that Katja would let her stay with her. Katja was so cut up about that.'

'About turning her sister away. Yes, I understand that. You know you'll have to come to the police station with me too.'

'Yes. I know.'

'I have to wait for Social Services to turn up and then I'll accompany you. An innocent man was murdered. A man whose worst crime was to be worried about a child.'

'He was a drug dealer.'

'No, he just had some cocaine on him for his own consumption and he gave that to the German guy. Still, that's irrelevant.'

'But it wasn't cocaine; it was heroin.'

Of course. I'd forgotten about that. From the toxicology report after the post-mortem, I knew that Piotr hadn't had heroin in his system. I was pretty sure that he'd believed it was cocaine he was giving to that German. That meant that maybe someone had been trying to kill Piotr. The same person who had swapped the drugs and got Sylvie Bruyneel to overdose. How very sad that those drugs had caused Piotr to die after all.

Gerard Campert looked at his watch. 'Sorry, I need to scrub up. I have one more surgery scheduled for today. Will you let me finish that?'

I nodded. 'Yes. Yes, that's fine. I'll wait.'

He left. I wasn't sure, I probably shouldn't have allowed him to do that, but I trusted him. Having been together on the night that Piotr was killed had created some link between us. I called Social Services to see when they would be coming. The woman said they were on their way. They would be there in ten minutes at most. I went down the stairs to the nursery area to wait for them to turn up. Even though this was absolutely not what Sylvie had wanted, it wasn't going to be as bad for Oskar as she had feared. A child needed to be looked after properly. We couldn't have him stay with a woman I suspected of being a murderer.

Vincent was standing by the side of the nursery's play area, looking frazzled.

'Social Services are coming for Oskar,' I said.

'Yes, they just picked him up.'

'No, they're on their way.'

'But the guy, he said . . .' Vincent pushed his hands to his mouth when he realised the mistake he'd made.

'What did he look like?' I said. 'The guy who picked him up, was he really good-looking?'

He nodded silently.

Chapter Thirty-Three

We rushed to the car park, Ronald and I. We had to go to Koen's flat. Koen, the child's father and Sylvie's lover. Katja had tried to protect her nephew but had killed the wrong man, and now her fears had come true and the drug-dealer father had kidnapped his son. Ronald still had my car keys. He got in the driver's seat. We didn't have time to argue, so I let him. He seemed surprisingly familiar in my car.

As he pressed down on the gas, I called it in. 'Suspect potentially armed and dangerous. Class A drugs on the premises.' I swallowed. 'And an abducted child. Approach with care. I'd like some medical back-up too.'

'Are we going to be in time?' Ronald said after I disconnected the call.

'We'd fucking better be.'

Traffic was horrendous and even though Ronald did his best to get some speed up whenever possible, it seemed we crawled to Koen's flat. He parked the car outside the block. I got out and walked into the shadows of the ten grey floors of apartments. We could not afford to let Koen see us, as that might spook him and force him into action. The wait for Ingrid, Thomas and back-up seemed endless. The wind floated calmly around the building, as if to mock the sense of urgency I felt inside. It carried the smell of dope. After ten minutes, I couldn't wait any longer. I called Thomas again and asked him how close he was. When he told me they were at least fifteen minutes away, I swore under my breath.

'Have you got a gun?' I asked Ronald.

He frowned. 'Of course I haven't. We should wait.'

'And let him kill a child? While we're standing here waiting because we want to be safe and careful?'

'Because we're being sensible.'

'I'm not going to let this child die.' I walked towards the elevator and pressed the button. The happy ping when it arrived set off alarms in my stomach. 'You don't have to come,' I said.

He followed me in. 'I know how you feel.' He spoke quietly. 'But don't let it cloud your judgement.'

'I've been so blind. I should have figured out that Oskar wasn't Petra's grandson.' The first and second floors went by.

'Then Koen wouldn't have tried to kill Natalie.'

I grimaced through the tension. 'Keys,' I said, and held out my hand. 'Give me back my car keys.'

Third floor. Fourth floor. He got them out of his pocket and handed them over with obvious reluctance. 'Natalie must have been discharged from hospital by now. We should tell her not to come here.'

'Leave it,' I said. The lift doors opened.

The wind tried to persuade us to go back. The wind tunnel of the corridor turned the gentle breeze from downstairs into a proper gale. I kept my gaze focused straight

301

ahead to stop myself from looking into the abyss on my right-hand side. I switched from holding the balustrade to holding the gun on my hip. It made me feel safer. My heartbeat was racing.

'What are you going to do? Ring the doorbell?'

I wished that Ronald wasn't sounding so much like my annoying inner voice. 'Have a better idea?' I was still torn between waiting and acting. One was sensible, the other necessary.

'Yes, wait until back-up arrives.'

As if his words had magically conjured them up, sirens became faintly audible in the distance. Ronald put a hand on my arm. 'Let's wait. Just a few minutes.'

'If he's drugged that child, every second will count.' The sound of the sirens would alert Koen. What would he do? I wasn't going to have another death on my hands. With every life I saved, I would alter the balance of my guilt.

The ping of the elevator sounded from the end of the corridor. I turned around and saw a thin woman with long blonde hair. Natalie. Perfect. She would have the keys. She'd come home to her boyfriend as soon as she was out of hospital. How stupid. It never ceased to amaze me that public transport was so much quicker than going by car.

'Stay away,' Ronald said. At exactly the same time as I shouted, 'Hurry up and give me the keys.'

She paused as if to consider, then dropped her bags, rushed forward and handed the keys over.

My hands shook as I tried to fit the key into the lock with my clumsy left hand. My right hand never left my gun. The outside door opened.

'Freeze! Police!' I shouted as soon as I was indoors.

'In here,' a calm male voice responded. Was there even relief there?

I wasn't sure what to expect. I just kept going on the route I'd started, rushing down the hallway with my gun pulled. I pushed open the door to the living room. The sound of the sirens was louder now, and we would probably be in time to save Oskar's life, if he'd been drugged. How much heroin would a small child survive? How would you even administer drugs to a toddler? Rub them into his gums?

As the door swung open, I sighted along the barrel of my gun and saw Koen sitting on the sofa. He raised his hands in the air. The ring on his thumb flashed golden. My eyes had to leave him to scan the room for the child. He was asleep in the corner, on the sofa opposite Koen.

'Ronald, get Oskar. Take him downstairs.' I fell silent to listen to the sound of the sirens. I identified the different tones. 'Have the paramedics check him over. I can hear an ambulance.' Thomas must have got me one. He was a good guy.

'I didn't hurt him,' Koen said. 'He's my son.'

'You abducted him. We'll just take him to the hospital.'

Ronald picked the child up from the sofa. Rudely awakened from sleep, the boy started crying and screaming. It was a very welcome sound. Ronald held him carefully, clearly used to carrying children, and took him out of the flat.

I waited for the rest of the police. My gun was trained on Koen's face. He didn't move. That sound of sirens so close was welcome. Back-up had only been minutes behind.

Maybe I should have waited, but whatever. The child was safe and I could breathe easily again. My heart rate slowed down. I had made up for my earlier mistake. I had atoned for Piotr's death.

I took a seat on the sofa opposite Koen, on the exact spot where Oskar had been sleeping. It was easier that way to keep my gun pointed at him. 'How did you know where Oskar was?' I said.

Koen frowned. 'I've always known. Sylvie told me. She said he was in a good place, so I decided to leave him there.'

'When did she tell you that?'

'When she came to my flat that evening.' He started to raise his hand to scratch his head but saw me looking and put it back on his knee.

'Did you know she'd had a baby?'

'No.' He shook his head. 'I had no idea.'

'Were you angry with her?' I kept my voice calm. Maybe he would admit to having killed Sylvie. He still hadn't asked for a lawyer. He seemed to think that we were just having a conversation, and I didn't want to destroy that illusion with aggressive questioning, whatever I might think about this man.

'No,' he said. 'She had no real reason to tell me.'

'I meant were you angry when she turned up on your doorstep?'

'She wanted me to pay for child support. She said she needed the money.' He stared out of the window for a bit. Then he shook his head. 'I wasn't going to give her any-thing, but Piotr cornered me. He was a good man. He asked me if I thought it was my child. I told him it probably was.

He said that I should take responsibility. That I should do my bit to help raise my kid.' He shrugged. 'I don't know, it made sense. So I called her.'

'You called her?'

'Yeah. I asked her to come back. Sit down, talk through what she needed. What we were going to do. That was when she told me that she was living with her counsellor and her husband. That they were a good couple but that she needed some space. She wanted to get her own place and needed money for that. Crazy girl, not registering the child under her own name. Having him without any help.' He leaned forward. 'But her parents were nuts. You know she was adopted, right? And she told me she didn't want that for her child. I said that if that was what she wanted to do, I'd give her some money whenever I had it.'

'And then you took some drugs?'

'Yeah, well. She told me she hadn't been using for a while because she didn't want to harm the baby. But she wasn't breastfeeding any more – trust me, that was too much information – so why not.'

'And she overdosed.'

'That was the weird thing. We just did a couple of lines. At the time it didn't make sense. It was only later that I realised what had happened.'

'What do you mean?'

'That she'd been given the wrong stuff.'

'That *you'd* given her the wrong stuff.' I did my best to keep my voice steady, but my heart was pounding. Maybe he was going to admit to having killed her.

'Me?' he said. 'No, not me.'

305

'But you know who it was.'

'What difference does it make?'

'You didn't think to go to the police?'

He laughed. 'I'm not really in the right situation to call in the police, now am I? Had I known, I would have phoned for an ambulance, of course. But I had to go to work and didn't find out until the next morning.'

'Work?'

'As a barman in a club. I start at midnight. Sylvie said she might come by later, but she never turned up.'

I stared at Koen. There was something not right here. This didn't make any sense. 'So you knew where Oskar was. What changed?' I kept the surprise out of my voice. 'Why take him now?'

'He'll be protected in hospital, won't he?' Koen said.

It was an odd phrasing that cut through my self-congratulatory thoughts. 'Protected from whom?'

Koen didn't have a chance to reply. A stream of police officers appeared. Thomas was the first in the flat, wearing a bulletproof vest and holding a drawn gun.

'I've got it,' I said. 'The situation is under control.'

'I guess I should say well done,' Thomas said. He hand-cuffed Koen and read him his rights. 'Are you going to wait for us next time?'

I stood up and holstered my gun. It was all over. Thomas threw a quick glance around the flat.

'We need to search this place for drugs,' I said. I wasn't sure how much of what Koen had told me would be admissible in court. 'Or maybe you just want to tell us where you're keeping your stash. Saves us time. Might make the judge like you more.'

Koen didn't reply; just sat quietly on the sofa. Resigned to what had happened. 'I want a lawyer,' he said.

'Of course you do,' Thomas said. 'We'll get you one. As soon as we get to the station.'

I felt giddy. This time we had been on time. This time I'd rescued the child and whatever reprimand I was going to get for it afterwards, it had all been worthwhile.

'So that's where the drugs were,' Thomas said. 'We were at the wrong flat. Instead of searching Piotr's, we should have come next door.'

He took Koen by the arm and helped him up from the sofa. I followed them out of the flat. As soon as Koen stepped through the door, he said, 'Where's Oskar?'

'He's fine,' I said.

Thomas led him down the corridor. 'Where is he?' Koen asked more loudly. 'Where's my son?'

I was surprised to see Ronald standing in the corridor. 'Is there a paramedic checking Oskar?' I said. 'You're back here quickly.'

'No, Natalie has him. She's just . . .' He turned around. I looked over his shoulder, but there was no sign of her. Natalie was gone.

'You gave her the child? Ronald, I asked you to take him downstairs.'

'I had to take a call. Sorry, Ilse called about the kids. Natalie helped me out.'

'No!' Koen screamed. 'What have you done? Go after her. She killed Sylvie. She tried to kill Piotr.'

307

What did he mean? Was it Natalie who'd swapped the drugs, not Koen? I wanted to stop and question him about that, but I had to get my priorities right. 'Where's Ingrid? Is she downstairs?'

'Yes,' Thomas said.

'She said she was going to take my son,' Koen shouted.

I got my phone out. 'There's a blonde woman with a small child. Stop her urgently,' I said to Ingrid as I started running towards the stairs. 'Now! Now!'

'She said she wouldn't kill him if I took her back. If we got back together. Please!' Koen was pleading with Thomas.

'That can't be right,' Ronald said.

I didn't listen to him but ran down the stairs.

'Where the fuck are you going?' Thomas shouted. He still had his hand on Koen's arm.

Chapter Thirty-Four

I bashed the lift button on my way past but knew there was no point. Natalie had taken it down. The lift was now on the ground floor. I could see her. I had to run down after her. As the staircase was open, I had a perfect view of the street. She was pretending not to be in a hurry and she walked calmly, carrying the child, as if she had all the time in the world. Just a mother with her toddler. That she could easily have dropped the child over the flat's balustrade was something that I pushed out of my mind. It hadn't happened.

I could hear the crying and screaming of the child over my heavy breathing and my echoing footsteps as I sprinted down the stairs. Sweat glued my T-shirt to my back. It was too hot to be running but I only went down more quickly, almost throwing myself down the steps, as if the sound of the child's cries was pulling me towards the ground floor. Footsteps echoed behind me but I didn't check who it was. Instead I kept watching Natalie. Everybody around her seemed to studiously ignore the crying. A man even smiled at her, as if to commiserate with her noisy child.

Where was Ingrid? Why didn't anybody stop Natalie? Behind her, to her left, I saw Ingrid with her hand on the arm of another blonde woman, with a child in a pushchair. I shouted, 'Wrong woman, wrong woman!' Ingrid looked in puzzlement at me, but before she could act, Natalie had reached a small grey car and my colleague was too late to stop her.

Only one more flight of stairs to go. I considered jumping over the open balustrade, but I didn't dare take the risk, so I kept running and finally pushed the door open to the street. I could see Natalie reversing her car out of her parking spot. I wouldn't be able to get to her before she drove off, and then I would be stranded on foot. Better to go for the safer option. I'd left my car on the other side of the road. I crossed quickly and jumped in.

I'd just fastened my seat belt and stuck my gun in the glove compartment when the door on the other side opened and Ronald slid in beside me. Not who I would have wanted to see, but probably better than nobody. I forced all thoughts of who was to blame for this out of my mind. Instead I jammed the car in reverse, screeched out of the parking space and sped after Natalie. We had to get Oskar back.

'Koen wasn't the one who swapped the drugs,' I said. A car was coming from the right. I didn't give way but accelerated across the junction. There were about four cars between me and Natalie. I was catching up with her.

'Maybe Natalie just wants to keep Oskar safe,' Ronald said.

'You're a misguided idiot.' My voice was harsh, trying to stop myself from saying that he'd handed a child over to a murderer. After all I'd done to prevent it. 'Koen had left to go to the club that night and Natalie gave Sylvie white heroin instead of cocaine. That's what happened.'

'Left! Left here,' he shouted.

As if I wasn't watching Natalie's car like a hawk. 'I see her. Call 112. Let them know where we're going.' I tried to sound calm, but my heart was racing. Sweat pooled on my upper lip and I rubbed it away with my shoulder without taking my eyes off the road.

Natalie pulled onto a main road. The traffic was moving faster here.

Ronald took his mobile out of his pocket. 'I'm here with Detective Lotte Meerman,' he said. 'We are in pursuit of a grey Nissan.' He gave the registration number, then slotted the phone into the holder and put it on speaker. A small car in front of us slowed down. I swore and used the gap in the oncoming traffic to made a quick evasive manoeuvre, swerving around it. My eyes stung from the intensity of staring at Natalie's grey car. I tried to ignore the sweat that ran down my forehead. I couldn't take a hand off the steering wheel to wipe it away.

'Where are you going?' a male voice said.

'We're in pursuit of a suspect with a kidnapped child,' I said. 'Ronald, can you give them the directions?'

'We're on the Transformatorweg.' He checked my sat nav. 'The S102.'

'How far down?'

Ronald tried to read the side roads. 'We're just beside a lot of building sites to our left. Looks quite industrial. Sorry, I'm not that familiar with the area.'

'Coming up to the Spaarndammerdijk,' I said. There were

now three cars between me and Natalie. I overtook one more. I was no longer careful not to be seen. From the way Natalie was driving, she surely knew we were chasing her. My fingers started to ache from the tight grip I had on the steering wheel. I couldn't let go. I could only clench even more strongly. 'Fuck, fuck, where's she going?'

'She could go towards the IJ,' Ronald said.

If she was headed towards the large body of water to the north of Amsterdam's Centraal Station, she would quickly run out of space. 'Anywhere you can block her off?' I asked the dispatcher.

'Not obviously.'

'Any cars in the vicinity to give me a hand?' Ahead, at the end of the road, I could see that we were coming towards the bridge. The barriers were closed and there was no way Natalie could make it through. The bridge was rising slowly.

'We've got her,' I said with relief. I unclenched my hands and stretched out the fingers of one hand and then the other. 'We'll block her here.'

About a dozen cars were waiting for the bridge on our side of the street. I was about to slow down and tell Ronald to get my gun from the glove compartment when suddenly Natalie veered onto the left-hand side of the road. She was overtaking the queue. I had no choice but to follow her. I could only hope that no car would pull out. At the barriers, she took a sharp right onto the street along the canal. I pulled the steering wheel hard and felt the car complain against the treatment it was getting. Even though I held on tight to keep myself upright, the centrifugal force swung my body into the inside of the car door.

312

I didn't even notice the first speed bump until I hit it too hard. I was thrown forward and the impact closed my mouth with such force that my teeth threatened to shatter each other. The street was littered with these obstacles so that cars wouldn't use it as a rat run.

Natalie didn't slow down and approached the next one at speed. Her exhaust pipe struck the road surface as the bump did its job. The car pulled right and hit one of Amsterdam's many small bollards with such a velocity that she seemed to bounce off it. She was struggling to control her car and it lunged sharply left.

I hit the brakes as hard as I could. I felt the wheels slip underneath me, then slowly grip again as I released the pedal. I could see the black underside of Natalie's car. I could see all four wheels off the ground. For a second she was airborne. There were no railings here. I could only watch helplessly as the grey Nissan plunged over the edge.

'Suspect's car has crashed into the canal,' Ronald said. I heard the shock in his voice.

'Westerkanaal,' I said. I left the car in the middle of the street, undoing my seat belt with one hand and pushing the door open with the other.

'Get us some help here!' Ronald shouted. 'Now.' He ran beside me along the side of the canal. Natalie's car was going under fast. There was no sign of a door opening. It had rolled when it hit the low edge of the canal and the wheels were up. It was sinking.

I kicked off my shoes. A loud splash next to me told me that Ronald had already jumped in. I wasn't far behind. The water here was deep. There was no risk of hitting the bottom; I just had to avoid the car. I tried to keep my head above water when I jumped in, to keep Natalie's car in sight, but the canal closed in above me. It was cool and took my breath away for a moment.

I fought against the drag of the water on my jeans and got my head back above water. I needed to get close to the car without being sucked down with it. I swam to the right. Not the driver's side, but the other side. Where Oskar was. I put my feet against the chassis and grabbed the door handle, pulling with all my might. It didn't budge. It was shut tight. Even though I knew there was no point, I jerked it a couple more times. I closed my eyes for a second. Panic wasn't going to help me. Panic was counter-productive. I knew the car had to fill with water so that the pressure equalised and we could open the doors.

There was nothing worse than knowing you had to wait. Seconds felt like minutes when you were so desperate to save a life. People were gathering at the canal's edge. The windows of the tall houses seemed like even more eyes staring at me to see if I was going to succeed this time.

'The door's open on this side,' Ronald shouted.

Natalie must have managed to open it before the car submerged. 'Can you see Oskar?' The door on my side still wouldn't move.

'I need to get Natalie out first before we can get to him.'

Let her drown, I wanted to say, but I knew we needed space or we wouldn't get to the boy. I swam around the car. It was tilting. It was sinking. From the size of the boats coming through, I knew it would sink deep. My legs were heavy from the weight of my jeans.

Ronald took a deep breath in, then dived under.

I couldn't watch him. Two police cars pulled up with sirens blaring and parked behind my abandoned car. The sun's rays blazed on my head. My eyes stung from the canal water as I waited for Ronald. I saw the movement in the water. The air bubbles where he was exhaling.

He came back up. He had Natalie in a tight grip. Her long blonde hair floated over his arm. The car was now submerged so deeply that only one of the wheels was still visible above the water. My colleagues who had just arrived could deal with the woman. I had a child to rescue.

I dived under. One stroke and I was next to the car window. The muddy-brown water closed above my head and it was hard to see anything. I felt my way to the open car door and pulled myself inside. Where had Natalie put Oskar? I saw it in front of me again. When she'd got into the car she'd been in a hurry. She'd had no time for a child seat. He could be anywhere inside the car. I felt around me. I didn't want to get stuck, but I needed to get Oskar out.

I wanted to breathe, I could feel my mouth opening reflexively. My lungs burned. I exhaled all the air I had inside. The child had been in the back. Surely he'd been in the back. My hand struck something soft like seaweed. It was hair. I knew they were blonde curls. I grabbed a handful and pulled. My other hand still held on to the door frame. Something gave. Thank God he hadn't been strapped in. My lungs were now so painful that I was starting to feel faint. I had to go up soon. I felt below the hair, found a T-shirt, a collar that I could grab hold of. I pulled him towards me, grabbed an arm, held him tight, pulled him out of the car and kicked my legs to get up to the surface.

I felt the blessed oxygen stream in through my mouth.

I lifted Oskar's head until his face was free of the water. I made sure his nose and mouth were clear. His eyes were closed. I wrapped one arm around his little body, under his arms, and looked around me, moving my legs to keep us afloat while I gently wiped the hair from his face. I hugged him to me and rested his head on my shoulder. He was a toddler, but half carried by the water he felt just the weight my daughter had been.

I didn't dare check for a heartbeat in case the knowledge killed me.

The boat for which the bridge had opened slowly pulled alongside me. It was a large sailing boat and it still had the rainbow flags strapped to its side. A man dressed in pink with a deep tan stretched out his arms towards the water. 'Hand the child to me,' he said. Two of his friends held him by the belt to stop him falling in. My arms were getting tired but I could just lift Oskar's limp body out of the water. I held on to the side of the boat and rested my forehead against it.

'He's breathing,' the man confirmed, his voice high above me. The relief I felt was enough to make my fingers release their grip on the boat. I let myself sink down.

Ronald was by the canal's edge, a distance away. 'You got the child out,' he said. His voice carried over the water. 'After I nearly got him killed.'

'I saved a life.' I pushed my feet against the side of the boat, floating on my back and letting the water support me. Letting it wash away my fears. I was slowly rebalancing the score.

Two policemen on the shore had hold of Natalie. We were done. Four hands grabbed me and pulled me out of the water and onto the boat. Someone handed me a towel. I'd never before been so happy to hear a child cry. I wrapped the towel, and then my arms, around him. I hadn't dared to hold a child in such a long time. It brought back memories and I allowed them to flood in. This time I wouldn't drown.

A small police boat pulled alongside us and a paramedic came across to check out Oskar as I held him. I wasn't going to let go. The sun shone on my wet skin and pulled it into pleasurable goose bumps. I ignored the fact that I was only dressed in a very wet T-shirt and sodden jeans. Maybe I should towel off so that I got dry sooner. Instead I closed my eyes and turned my face to the sun in the cloudless sky, treasuring that feeling of having a child in my arms again. Water dripped from my jeans onto the deck. I rested my chin on top of Oskar's head and watched as Ronald climbed out of the water and sat down next to Natalie.

Chapter Thirty-Five

Oskar was taken into care. Luckily he suffered no adverse consequences from his bath in the canal. Ingrid and I had another go at interviewing Katja. I knew that Bauer and Tim were watching us from the other side of the mirror. It seemed to make Ingrid more nervous than it did me. She kept throwing glances at the mirror. Bauer was still pissed off with me and I knew that he was sitting there trying to find fault with whatever I did. Even all the drugs we found at Koen and Natalie's place didn't make him happy. I remembered that time we'd searched Piotr's flat and I'd heard the disturbance next door. I'd gone to Koen and Natalie's flat and I had wondered why Koen hadn't opened the door wider. Now I knew that what had kept Natalie so long wasn't that Koen had hit her and she was putting on new make-up, but that she had to put their stash back in its hiding place.

'I think you should finally tell us what happened.' I said to Katja. 'I know you tried to make sure that Oskar would stay with Petra and Gerard, but now you need to tell us the truth.'

'I found out that Sylvie had been living with Petra and

318

Gerard. So I thought she'd killed herself and had selected Oskar's new parents for him. She wouldn't want him to be adopted by people like our parents. You've met them. You know what they're like. I love him so much.' She smiled. 'From the very first time I met him and smelled his apple shampoo. That toddler smell. His life was in front of him and mine was nearly over. I had to look out for him. I thought I had killed my sister. I thought that because I hadn't let her into my flat, she'd committed suicide.'

'I think Sylvie came to you because she wanted to move out of Petra and Gerard's place. I don't know that for sure, but I think that's why she went looking for money. From you and then from Koen.'

'It's ironic that it was only when Piotr turned up and started to ask all those questions that I realised it wasn't my fault.'

'What did he ask?'

'He wanted to know if Sylvie had ever done heroin. He said that a heroin overdose seemed out of character.' She shrugged. 'That they'd been doing lines of coke before she turned up and that the heroin overdose sounded wrong. And where was the child.'

'And those questions didn't make you think that maybe he had nothing to do with her death?'

'They sounded like a threat to me. That he was looking for his child. That's what Natalie told me.'

'Natalie killed your sister. She was the one who swapped the drugs. To keep Sylvie out of Koen's life. Koen cheated on Natalie with Sylvie. She's insanely jealous.'

'I know she lied to me now.'

'So why kill Piotr?'

'I thought that if he was the father, maybe he should get to know his son. Petra disagreed vehemently, said it was too risky, that he could shop us to the authorities. But I would have loved to know my father. I thought we should give Piotr that chance. Introduce him to Oskar, maybe give him some visitation rights. Gerard agreed with me.'

'But you changed your mind when he gave those drugs to the German.'

'Yes. The guy with the beard. It brought back to me that he was a dealer; how could I introduce Oskar to a man like that? I called Petra and said I couldn't do it. That she should leave with Oskar and hopefully Piotr would be happy now that he'd seen the photo. I would give him some other updates, I don't know. But she insisted that we should go ahead. That I should bring him to the car. And she would take care of everything else.'

'And then she killed him.'

Katja nodded. 'He never expected a thing. I never expected it either.'

'You drove off?'

'She stabbed him, I got in the car, and we left.'

'Did Petra ask you to take the fall?'

'No, it was my decision. I wanted Oskar to stay at the house where he was so happy. He could go on being Petra's grandson.'

'Someone would have found out.'

'It was a risk worth taking.'

Chapter Thirty-Six

We sat together in the restaurant. I hadn't been here before; restaurants with white tablecloths and as many glasses as there were sets of cutlery around my plate weren't really my thing, but my lemon sole was cooked to perfection, its skin a crisp brown and a butter and dill sauce that added to the flavour but didn't overwhelm. The simplest way of cooking fresh fish was often the best. The skin crunched pleasingly between my teeth. I wore my new green dress.

'How's yours?' I felt that the surroundings meant I should eat the potatoes as they were, not mash them together with my fork in the sauce. I speared a piece.

'It's very nice,' Mark said.

A silence fell. It felt awkward. At the table next to ours, an overweight man and a super-skinny woman both looked down at their phones while having their dinner. The woman smiled at the appliance, put her fork down and wrote something back. She held her phone up to her dining partner, so he could read what was on the screen too. At least she didn't just forward the message to him.

A waiter came to our table and refilled the glasses from a bottle of mineral water. When I'd asked for tap water, he'd said that they didn't serve that here. Now I wished I'd argued with him about it. It would have released some of the tension.

I had been nervous before coming here, with the kind of butterflies in my stomach that would be more suitable for a first date than for this dinner. The only sound was the noise that Mark's knife made cutting his steak. I pulled a piece of fish away from the bones.

'I've done some thinking.' He took a sip of his wine. 'I haven't been fair on anybody.'

I didn't respond, but continued dissecting my fish. Its eye stared at me from the top of its head. I had been fascinated by these fish when I'd been a kid: how when they were young their eyes were on either side of their head, like normal fish; then, as their bodies flattened out, their eyes travelled upwards until they were both at the top of their head.

Mark looked down at his plate. 'Lotte, what do you want from me?'

I swallowed the mouthful of fish and looked up sharply to meet his eyes. I rested my elbows on the table and took a couple of breaths in. I was saved from having to answer by the waiter, who just then turned up by my left elbow and asked if everything was okay. I responded tersely that every-thing was just fine. He left as quickly as he could.

'I want to apologise. For everything. For arresting you, for stalking you, for drunkenly texting you.' I smiled uncom-fortably. 'It feels too light, those words. If I'd been Asian, I would have knelt on the floor to beg your forgiveness.'

'I got used to seeing you outside my house. Maybe I've missed it. Maybe I liked it.'

'You're crazy.'

'I just had to get over being angry with you. Even though I knew you'd only done what was right, I was still angry with you.'

'Why didn't you stay?' I said. Two people came past outside, arm in arm, walking their dog. They stopped to look at the menu, then seemingly at my plate. I looked back at Mark. 'At the bar? Why did you leave?'

He put his fork down, giving me his full attention. 'I think I freaked out. For you this is probably normal, but I've never seen anybody get killed before. I was . . .' He hesitated. He picked up his wineglass and took a big gulp. 'Okay, I might as well tell you. It seems I've got nothing left to lose anyway. I was scared, okay?'

'That's perfectly sensible.'

'Then there was the smell of blood. I've never seen someone get killed before,' he repeated. 'You think you know how you're going to react, but really, it's totally different. I just froze. And you acted, you tried to save him. I just felt stupid. Completely useless. Like I said, for you this is normal, but for me—'

'It's really not normal for me either.'

'You were . . . I don't know, completely in control of the situation.'

I frowned. 'And you think that makes it easy?'

'You looked as if you didn't need me there.'

'Need? No, I guess you're right. I didn't need you there.' I saw that he flinched but I couldn't stop myself from being

323

honest, whatever my mother might say. My heart was thumping in my mouth. Here was where I had to be brave. I took a breath and added, 'But I would have liked you there.'

'What for?'

'You could have asked me if I was okay afterwards. Given me a hug. Whatever. That would have been nice.'

He looked down at his plate. He pushed the steak further away from him. Instead he ate a couple of chips with his fingers. 'Do you want to start again?'

I really shouldn't have been as happy as I was. Maybe I should even have played hard to get. But I couldn't be bothered. 'Of course,' I said.

Chapter Thirty-Seven

'Why did you do it?' I asked.

'He was going to leave me,' Natalie said. With her hair bedraggled and her face free of make-up, she looked very young. Two days in the holding cell had stripped the glamorous veneer away. 'It had already changed before Sylvie came back. I love him so much, I can't imagine life without him.'

'What happened with Sylvie?'

'It was so easy to swap her drugs. She needed a bit of persuading to do a line, but of course she did in the end. They always do. I gave her white heroin instead. We kept that for a couple of regular customers.'

This needed to be clear on the tapes in order for another case not to fall apart. 'So can you confirm that you swapped the drugs on purpose?'

'I heard about that dealer who killed all those people. Giving them white heroin instead of cocaine. It seemed such an easy way to kill somebody. To be honest, I never thought it would work so well. I think I could have saved her life but I didn't want to. The lying bitch.'

'Did Koen cheat on you with her?'

'No, he cheated on her with me. But I really loved him so I kicked her out of the flat and framed her for theft. It was all really easy. I didn't know she was pregnant.'

'And Piotr kept asking questions.'

'Yes, he wanted to know why the bitch had OD'd. And where the child was. He recognised Katja from the funeral. Luckily she came to me to ask questions and I told her that Piotr was the boyfriend.' Natalie laughed. 'It was almost funny when they killed him. I hadn't expected that, but it made things easier for a bit. But then Koen started to suspect what I'd done. He was so angry with me. He said that he couldn't be with a woman like me any more. He called me insane. He said that on the way to Piotr's funeral, can you believe it? That's why I hinted that his child wasn't safe.'

'Koen said you threatened to take Oskar.'

'I saw that counsellor in the hospital after they'd pumped my stomach. The one with the ghastly hair. She talked to me. No, she screamed at me that I'd killed Sylvie. I wondered why she cared so much and then I realised she knew about the kid. So I called Koen to say that I'd figured out where the boy was. I wouldn't have killed his son, I'm not capable of doing that. But he would have stayed with me to protect his child, and in time he would have loved me again. Don't you think?'

I slowly shook my head. Love wasn't like that.

Natalie had been lying to us constantly. Had she told us the truth this time? I decided it didn't matter. She had killed Sylvie and had got Piotr killed. She had abducted Oskar. Plus what she had just said during the interrogation would keep Bauer's case intact.

I left the interview room.

Bauer came out of the observation area. 'Thank you, Lotte,' he said. I could even hear a little bit of contrition in his voice. 'Good job,' he added, as he had been saying before.

I nodded. 'You're welcome,' I said. Because this time it really had been.

Acknowledgements

Even though this book is a work of fiction, it was partially inspired by real events that took place in the Netherlands. I have changed the number as well as the nationalities of the victims and, of course, everything about the people who were involved with this case.

In 2014 and 2015, three people died in Amsterdam and over a dozen more victims were treated in hospital after they used white heroin that they thought was cocaine. At that time, large boards all over the city warned cocaine users to make sure they trusted their dealers and knew where they were getting their drugs from. After three Danish tourists barely survived, their dealer was caught on CCTV. The man, Flip S., came forward after he recognised himself. It could never be proven that he had dealt drugs to the other tourists as well. Even though it was shown that the drugs came from the same batch, the surviving earlier victims described their dealer as a man in his early twenties, whereas Flip S. was in his early forties. Therefore the judge convicted him only for dealing drugs and for not ensuring that the drugs he sold were 'safe'. In other words, he should have been more careful about what he was selling, as he must have been aware that white heroin was being sold as cocaine. He was given a one-year prison sentence. It has never become clear what the original source of this batch of drugs was.

There have been no more victims since Flip S.'s conviction.

Many people helped me with this novel and I'm grateful to you all. My agent Allan Guthrie is as supportive an agent as I could wish for, as well as a fantastic writer. I'd also like to thank my editor Krystyna Green and all at Constable and Little, Brown for helping me make this novel the best it could possibly be.